DOPPELGANGER

Also by David Stahler Jr.

A GATHERING OF SHADES

TRUESIGHT

DOPPELGANGER

DAVID STAHLER JR.

An Imprint of HarperCollins*Publishers*

Eos is an imprint of HarperCollins Publishers.

Doppelganger
Copyright © 2006 by David Stahler Jr.
www.harperteen.com

Library of Congress Cataloging-in-Publication Data
Stahler, David.
Doppelganger / David Stahler, Jr.— 1st ed.
p.   cm.
Summary: When a sixteen-year-old member of a race of
shape-shifting killers called doppelgangers assumes the life of a
troubled teen, he becomes unexpectedly embroiled in human
life—and it is nothing like what he has seen on television.
ISBN-10: 0-06-087232-2 (trade bdg.)
ISBN-13: 978-0-06-087232-8 (trade bdg.)
ISBN-10: 0-06-087233-0 (lib. bdg.)
ISBN-13: 978-0-06-087233-5 (lib. bdg.)
[1. Family problems—Fiction. 2. Conduct of life—Fiction.
3. Football—Fiction. 4. Child abuse—Fiction. 5.
Supernatural—Fiction.] I. Title.
PZ7.S78246Dop 2006   2005028484
[Fic]—dc22   CIP
                                                  AC

Typography by Christopher Stengel
1 2 3 4 5 6 7 8 9 10
❖
First Edition

For my brothers, Daniel and Nathan

PROLOGUE

He had been watching for most of the day, watching the far mountains as they faded in and out of clouds, then the trees closer by as they came and went amid the mist as well. Later he began watching the strip of gravel road that wound its way up to the cabin, waiting for her to get home so she could feed him. He was hungry. He'd been hungry all day, and yesterday, too. In the end, he settled on watching the rain patter against the glass, watched the drops as they puckered and trickled, splitting up or drawing together in patterns he couldn't understand. Then finally, as even the drops began to fade against the encroaching darkness, a pair of headlights at the corner, and soon a station wagon pulling up to the house. It was a new car. She usually came back with a new one.

He left the window, ran behind the chair, and crouched in the darkness. A minute later, the door opened. There were footsteps—six slow ones—followed by light in the cabin, causing him to pull back, blinking, even further into the shadows. Footsteps again, closer now. Then the face, illuminated by the overhead light as she bent down to stare into the hollow place behind the chair.

"It's not much of a game if you always hide in the same spot," she said.

He didn't reply. He just pulled his knees in tighter to his chest and studied the face.

It was a full face, smooth and pale, with the slightest hint of a double chin. Its eyes were round and blue, and its hair was yellow like the sun. He liked this face better than her last one. The last one was old. Old and mean, with squinty eyes and a cruel mouth. This face wasn't mean. It even looked like the face of somebody's mother, one that could be warm and kind if the wearer wanted it to be. And maybe with a face like that, the wearer would want it to be.

Still, even though he liked it better, he didn't move. He never moved when she first came back, until she made him. She thought it was a game, but it wasn't—he just had to be sure.

"You can come out," she said. "Come out of there."

He shook his head, stubborn. She looked away, sighed, and then looked back. There was a twitching along the corners of her jaw and hairline, followed by a ripple, as if her face were a pool into which he'd thrown a pebble. For a moment he could see the old eyes, lidless, round and cold; could see the gray skin and nostril folds. It both comforted and terrified him.

She turned away and went over to the woodstove.

"The lights were off," she said. "Were they off yesterday, too? Did you never turn them on?"

He crawled out from behind the chair and shook his head, even though she wasn't looking.

"It's freezing in here." She opened the stove door and peered

in. "You let the fire go out." She glanced back at him in disgust. "And after I showed you how to do it."

"I wasn't cold," he said. It wasn't true. He was cold last night.

"Well, I'm cold, and it's only now getting dark. Sit at the table. You probably didn't eat, either."

He sat at the table and waited while she built a new fire. Soon it was warm in the cabin again, and his mouth watered at the smell of the bacon she was cooking to go with the beans.

When she finished, she put the food before him and sat at the table watching him eat. The rain had stopped throbbing against the metal roof, and the quiet, coupled with the warmth of the fire, had coaxed a cricket out of hiding, and then another. He'd listened to the pair the night before, sometimes chirping together, but usually taking turns. Lying alone in the house, he'd wondered if they were trying to outdo each other or if they were just talking. Now, as they set to chirping once more, he smiled vaguely at their song.

"You've got to do a better job taking care of yourself," she scolded as he shoveled beans into his mouth. "Otherwise you'll never survive."

"I'll try harder next time."

"Do," she said.

She left the table for a while and came back as he was finishing up, opening her hands to set the two crickets on the table. He watched them take a few tentative hops. They'd stopped chirping, suddenly shy.

"Dessert," she said.

"I don't like crickets," he whined. "They tickle in my mouth."

"That's because you don't kill them first," she said.

From the corner of his eye, he watched her pick one up and pinch its head precisely. Only when its legs stopped their frantic squirming did she pop the black-shelled creature into her mouth and crunch down on it.

"Just like that," she said. "Now you try."

He reached out for the remaining cricket, but it hopped out of reach. She retrieved it for him and held it out, dangling by one leg. Taking it from her, he held it tight until it stopped squirming. Then, looking away, he pinched, closing his eyes at the crush. His eyes still closed, he thrust it in his mouth, feeling it break apart as he chewed. She was right—they did go down better dead.

Opening his eyes, he looked back at his mother. She had the same look of disgust on her face as before.

"We've got a lot of work to do," she said. "It's ridiculous, a boy your age, can't keep a fire going, can't even kill a cricket without squirming. And how old are you?"

"Five," he whispered.

"That's right. Five years old. Shameful."

I met Amber two days after I throttled her boyfriend, Chris Parker. A week later we were in love. Or rather, I was in love with her. It took a while on her part. After all, she thought I was him.

Let me explain—I am a doppelganger.

Not many people have heard of us before. We're a pretty secretive race. So secretive, in fact, that I don't even know that much about us myself. Most of what I know about my kind I learned from my mother, and she wasn't all that informative. I can't even tell people my name. I don't have one. Not one I was born with, anyway. My mother always said names are worthless to a doppelganger. So the whole time I was growing up, she was she, and I was me, and that's as far as it ever got.

The problem is that doppelgangers are loners. We don't keep in touch. We don't call each other or send postcards. We would never e-mail. There's no annual doppelganger convention or home base or family reunion. When you're a doppelganger, you're on your own.

Maybe there just isn't much to know about us. We're pretty simple, actually—primitive, one might say—which is how we've managed to survive for so long.

But there are a few things to know. The most important is that we're shape-shifters. We can change the way we look, the sound of our voice; we can even change our sex, though we usually prefer not to. We're like chameleons, but taken to a higher level.

And it's a good thing we are shape-shifters, because in our natural state we're ugly as sin. Really hideous, to the point where we can barely stand to look at ourselves, let alone others of our kind. A doppelganger mother will even turn from her own child in disgust. I'm sure it's hard to imagine such a thing—after all, a human mother will love even her ugliest child—but with us it's true. It must be an evolutionary thing or something. If so, it works pretty well—a doppelganger can rarely be found in its natural form. I can count on one hand the number of times I saw my mother in her own skin. Who knows, maybe I've just blocked the other times out of my head. Between the mottled, almost transparent flesh, the bulging eyes, and a face with no nose or mouth other than a few slimy slits, you've got the makings of a real freak. Actually, all those drawings of aliens recreated from people's so-called abductions—those things with the egg heads and spindly arms—they're not aliens, they're doppelgangers. And those people who *think* they were abducted didn't go anywhere—they were just lucky enough to have survived. That's my theory, anyway.

Which brings me to another important doppelganger fact: We're killers. Of people, that is. We prey on your race—stalking you, watching your moves, the places you go, learning the patterns of your life. Then, when we think we've got it down, we find a nice quiet little corner to strangle you in and take over. At least that's how it's supposed to work. Sometimes things get a little messy.

But if we're really good, no one can tell it's not you. We look like you, sound like you, even act like you. We take your life and live it in your place. And then, when we get bored or someone seems to be getting too close to the truth, we move on. Though, to be honest, we can only hold a form so long before we start to lose it. It takes a lot of strength to hang on to somebody's life. After a while it even starts to hurt.

Of course, the letting go can be just as bad. Trust me, I know.

Does this sound awful? Are we evil creatures? Monsters? I've been asking myself the question since I was old enough to wonder, and I still haven't figured it out. My mother would say no. In her view, our people have nothing to do with the concepts of good or evil. "Foolish human conventions," she once called them. In her mind, we do what we do because that's who we are.

"Are we bad?" I remember asking one afternoon as I watched her break the neck of a rooster for our supper. I was eight, I think, and had recently learned the truth about doppelganger ways. "Are we bad for killing?"

She looked at me in disgust. "You've been watching too much TV," she said, tossing me the limp bird to pluck. "That's a foolish question. The kind a human would ask."

"Well, are we?" I pressed.

"Is the tiger evil when it kills the zebra? Is the shark

3

malicious for biting the swimmer? Does the bee sting out of wickedness?" she said.

I took her meaning. She felt it was our nature to kill—nothing more, nothing less. And it's true, it's not like we doppelgangers want to take over the world or enslave the human race or anything like that. Far from it—we prefer to live quietly, below the radar. Still, it troubled me. Not because I didn't believe her, but because I did. Because I believed a doppelganger was supposed to obey its nature. That's what bothered me. For even back then, I wasn't sure if I'd be able to live by killing. Not like her.

Anyway, that's about it. There's only one other important thing to know about doppelgangers that I can think of. Since we keep to ourselves, we don't run into each other very often, but when we do, we know it. Even in human form, we can tell. It's like we can sniff each other out. If two doppelgangers of the same sex happen to meet, they'll more than likely ignore each other and move on. But if a heganger and sheganger come together, they're going to mate. It's practically unavoidable—nature's way of ensuring the continuation of the species, I guess. My mother told me all about it not long before she kicked me out.

"Even if you don't want to—and you won't—you're going to couple," she said, "and she will bear an offspring, just as I bore your miserable excuse of a being."

"What was my father like?" I asked.

"Weak," she said. "The males always are. But he was there, for that day of our coupling at least."

"Did you have another child before me?" I asked her. I'd always wanted to know, and since she was in a rare talking mood, I figured I'd ask.

"Once. A long time ago," she said.

"A boy or a girl?"

"I hardly remember."

My mother wasn't exactly the warm and snuggly type. I didn't take it personally. I knew that's just how she was. She told me we were all that way, and since I'd never met another one of us, I took her at her word.

I also knew, without her even having to tell me, that I was a hindrance. Putting aside the fact that—as she often put it—I was an embarrassment with no prospects, there was the simple matter that she'd been holed up with me in our cabin for the last sixteen years, rarely leaving except when the urges got too great to bear. Then she'd disappear for a day, maybe even two or three, and come back as someone else. It was enough to calm her, but not enough to truly satisfy. She wanted to be on the road again and alone, but she couldn't leave me. For though her urge to kill was strong, equally strong was the urge to make sure her offspring survived. Nature is funny that way.

Still, she must have been convinced I could make it on my own because she eventually got rid of me. I remember the moment she called me out one night onto the porch as she was preparing to leave.

"I'm going," she said, watching me in the light of the open doorway. "There's a pack with some food in it on the counter. Enough for a few days. When I get back, you'd better be gone. I've babied you long enough." She shook her head. "When I was your age, I'd already gone through three forms."

"Where am I supposed to go?" I asked.

She shrugged. "Wherever you want—I don't really care.

Just don't do anything stupid. And for heaven's sake, don't travel in the daylight, at least not until you've taken a form. I've had to look at you for sixteen years now—you're not a pleasant sight."

"I guess this is good-bye, then," I said. I tried to decide if I should thank her.

"Spare me the sentiment. And don't bother thanking me," she said, as if reading my mind. "I tried to teach you, but as far as I can tell, it was a waste of time. You're my only failure in life. You're a weak one, even worse than your father."

"I'm sorry," I said.

"I suppose it's my fault. I shouldn't have let you watch all that TV. I figured it would keep you occupied, but it only made you soft, like a human. Still, you're a clever boy in your own way. Who knows, maybe you'll get by."

With that, she headed down the porch steps. A minute later she'd driven away, and I haven't seen her since.

I went inside and saw the pack on the counter. I'd noticed it earlier in the afternoon, but hadn't thought anything of it. It had been sitting in front of me the whole time, waiting—the signal of my departure. And now it was time to go.

I didn't feel too bad about it. I'd only left my immediate surroundings a half dozen times in my entire life. A change of setting was called for. And really, there wasn't much I'd miss there, least of all my mother. I even contemplated burning the place down before I left, just to spite her, but I realized it was pointless. Somehow I knew she wasn't coming back. Besides, I didn't want to toast my books. I'd read everything I could get my hands on—

trashy paperbacks, supermarket tabloids, schoolbooks, even instruction manuals—and had amassed quite a little library in one corner of the cabin. Whenever my mother came back with a new car, I'd comb through it, looking for reading material. I almost took a few of the books with me, then decided against it. To bring some and not others—it didn't seem fair.

What I really hated leaving was the TV. I liked my books well enough, but I'd miss our television the most. I took one last look at it before I left. I'd spent most of the last seven years watching it. It didn't matter what time of day it was or what was on—soap operas, cartoons, news— I took it all in. And my mother was perfectly happy to let me—it made her life easier, that's for sure.

I didn't really know where to go as I left the cabin, so I followed my momentum downhill, walking the half mile or so of our driveway to the main road, then crossing into the woods where I kept on walking. Night had fallen, but it wasn't bad going—with our bulbous eyes, doppelgangers can see almost as well in the dark as we can in the light. The rain had stopped, and it was actually quite peaceful in the woods. The night birds were calling to each other, and I could see a pair of deer drifting between the trees a ways off.

Maybe I could just stay here, I thought. But I knew it was foolish. Necessity would drive me to civilization. Already I could feel it pulling me, like gravity, toward the lowest spot.

As I headed out into the world, I had no idea what lay ahead of me. I didn't know anything about Chris Parker, his sister, Echo, or his parents. I didn't know about the kids at school, the teachers, the coaches, or any of that. Most of all, I didn't know about Amber or have a clue that in a few short weeks I would be in love with her. Why would I? Doppelgangers aren't supposed to fall in love. But then, like my mother said, I always was different. The question was—could I be different enough?

CHAPTER TWO

It took me about three days to get out of the mountains. It wasn't hard at first, because in the woods I could still walk during the day. But as the trees began to thin out and I started coming across fields and the occasional house, I had to be more careful. By the time I hit the first town, I was pretty much forced to walk at night and find some place to lay low before the sun came up. It wouldn't have been so bad if I'd been able to sleep, but I was always on edge. I was still in my natural form. If I got caught, who knows what they'd do to me. After all, I'd seen *E.T.*

Of course, there was a way out of this predicament. And when I came across a man stumbling drunk down a backstreet at two in the morning, or spied a boy on his lonely way home from school, I'd be lying if I said I didn't feel the urge. It's a strange feeling, like hunger, only deeper, a sort of inner clenching that comes in waves and leaves longing in its wake. But I wasn't ready yet to assume a form. That's what I told myself, at least.

I couldn't figure out what my problem was. I mean,

after all, I was a doppelganger. I was supposed to follow through on the urges. And it wasn't as if I hadn't been trained. My mother had taught me all the tricks, all the signs to look for, the right way to go about making a proper kill. So what was I waiting for? Maybe my mother was right. Maybe watching too much TV had spoiled me. It was the news, I think, that did it. All those sad stories of human failings or plain old bad luck. I couldn't help it, I just felt sorry for them.

I remember once—I'd say I was around ten or eleven—seeing two parents being interviewed on the local news. They were both crying, taking turns breaking down. Their daughter had disappeared. They showed her picture on the screen—a pretty girl, about my age, with dark pigtails and green eyes.

"They should just be glad they don't have to feed her anymore," I heard a little voice say. I whirled around to see the girl standing there in real life, right behind me. Her clothes and hair were different from the picture, but it was her. I jumped back, almost knocking the TV over, but the girl just giggled and shook her head.

"There's a whole pile of schoolbooks in here," she said, throwing a loaded backpack onto the floor between us. "Since you finished the other ones, I figured you could start working on these. She looks to be about your age, after all."

I nodded but couldn't look her in the eyes. I just took the textbooks out of the pack and began studying them, not wanting to seem ungrateful. Later I realized it wasn't my mother I felt I owed—it was that girl's frantic parents, and the little girl herself. Her form hung around the house for the next two weeks, cooking my meals and splitting wood.

Deep down I knew I would've been in trouble, even without the TV. My squeamishness went way back. When I was younger, I had trouble killing even the smallest of creatures. It didn't matter if it was a squirrel, a hen, or even a cricket that my mother caught for me, I always resisted, holding out until I didn't have a choice. The worst was when she brought home a puppy. I'd seen dog food commercials on TV and was excited to have a pet. She let me play with it three whole days before making me strangle it.

Still, in spite of my hesitation, I knew I'd have to pick a mark sooner or later. The urges would only get stronger, and I couldn't hide from the world forever. Food wasn't really a problem—doppelgangers are hardy creatures. We can go a long time without eating and can gobble down almost anything. Worms, insects, grubs—it doesn't matter. But shacking up behind a Dumpster every night is no way to live. Besides, part of me was eager to prove myself, to show my mother she was wrong. I wasn't weak. I could take care of myself.

I reached the city a week later, following the lights as they got brighter each night until they finally blotted out the stars. Fall was coming, and the air was getting colder. By the time I reached the outskirts of the city, I was feeling pretty low. For the first time, I missed the comfort of my cabin. And the trees, too—spires of fir softer and warmer than these city towers—that had stood between the other mountains and me. I longed for my TV most of all and kept thinking of the shows I watched. All those characters who had joined me every week or every day—it sort of caught me off guard how much I missed them. I found myself thinking about them, worrying about the difficult spots I'd left them in, the problems that dogged them from episode to episode. And now they were all gone. Actually, they were still out there, going on without me. I was the one left alone.

At my lowest point, I even missed my mother. At least she'd been someone to talk to. I was in a train yard at the edge of the city. It was late. Most of the windows in the nearby skyscrapers were dark. There was a full moon out, and I was shivering from the cold snap as I wandered between the glowing boxcars scattered along the tracks. I'd started thinking about her, wondering where she was now, what she might look like, when I saw a light ahead and made my way toward it. Soon I could make out a group of men in the distance. From where I stood, peeking around the corner of a coal car, I could barely tell the four of them apart. They were wrapped up pretty tight against the cold, standing around a barrel fire, like four bundles of rags, passing bottles around, talking loudly. They seemed pretty lit.

I wanted some of that fire. I remember thinking they might just be drunk enough for me to put in a late-night appearance, maybe even scare them off, when I heard a loud cough behind me and nearly jumped out of my skin. I ducked into the shadows and looked around. The cough had come from right behind me, but there was no one in sight.

I heard it again. This time it came in a long spasm, and I realized the sound was coming from a nearby boxcar, its door ajar. Sticking to the shadows, I sidled up to the door. I could hear rattled breathing coming from inside and someone mumbling to himself. The noise made me shiver worse than the cold.

I stole a glance inside. The moon shining into the car illuminated a figure lying on a pile of blankets against the far wall. It was an old man. I could see his beard, a white blaze in the moonlight. He coughed again, even more fiercely. His whole body stiffened and shuddered with the effort, as if every muscle was working to get out whatever was filling his lungs. This was the closest I'd ever been to a human. It was an awful sight.

But I was curious. I paused in the doorway and took a look back. There was no sign of anyone. Either the men at the fire hadn't heard the coughing or didn't care.

I pulled myself up into the car and plopped down next to the old man, shifting so that the light could still shine down on his face. The stench in the car was overwhelming.

"That you, Ridge?" he rasped. His face was covered with sweat.

"No," I said.

He blinked and looked over at me, his eyes widening for a second. My back was to the moon, so he couldn't have seen more than my silhouette, but it was enough.

"Who are you?" he asked.

"Nobody," I said. "Just me."

"What are you?" he asked. He didn't sound afraid. "Are you an angel?"

"Something like that."

He nodded. It was weird. It was like he had been expecting me or something. It was then that I realized what

I was there for, why I'd climbed in there to begin with. The old man had figured it out before me.

"I'm in a bad way," he moaned.

"So it seems," I said.

"Hand me my bottle, will you?" he asked, and gestured toward the corner of the car. He started coughing so bad he could barely get his words out. "It's in that bag there," he said.

I went over and poked around the shadows until I found the shopping bag with the bottle in it. I pulled it out and brought it over to him. For a moment he just rested it on his chest, pointing it at the sky. Its curved glass reflected the bright square of the boxcar's open door, a window for the moon. The bottle was empty but for a small bit at the bottom.

"Been saving this," he said. "It's the good stuff."

He was wheezing pretty heavily. Then he glanced my way. "Got no regrets," he said. " 'Course I got no family nor no money, neither. But I got no regrets."

"That's good," I said. I suddenly didn't want to look at him.

He struggled to pull himself up until he rested on one elbow, and then unscrewed the cap. I had never smelled anything like it before. To this day I still can't stand the smell of whiskey.

"Cheers," he said, raising the bottle to me.

"Cheers," I whispered.

He tipped the bottle and emptied it in one swig, then sank back to the floor, gasping. "Better."

Though the rattle in his chest didn't diminish, his breaths came slower and he seemed to relax a bit. He'd closed his eyes and I thought he'd fallen asleep when I heard him say something. I told him I hadn't caught what he'd said, so he said it again, and this time I leaned way down so that even breathing through my mouth I could smell the rotten, boozy odor of his breath.

"Mercy," he whispered.

I won't describe what happened next.

I can hardly recall it anyway. I just remember being surprised at the strength with which the old man kicked out before it was over and the grip he had on my arms. Most of all I remember thinking over and over again, *Please don't open your eyes.*

Then he was gone. Moving back to where I'd been sitting earlier, I watched the light play over his body. He looked better in death.

It hit me all at once. I could feel myself stiffen, overwhelmed both by the rush of killing and my revulsion at the deed, and I shuddered the way he had at the end. I felt disgusting and full, like I'd just eaten too much of something sickly sweet.

"There you go," I said to her, even though my mother wasn't there. Good thing, probably. But I could still hear her voice in my head—"*Well, he was just about dead anyway. Where's the challenge in that? And he practically wanted you to. You did him a favor.*" I don't know, maybe it was what I wanted to hear right then.

I reached over and placed my hands on his chest the way she'd taught me. Soon enough I could feel him drawing into me. I gasped. I didn't think it would hurt that much. It was worse than any pain I'd felt before—like my whole skin was on fire, like a part of me was being torn away, though really it was just rearranging. It didn't take long. A lot less than the actual killing part.

I looked down at my worn hands, the nails dirty and cracked, then picked up the bottle and turned to face the moon. There he was in the glass, his scraggly face staring back at me, wrapped around the bottle's curve like a label.

Voices called out and I ducked back inside, pressing into the darkened corner of the car.

"Loamer!" they cried. A minute later, one of the men from the fire poked his head in.

"There he is," he said. He climbed in and went over to the old man. "Come on, Loamer. Get your ass up."

Another man stood outside and peered in. "He sleeping?"

The first man prodded him a little with his foot. "Nope. Old geezer's kicked the bucket."

"I get his stuff," said the man looking in.

"Screw you, Myers. I found him first."

"Yeah, well, I loaned him five bucks last week and he never paid me back, so call it collateral."

It went on like this for several minutes before they finally agreed to split the old man's belongings. Watching them go through his stuff, I could feel myself grow more and more nervous—I had no idea what I'd do if they saw me. But it wasn't just that. I needed the old man's clothes, and I was afraid they'd take everything.

Fortunately they didn't bother with Loamer's clothing—it must have stunk too much even for them. I breathed a sigh of relief as they left, then crept from the shadows and dressed myself in the remaining rags as quickly as I could before covering the old man with a blanket. It didn't seem right leaving him all naked like that, dead or not. I was about to cover his face, when something around his neck caught the moonlight.

I'm surprised the two bums missed it. I took the necklace off and held it up to the light. Attached to the chain was a tiny medallion with the picture of a robed man on the front with a halo over his head. "Saint Jude" was engraved on the back in small letters. I didn't know who that was, but it was kind of cool. I put it around my own neck—a memento of my first time.

The coast was clear, so I dropped out of the boxcar and began stumbling down the tracks, surprised at how stiff my legs felt. I was a bit numb from what I'd just done, but that wasn't the reason I was lame. Though the change is mostly skin deep, you still take on a little bit of the person you become. And here I was, a sixteen-year-old doppelganger in prime shape suddenly with an old man's body—it took a bit of getting used to.

After everything that had happened, I was tired and sick. Sick of myself and sick of this place. So an hour later, when the first train came along and I spotted an empty boxcar, I hopped on board. As I watched the city fade and the stars come back, I felt a strange kind of relief. I'd gotten it out of the way, and maybe I'd even helped the old man by doing it. Most of all I was just relieved to stop moving, to finally sleep and let the rocking train decide my destination for me.

CHAPTER THREE

For the next couple of weeks, I rode the trains, bumming my way across the country. It wasn't bad. I saw some pretty interesting places. Eventually the mountains shrank to a tiny row of bumps on the horizon, and I crossed the plains and saw fields of wheat ready for harvest, rolling out from the tracks like golden sheets of silk. Then the plains ended and the land turned green and hilly, dotted with farms and the occasional town.

Every few days I'd hop off the train and head into a new town. It took me a while to work up the courage the first time. I had to keep reminding myself who I was—or rather, who I looked like. Though I felt bad about what I'd done to the old man, it was nice to walk out in the open and pass people on the street. 'Course, looking the way I did, they still gave me nasty glances, but at least they didn't run away in horror or try to capture me.

It's funny—some of them actually helped me. I was sitting near a street corner the afternoon of my first excursion, back against a building, just watching people go by and minding my own business, when someone dropped a dollar at my feet. I remember picking it up and looking at it sort of confused. I almost jumped up and ran after the guy to return it. But then another person did the same thing, and some others threw some coins down. Before long I had more than ten bucks. Then there were people who called me names and said all sorts of rotten things. One person did both—first he called me a filthy beggar, then he gave me a five-dollar bill. Humans can be strange.

After a while I had enough money to buy some food. I found a grocery store and stocked up on candy bars and cans of tuna. I even bought some beans. My mother always fixed me beans from a can, to the point where I swore I'd never eat beans again when I was on my own, but for some reason I missed them. Since the old man had nothing left for supplies after his friends had gotten through with him, I bought a new spoon, a can opener, and a lighter with the last of the money. Then I hit the road again, catching another train out of town.

And that's how I ended up in Bakersville. It was the fourth town I stopped in, and as far as I could see, it looked like all the others—the same kind of main street with the same kinds of stores, parks, churches, same everything. It was a warm afternoon, and I was on the corner, doing my best to look down and out, which wasn't too hard. I had the whole thing down to an art at this point and was raking in the dough, when these three guys wearing football jackets came by and stopped to check me out. The one on the left was short with curly brown hair. The name stitched on his jacket was Josh. The one on the right was taller and blond. His name was Steve. The kid in the middle had black hair combed back and a sharp nose. That was Chris. He was a good-looking guy—like the kind I used to see on soap operas—but there was an edge to him, as if there was a storm brewing behind his eyes. I sensed trouble.

"Hey, Chris," Steve sneered, "since when do we have beggars in town?"

"Since never," said Chris.

"Man, I can smell him from here," Josh said.

"Spare some change?" I murmured, and held out my hand. I could see it was shaking a little.

"Get a job," Chris snarled.

I'd seen jocks on TV before. These three didn't seem much different from them, maybe a little meaner. But I knew they liked to joke around and give each other a hard time.

"Sure," I said. "Just tell me where your mother lives and I'll be right over."

Looking back, I guess it was a stupid thing to say. But at the time, I was just trying to get along, maybe draw a laugh. Jocks are always talking about each other's mothers.

It sort of worked—the other two laughed. Unfortunately, Chris didn't.

"You stupid old bastard," Chris snarled, and took a step toward me. Both his friends grabbed him by the arms and yanked him back.

"Forget it, Parker. Come on," Josh said, nodding toward the corner.

Shaking his friends off, Chris scowled at me for a second. Then he glanced both ways down the sidewalk and, seeing no one nearby, turned back and spit on me.

It hit me on the arm. I looked down at it and did nothing. But as my heart started to pound, I could feel a little prickle along the back of my neck where the hairs were standing up.

As they walked away, Chris looked back and glared, then the three turned the corner. I was glad to see them go.

I forgot all about Chris and his pals until they showed up later that night. I'd made my way out of town to a deserted meadow off the tracks. I had a little fire going and was trying to enjoy my beans. But it was hard—I was starting to feel a bit at odds with my form, sort of itchy and a bit ragged around the edges. I mean, it wasn't horrible or anything, but it just depressed me because I had no idea how much time I had before it would get too uncomfortable to bear. And when it did, I'd be right back where I started.

I was in the middle of eating when I heard their voices on the tracks. I glanced up and saw them coming out of the dark. I knew who they were right off—their jackets gave them away.

"Well, look who it is," Steve shouted.

"So this is where bums go at night," Josh pitched in.

Chris didn't say anything. He just smiled when he saw me. As they drew in toward the light, I could see he was carrying a bottle. It looked just like the one the old man had owned and was just as empty. Between the bottle and their weaving, I knew I was in for a rough time. I thought about making a run for it, but I figured I didn't have a chance outrunning the three of them.

They walked up to the fire and surrounded me. For a minute they didn't say anything. I could see the other two

21

looking over at Chris. It was like they were trying to decide what to do. Whatever it was, I was sure it involved kicking my ass.

"You guys want some beans?" I asked, and held out the can with the spoon in it. I wasn't sure if being friendly would work, but I didn't know what else to say.

Chris kicked the can out my hand. *So much for that,* I thought.

"Shut up," he said. "Don't talk."

Steve threw the rest of the wood I'd gathered on the fire. The clearing darkened. Then Chris poured what was left in the bottle onto the fire. There was a *whoosh!* as the flames leaped up, and for a moment everyone froze, squinting at the light.

"Hey, what are you doing!" Josh hollered. "What a waste."

"Shut up," Chris snarled back.

"I'll buy you some more if you want," I offered, rubbing my hand.

"I can get it whenever I want," Chris said, whirling around to face me. "And I told you to shut up."

He chucked the bottle. I saw it spinning at my head and turned so that it merely glanced off my shoulder. They all laughed.

I shrank into myself as they closed in, but a part of me was starting to get pissed off. I could feel my heart begin pounding the way it had back in town when Chris had spit on me. Still, I didn't want any trouble. I just wanted them to go away.

"Why are you doing this?" I said, looking up into each of their faces. "I'm nobody."

"That's right," Chris said. "You are nobody. A useless piece of shit. So who cares?"

He pushed me backward, then gave me a kick. I rolled over onto my stomach. Then Steve joined in, and pretty soon the two were taking turns kicking me while Josh stood back and watched. I tried crawling away, tried pleading with them to stop, but they just hollered and laughed and kept on going. It didn't really hurt that much, at least not at first. But toward the end, they started kicking harder. Then came the big blow.

I remember seeing Chris come at me with the bottle, but before I could react, Steve nailed me in the side with a good one and I got distracted. The next thing I knew, I felt a shock and heard the sound of breaking glass. I collapsed and sort of went limp for a moment, trying to remember where I was and what was going on. Finally I managed to open my eyes a crack and saw the fire burning, and it all came back to me.

"Dude, you killed him," Josh said. He sounded scared.

"No, look. He's still breathing," Steve said, but he sounded just as scared.

"Hardheaded bastard," I heard Chris say.

"Good thing," Steve said. "Come on, let's get back to the car."

"Yeah, I'm bored," Josh said. "Let's go, Parker. It's getting late."

"What are you talking about?" Chris said. "We're just getting started."

"Funny," Josh said. "I'm out of here. Coming?"

"Yeah," I heard Steve say.

"Don't be a pussy, Josh."

"Screw you, Chris," Josh said. "You're whacked."

Chris laughed. "Go ahead," he said. "I'll catch up with you guys in a few minutes."

I turned to watch Steve and Josh head back toward the tracks. A minute later they disappeared into the darkness. Chris and I were alone.

I managed to push myself back up. I was feeling a bit spinny and there was a pretty good lump rising on the back of my head, but nothing seemed broken. As for Chris, he just sort of paced back and forth in front of me, glaring.

"You got what you came for," I gasped. "Go back with your friends and leave me alone."

"Take it back," he said.

"Take what back?"

"What you said today. About my mother."

It took me a moment to remember what he was talking about. "All right," I said. "I take it back. I'm sorry."

I figured maybe now he'd go, but he just started pacing faster and breathing sort of funny, like he was huffing through his cheeks or something. It kind of creeped me out.

"No, really," I said. "I shouldn't have said it. I'm sorry."

He crouched down and stared into the fire. He wouldn't look at me. It seemed like he was calming down, like maybe I could talk to him.

"You're right about not talking about someone's mother," I said. "I just wasn't thinking. If you knew my mother, you'd probably understand," I tried joking. "You close to your mother?"

"Not really," he muttered.

"Or maybe your father?" I offered. "I never knew my father."

24

He stood up and loomed over me. "What the hell do you care? You don't know the first thing about my family."

"Okay, okay," I said, raising my hands. His shoulders sank a bit as he turned away. "You know, you shouldn't be so mean," I said to him. "Maybe people would like you better."

"People like me," he snapped. "Everyone likes me."

I found that hard to believe, but I wasn't about to argue with him. "Then what are you so pissed off about?" I asked.

He bent down and picked up a shard of glass from the broken bottle, almost losing his balance as he stood back up. "Because the world's a crappy place," he said, looking down at the shard.

He kept on going, his voice rising. "A crappy place, filled with crappy people like you."

I could tell he was getting pretty hot, but I wasn't in the mood to try to soothe him anymore. My head was really starting to pound, and all his talk just made it beat harder.

"And what about you?" I said, pulling myself to my feet. "I'd include you in that category."

"Yeah, me too," he said, advancing on me. I could see the hate returning in his eyes, only this time it wasn't for me. But as I watched his fists clench, I wondered if it even mattered. "I'm as crappy as they come. The worst."

"Why?" I said. "Is that what you want?"

"What I want?" he asked, his face crinkling in disbelief. "What does that have to do with anything?"

He tossed the shard aside and stepped up to me, so that I could smell the whiskey on his breath. My stomach churned as I thought of the old man again. I pictured him right there before me, gasping out his last moments. His final word echoing in my head.

"Mercy."

I must have said it out loud. There was a brief look of shock on Chris's face. Then the storm in those eyes erupted. It was as if it enraged him that I dared make such a request, that I dared ask for something like that from him. Without a word he hauled off and punched me in the face, and suddenly I was falling back again. I had barely hit the ground when he jumped on top of me and began punching me over and over again, screaming.

Just like back in the boxcar, everything became a blur. I remember the blows—heavy, with a viciousness the previous beating had lacked. I remember just wanting him to stop, and trying to tell him so through the pain. Then something in me snapped. I grabbed his falling fist with one hand, his throat with the other, and the next thing I knew, we'd flipped over and I was on top of him. The old, withered flesh of my arms started to ripple and melt away as I squeezed harder and harder, with both hands on his throat, no longer a weak old man. His eyes widened as the shell of my adopted form fell away for good—a look of incomprehension that slipped into pure, unadulterated fear, then slipped further, at last, into nothing.

When it was over, I rolled off him onto my back and just lay there next to him, panting.

The fire had died down some, and the dark had crept in closer by the time I sat up. Seeing Chris staring at the sky with his mouth still open, I could feel my heart start to pound all over again. That same sweet sickness as before filled me, and my stomach heaved.

"You idiot," I muttered, staring down at him. "You stupid idiot."

I just kept saying it over and over again, every time I looked at him. For the first time in years, I wanted to cry. But I didn't. I guess doppelgangers don't have the ducts for it.

I looked down at my body. There it was—the familiar gray skin, the floppy feet. I'd lost Loamer for good.

Kneeling down beside Chris, I knew what I had to do, but I just couldn't bring myself to do it. Once again my mother's voice sounded in my head. *Well, for God's sake, don't waste him. Make a go of it this time. You've already got the hard part out of the way. Just follow through for once.*

"But I'm not ready," I said. "I haven't had any preparation. I don't even know where he lives." But I knew she was right. It would be a waste.

I placed my hand on his chest. A moment later it was done. The pain wasn't bad this time—I hardly felt anything. Drawing back, I marveled at the skin—firm, pink, the joints supple. It felt good to take on someone my own age.

I removed his clothing and dressed as quickly as I could in the cold. Pulling his wallet from the pocket of his jeans, I opened it and looked inside at his driver's license. His face—now mine—stared back at me with a smile. It looked so different from the cold visage next to me. I covered the picture with my thumb and focused on the information. There it was—his name, date of birth, height, weight, eye color, sex, and, most importantly, his address—all the details of his life squeezed onto a two-by-three-inch piece of plastic. There wasn't much else in the wallet—a few dollars, a fake ID, some random cards.

And then I found her, tucked into a back fold. I pulled the picture out and held it up to the light. She was a little scuffed, but I could still make out the ringlets of red hair and the eyes that sparkled even in the worn photo. I had seen plenty of beautiful women on TV, but never anyone so beautiful in quite this way. I flipped the picture over and saw—written in smudged round letters—"Amber."

I stuck the picture back in the fold, slipped the wallet in my jacket pocket, and stood up.

I knew I had to get rid of the body. Mother always told me it was one of the most important parts. I didn't have the time or tools to bury him right now, so I'd have to stash him somewhere where nobody would find him. This is why it helps to prepare ahead of time, but once again I'd messed up. Of course, it's easier to hide someone when no one else knows they're supposed to be looking for him. Still, I didn't want to just dump Chris in the woods—who knew what might get after him. Suddenly I got an idea.

I jogged over to the tracks and walked along the bank, and pretty soon I found what I was looking for. The culvert—a corrugated drainpipe running under the tracks—was less than three feet in diameter. It wasn't ideal, but it would do.

I went back to my pack and pulled out a rolled-up sheet of plastic that I'd found last week in an empty boxcar. I had been using it as a groundsheet to keep the moisture out as I slept. It had worked pretty well, but I wouldn't need it anymore.

The hardest part was getting him to the culvert. His license said 175 pounds, but he felt a lot heavier than that. I carried him over my shoulder at first, but then it got to be too much, so I just put him down and dragged him the rest of the way over grass already soaked with dew. It seemed to take forever, and I kept waiting for Josh and Steve to show up, wondering where their buddy was. Finally I got him over there, laid him out, and wrapped him up. After I finished, I just looked down at him for a minute. I couldn't really see him through the plastic, but I knew the expression on his face hadn't changed.

"Sorry things turned out this way," I said, standing over him beneath the cold stars. I felt like I should say something, like I should try and reassure him.

"I'll try not to screw it up too bad."

I was worn out after hauling him all that way, but I managed to get him stuffed in there pretty well. I put him in headfirst and pushed and pushed until he was out of sight.

Then I said good-bye one last time, climbed up onto the tracks, and headed for town.

Steve and Josh were waiting about a half mile away where the tracks passed an empty lot. I took a few deep breaths and walked up to them.

"Hey, guys," I said. They jumped at the sound of my voice. They'd been talking and hadn't seen me.

"Christ, you scared the crap out of me," Steve said.

"Good thing you showed up," Josh added. "We were just about to leave your sorry ass."

"How's the old man?" Steve asked.

"He's gone," I muttered.

"Got rid of him, huh?" Josh said.

"Well . . . ," I said.

"I don't want to know," Josh said, holding up his hands and laughing nervously.

"Let's get out of here," Steve said. We left the tracks and headed down to Steve's car, a beat-up Ford Escort parked in the corner of the lot. I sat in the backseat as we drove off, not saying much of anything. Not that it would have mattered—with the music thudding from the zillion speakers Steve had in his car, they probably wouldn't have been able to hear me anyway. A little while later, they pulled over in front of a house partway down a crowded street. The lights were out in all the houses. A street lamp cast the only glow around. Josh clicked off the stereo, and the car suddenly went silent and still.

"Here you go, pal," Steve said, glancing up to look at me in his rearview mirror. "Try not to look too hung over tomorrow. We've got a big practice."

"Yeah," I said, nodding, "big practice."

I got out of the car. As I was heading across the lawn toward the house, Steve rolled down the window and called out, "Need a ride in the morning?"

That's right. School.

"No thanks," I said. At this point I didn't see myself making it to school. Not tomorrow, anyway.

"All right. Later."

I watched them speed off, then turned and looked things over. A bike was lying on the scraggly lawn in front of me, the grass growing up between the spokes of its wheels. The house was a single-story ranch. Even in the semidarkness, I could tell it looked sort of run down.

Chris Parker, I said to myself, *welcome to your life.*

CHAPTER FOUR

The front door was locked, so I went around to the back porch off the kitchen and tried the sliding glass door. It opened, and I poked my head in. A light over the sink glowed weakly, but it was enough to see by. The house was quiet. Everyone seemed to be asleep, but I didn't want to stick around the kitchen long enough to find out. I had to find Chris's room and just pray no one else shared it.

I stepped in and slid the door shut behind me as quietly as I could. The first thing that struck me was the smell. It was the smell of a human home—a heavy mix of foods, soaps and cleaners, cigarette smoke, and body odor. And there was something else.

A sudden jingling noise startled me. I froze with my back against the door, and a second later the source of that strange odor appeared as a dark shape glided into the kitchen. The next thing I knew, I was face-to-face with a black dog. A big black dog. Seeing me, it pranced forward, wagging its tail in welcome, then stopped three feet away, its entire body stiffening. Dogs—they're just like doppelgangers. They can tell who's human and who's not. They can smell it.

The last time I was this close to a dog was when I'd had that little puppy my mother brought home. I still remember her taking its limp form from my hands and pitching it into the woods. I'd looked for the body the next morning, but it was gone.

I bent down on one knee and reached out to pet the dog, wondering if it was Chris's or if it belonged to the whole family.

"Hey, boy. How ya doin'?" I said. I didn't know if it was actually a boy or not, but that's what people always say on TV.

The dog cocked its head at the sound of Chris's voice. Then its hackles raised. The poor thing was so confused, it didn't know whether to attack or jump up and start licking me. After a few seconds, it just gave up and slunk away, giving me one last skeptical glance before disappearing.

I went from the kitchen into a hallway. The living room opened out to my right, while the hall continued to my left with doorways on both sides. The little bit of light from the kitchen revealed a set of photos on the wall, and I paused to meet my new family. I found Chris in one of the pictures—looking a few years younger, dressed in a baseball uniform, smiling, with a bat over his shoulder. Beside it was a family portrait. Just what I was hoping for. There was Chris, flanked by a man and a woman on one side and a girl who appeared a good deal younger than him on the other. They all resembled each other—two parents, two kids, one big happy family. At least, that's what it looked like.

I headed down the hall and passed the open door of a bathroom with a closed door directly across from it. Beyond them, at the end of the hall, were two more doorways. I went to the end of the hall and tried the door on my left, opening it a hair and putting my eye up to the crack. I could make out a double bed with two people sleeping in it. One of them stirred. I shut the door as quickly as I could.

I heard the bed creak on the other side of the door, followed by footsteps. Without thinking, I opened the door behind me, ducked inside, and pulled it closed. I spotted an empty bed and jumped in, throwing the sheets over me and praying nobody would come in.

It wasn't so much that I was afraid of getting in trouble. I just didn't want to talk to anybody right then. I was still pretty rattled from everything that had happened and wanted some time to settle down and ease into my new life. Get a lay of the land.

For a whole minute, I waited in bed, facing the wall as my heart pounded in my ears. Suddenly a toilet flushed, and I breathed a sigh of relief. A moment later the door opened and a slit of hallway light flashed upon the wall before me. I froze, resisting the urge to turn and see who was watching me, focusing instead on the shadow my head cast against the wall. Finally the door closed.

I waited until I couldn't feel my pulse throb anymore before slipping out of bed and switching on the desk lamp. Chris's room was pretty spare, almost as bad as mine had been at the cabin. At least I'd had an excuse—I was pretty much a shut-in. Chris might as well have been. I looked around at the mostly bare walls, trying to get a sense of things, and guessed there wasn't too much to this kid. It didn't appear that he had many hobbies or special skills I was going to have to deal with. That's one of my recurring nightmares, by the way—I take on a form only to discover that the person is, like, a master bagpipe player or something ridiculous like that. As far as Chris was concerned, there was sports—football, basically—and that seemed to be it. All to the good, I thought—it was going to make my life simple.

There were a couple things on the wall—an AC/DC poster, another of some sports star—but not much else. No real toys that I could see, aside from a football on top of the bureau next to a piggy bank. There was a stereo with maybe a dozen or so CDs in beat-up jewel cases. And then there was the TV—a nice one, bigger than the one I used to have. I went over and flipped it on, turning down the volume until I could barely hear it. It was incredible—the image so sharp, the colors like real life. And the channels. My old set had had an antenna that picked up four, sometimes five, channels with varying degrees of success, depending on the weather, my patience for fiddling around with it, or the mood it was in. This TV had channel after clear channel. And there were channels just for news, sports, food, all kinds of different things.

I plopped myself down on the floor and settled in for a good hour or two of TV time. I had a bit of catching up to do, and it helped take my mind off all the night's ugliness. After a while, though, I started getting sleepy, so I grabbed the remote, got up, and went back over to the bed. I was about to get in when I noticed the sheets.

Race cars. Chris had race car sheets. It struck me as a little funny at first, and then sad as the memory of what had happened around the fire came back to me. I tried to imagine that same drinking, swearing, screaming boy coming home and curling up in his race car sheets to go to sleep.

But not tonight. Not any night, not anymore. Instead it was me who was curling up with the race cars. Chris was out there in a musty old culvert, by now as cold as the plastic he was wrapped in, not even able to see the sky. And I was the one who had put him there.

I picked up the remote and flipped around until I came to a rerun of *Gilligan's Island*. It seems like there's always *Gilligan's Island* playing on some station. Even growing up with only four decent channels, I was able to see it pretty regularly. As a little kid, I didn't like the show. I felt scared for the castaways—lost, confined to an island with not much to live on. But to them everything was a big joke. It irritated me that I had to worry for them. Oh sure, they wanted to go home, but when every episode ended with them yukking it up, how serious could they be? As I got older, I lightened up. I figured maybe they were on to something. Maybe sometimes, to survive, you just have to make the best of what you've got.

"Chris, it's time to get up."

I opened my eyes to see Chris's mother standing over me in a pink bathrobe. She didn't look as good in real life—her eyes drooped with dark circles, her brown hair was going in all different directions, and her skin seemed pale and gray. Almost like a doppelganger's.

She walked over and turned off the television set.

"What were you doing watching TV?" she asked. She seemed pretty annoyed.

"I got up in the night," I said. "I was having trouble sleeping."

"Well, you got over it pretty well. It took me three tries to wake you."

"Sorry."

"Anyway, you better get up. Your father's already in the shower, so you'll have to wait. You're going to be late. Again. And this time I'm not going to write a note for you."

"I can't go to school," I said. I almost added "Mom." I wasn't sure what to call her—Mom, Mother, Ma?

"What's the matter this time?" she said, frowning.

"I don't feel good," I said. "I'm sick. My stomach really hurts." It wasn't true, but I knew as soon as I opened my eyes this morning that there was no way I could leave the house today. I needed more time.

She came over and felt my forehead.

"You don't have a fever." She grabbed my chin. "You got in late last night. Were you drinking?"

"No!" I exclaimed. It wasn't a lie—not really, anyway. "I just have a stomachache. Please let me stay home today?"

"Fine." She sighed and turned away. "I don't care, anyway. I've got to be at work in an hour." She paused in the doorway. "But you're telling your father. Not me."

"Okay," I said.

She frowned again. "You must be sick after all," she said, and disappeared.

I lay back in bed and looked up at the ceiling, trying to decide how that had gone. She didn't seem to suspect anything, other than some questionable activity on the real Chris's part. Fair enough.

"What the hell are you still doing in bed?" barked a voice so loud I nearly jumped out of my skin—literally. I looked over. This time it was the man from the picture standing over me, wearing nothing but a towel around his waist. Like Chris's mother, he didn't look so hot compared with the picture. He'd just gotten out of the shower, so his black hair was all messed up, and there was a trickle of blood running down his neck from where he'd cut himself shaving. Whereas Mrs. Parker had just seemed annoyed, Mr. Parker seemed mad as hell.

"I don't feel good," I croaked, trying to sound as sick as possible.

"Big deal," he said. "I feel like crap every morning, but I still get up and go to work."

"I can't go to school today. I really can't."

"But you felt good enough to go out last night and get drunk. And don't bullshit me, either. I know when you got in."

Now I knew where Chris had gotten his scintillating personality.

I figured there was no point arguing, so I just shut up and waited for him to decide what to do. As he stood there glaring, a girl dressed in school clothes appeared behind him in the doorway, looking in at me with quiet eyes. It was the sister.

"What's the matter with him?" she asked. Her voice was subdued, almost a monotone. There was something about her that creeped me out. I don't know what it was. I just wanted her to go away.

"Little baby says he's sick," Chris's father said.

"I'm sick, too," the sister replied.

"No you're not, Echo," he said, whirling around. "Now get your ass back in that kitchen and finish your breakfast before the bus comes."

Echo jumped and disappeared down the hall. Chris's father turned back and eyed me one last time.

"You'd better not leave the house today. I'll know it if you do, believe me. In fact, don't even get out of your goddam bed until I get home."

I shrank back and looked away.

I could feel him staring at me for a moment, like he was waiting for me to challenge him. When I didn't say anything, he turned and left, slamming the door behind him.

I sat up in bed shaking, trying to understand what had happened. I mean, this guy was even worse than Chris. My mother may have been cold, but even on her worst day, she had never gotten in my face. Then again, I'd never had a father before. *Maybe they're all like that*, I thought.

I waited in my room, listening to the Parkers as they dressed, ate breakfast, bickered, and hollered. Then one by one they left. Dad was the last to go. He stuck his head in one last time before heading out the door.

"And no TV," he snapped.

"Yeah, right," I said after the door shut.

From my bedroom window, I watched as Chris's father backed the car out into the street. Then he was gone. I had the place to myself.

I spent the rest of the day poking around, trying to learn as much as I could about my new home. Trying to forget how I'd gotten there to begin with. It wasn't easy, on either end.

I opened all of Chris's drawers, hoping to stumble

across a journal or diary, something to help me get a better sense of who this kid was. I came up empty. Searching his closet yielded nothing but a collection of porno mags hidden under a stack of sweaters. I admit I spent a bit of time poring over those.

There was nothing else of interest until I looked underneath Chris's mattress. There she was again. This time, instead of being scratched and jammed between the folds of a wallet, she was tucked inside a birthday card, smiling out of a glossy photo with trees and hills in the background. Amber was even more beautiful in the daylight.

I glanced at the card. There was that same handwriting from the back of the wallet photo—a loopy stream of letters. I read the note, dated last April. It was six months old.

> *Hey Chris,*
> *Happy Sixteenth Birthday. You took this picture, remember? Our first picnic together. It was so perfect. Why don't we do it again? Pretty soon school will be out. No more stupid practice. We can go to the lake and to the fair, okay? Things haven't always been perfect, but I forgive you, even though you're a jerk sometimes.*
> *Love, Amber*

It was nice. I put the picture up on the windowsill and slipped the card back under the mattress. Then I took it back out and read the card again, trying to imagine what her voice sounded like.

I went through the rest of the house. It may not have

been as big as most of the other places on the street, but it was bigger than the cabin I grew up in, and it took a while to go through all the rooms, especially since I had to be careful to put everything back exactly as I found it.

Echo's bedroom was across from the bathroom. Unlike Chris's bare room, it was full of all kinds of strange stuff. Dolls, toy ponies, snow globes, costumes—I went over everything, touching each object, picking things up, then putting them back. A few of the toys were familiar—I'd seen commercials for them on Saturday mornings in between the cartoons, but it was different seeing them in real life. Scattered across the floor or lying still upon the shelves, they seemed smaller, almost dead somehow.

The strangest thing in the room, though, was the frog. There was a terrarium in the corner of her room with a big green frog in it. It seemed like a funny thing for a girl to have. I went over and knocked on its glass, but the thing never moved from its rock in the corner of the glass cage. It just blinked its eyes a few times and that was it.

The parents' room was dark with the shades drawn, so that I had to turn on the overhead light to see. The first thing I noticed was a picture of Elvis on the wall above the bed—I recognized him right away in his rhinestone suit and flower necklaces. There were a few bottles of perfume on the bureau beside a cardboard box of jewelry and some photographs, including one that lay facedown. I picked it up to see what was in the frame—a wedding picture—and noticed the dark rectangle underneath where there wasn't any dust. I put the photo back down on its face and moved on.

It was while poking through the father's underwear drawer that I found the gun. If he was trying to hide it, he hadn't done a very good job. The pistol was wedged against one side, held in place with a pile of boxers, and I spotted it as soon as I opened the drawer. I pulled it out and studied it. I was pretty excited. I'd seen all kinds of guns on TV before, and now here was one in real life. I remember being surprised at how heavy it was. And at the smell—that strange mix of metal, oil, and powder. After fiddling with it awhile, I managed to get the clip out. No bullets.

The living room was plain: TV against the far wall. No books to speak of. A desk in the corner stacked with bills and other papers. I noticed some burn marks on the plaid couch, and there was a pile of newspapers and a dirty ashtray on top a frail-looking coffee table. The dog lay curled up on a gray comforter like it was just another piece of furniture, watching me out of the corner of its eye.

"Just you and me today," I said to it.

The dog sort of sniffed and looked away.

"Come on," I said, "don't be that way."

I went over to pet it, but as I drew closer, its ears flattened, its eyes flicked up toward me, and the lowest murmur rumbled in its throat. Not quite a growl, but I decided not to take any chances.

"Another time then," I said, backing away.

I found out later that the dog's name was Poppy. Old Poppy never did warm up to me. Maybe he knew what I'd done.

I turned to the desk and looked through some of the papers, mostly money stuff—bills, a few paycheck stubs, things like that. I learned that Chris's father's name was Barry and that he worked at a plumbing supply store. The mother's name was Sheila. She worked at Wal-Mart.

The only part of the house I hadn't explored yet was the basement. I found the door to it in the kitchen and headed down the wobbly steps. The heavy odor of concrete filled the space, and the two naked bulbs at either end cast a feeble light. The air seemed thick. There was the furnace and water heater in one corner. A freezer chest, washing machine, and dryer in the other. The third corner was full of messily stacked boxes and bins. I didn't feel like going through them. *Later*, I thought.

The fourth corner was blocked off by a pair of sheets hanging from a clothesline nailed to the joists. I poked my head in and saw a tiny table with chairs around it. Some of the chairs had stuffed rabbits and bears in them, a few were empty. There was a little lamp in the corner next to a toy carriage and beside the carriage was a box full of toy tractors, dump trucks, bulldozers, and cars. I turned on the lamp and looked through the box. The toys inside were all pretty beat up, but neatly arranged. In fact, the whole corner was tidy, with everything, even the chairs, symmetrically ordered. There were some pictures on the wall that I guessed Echo had drawn. They were cute—pictures of her stuffed bears and her frog, all playing in a field with the sun shining down, a big yellow circle spiked with orange. Other scenes were at night, with the bears dancing beneath the moon. The whole thing was kind of weird, but so far it was my favorite place in the entire house.

I turned the lamp off and headed upstairs. All in all, I wasn't sure what to make of the Parkers' house. I'd seen plenty of family homes on TV, especially in the sitcoms, but this was different. It wasn't so much the clutter, or even the smells all stirring together. There was a dingy feeling about the place, as if a layer of some kind of poisonous dust had fallen over everything in the house: invisible, but palpable. I don't know what I'd been expecting, but somehow the whole place seemed less real than the homes I'd gotten to know on all my favorite shows.

I went back to Chris's room for some daytime TV. *Gilligan's Island* was on (of course), but I didn't watch it. There was a football game on one of the sports channels, so I watched that instead. I decided I should bone up. Who knew what position Chris might play? It felt good to study the game, to take note of what all the players were doing. I was getting a grip, taking control. I could do this.

At halftime I flicked to a local channel in time to catch the news flash. The caption in big letters along the top— "Body Found"—made my heart start to pound. The anchor was talking, and beneath the caption was a box showing footage of police carrying a blanketed stretcher. I turned up the volume and listened.

" . . . today recovered the remains of twenty-six-year-old Jill Vitelli, last seen on Friday. Her body was discovered this morning outside of Springfield by a fisherman along the banks of the Killmartin River. There is no word yet on whether foul play was involved, but local police have begun an investigation. Channel Six News has learned that Vitelli's car, a 1998 white Subaru Legacy, is currently missing, though police at this time have not officially confirmed this. We will, of course, follow up on this breaking story at the six o'clock hour. Now, back to *One Life to Live*."

I lay back and breathed a sigh of relief. Springfield was a ways away from here—the train had brought me through

43

there a few days ago. I flicked back to where the game had restarted, but I just couldn't pay attention. The news still had me rattled. I suddenly thought of my mother. An image of her driving down the road in a Subaru flashed through my head, and I wondered where she was now, what she looked like.

I heard a noise outside and looked out the window to see a big yellow school bus pull up to the curb across the street. A minute later it drove away, leaving behind a whole crowd of kids. I spotted Echo in the group. She was talking to a few other girls as the others dispersed. Pretty soon it was just Echo and another girl, and then that girl left and Echo was all alone. She poked around on the sidewalk for a few minutes, looking smaller now, with her black jacket tucked under her arm. Finally she crossed the street and let herself into the house, coming in through the back door like I'd done last night.

I turned the TV's volume down and listened to Echo bustle around in the kitchen. Part of me wanted to go out there and talk to her, maybe feel her out a little bit. What kind of brother was I? How was I supposed to treat her? What did she call our parents? What did she think of them? But I held back and closed the door instead.

A half hour later, there was a knock. I could hear Echo call my name, but I just got into bed and pulled the sheets over my head until she went away.

I know. I'm a real coward sometimes, but there was still something about Echo that bothered me. The image from this morning of her standing in the doorway came back into my head, and I suddenly realized what it was. It was that girl, the one I'd seen on TV back when I was Echo's age, the one whose form my mother had taken on, whose schoolbooks became my schoolbooks for the next year. Echo looked just like her—not so much the face, but the hair and the clothes, the backpack. It was all so familiar. Those parents probably never found their daughter, just like at some point Echo's brother would disappear and she and her parents would never find him. It was only a matter of time. And I was the only one who knew it.

Of course, my mother would have a different take. *"You're overthinking things,"* she'd probably say. *"Just become the form. Forget about your own miserable self for once."*

And she would probably be right.

Later that evening Echo knocked, then poked her head in. I hit the mute button.

"Supper's ready," she said. "Mom told me to get you. She made yellow meal."

"Okay," I said, wondering what "yellow meal" was. I got out of bed and followed Echo down the hall.

"Yellow meal" turned out to be frozen fish patties heated in the oven, Kraft macaroni and cheese, and canned corn. Apparently it was my favorite. To be honest, it was pretty good, if a bit monochromatic, and I was hungry, too, having eaten only half a can of beans in the last two days. Still, I was supposed to be sick, so I poked the food around the plate a bit at first. I figured sick people weren't supposed to seem too eager.

"Still not feeling great, huh?" Sheila asked, watching me. "By now you've usually inhaled your first plate and reloaded for seconds."

Before I could answer, she turned and hollered into the living room.

"Barry, get in here! Your supper's getting cold!"

A minute later Barry came in, the smoke from the last drag of his cigarette still trailing from his nostrils. He swigged the remnants of his beer and set it down next to the two other empty cans on the counter.

"You left the TV on, Dad," Echo said. Barry turned to her but didn't say anything, and after a second Echo looked down at her food.

"How was work?" Sheila asked.

"A bitch. Big delivery in the morning, then a bunch of pipes broke at the hospital and I had guys coming in all afternoon looking for this and that. I told Mitch, another day like that and he could find himself a new manager."

"Careful," she said, "he might take you up on it."

"Funny, Sheila," he said. "He knows he could never make it without me there to run things for him."

"I suppose," she replied.

"No supposing," he said.

Then nobody said a word. We all just ate, staring at our plates, glancing up from time to time to see if anyone else was glancing up, and then ducking our eyes back down. Finally Barry broke the silence.

"And what about you?" he said, turning to me. "Is the little pansy going to be feeling good enough to go to school tomorrow?"

"Barry, stop it," Sheila said.

"Well, the game against Waterbury's coming up this

weekend. I don't care how good a linebacker he is, if he misses another practice, coach might not start him."

"I'm feeling better," I said.

"Well, start acting like it. You know, you look kind of funny. All pale and everything. Jesus, no wonder Amber doesn't call anymore." He started laughing.

"Barry, leave him alone," Sheila said. "Things are going fine with Amber. Isn't that right, Chris?" She turned and looked at me expectantly.

"Swimmingly," I said. I'd heard people say it in the movies before, and I always liked the sound of it. Unfortunately it didn't go over well with Barry.

"Swimmingly?" he said, scrunching up his face. "What are you, a faggot or something?"

"No," I said. "I just meant things were all right, that's all."

"Swimmingly," Echo said, then giggled to herself. She liked the word too.

"Shut up, Echo," her father barked.

"Swimmingly," Echo said again, laughing harder.

"Jesus Christ," he said, getting up. He grabbed his plate and went back into the living room. Sheila sighed and shook her head.

"Swimmingly," Echo murmured, smiling down at her plate.

"God, Echo, would you just shut up," Sheila said, slamming her fork down. Echo jumped at the noise, and I admit I did a little too. We watched as Sheila got up from the table with her plate, went over to the sink, and started doing the dishes, her face set hard.

Echo and I finished eating dinner alone. Neither of us spoke until the end.

"By the way," Echo said, "Amber did call. This afternoon."

"She did?" I said, snapping to attention.

"I tried to get you, but you wouldn't open your door."

"So what'd you do?"

"I told her you were sick."

"What did she say?"

"She said 'good.'"

As I lay in bed that night, I thought back over my first day
as Chris Parker. To be honest, I was a little disappointed.
Not so much with myself. Things hadn't gone perfectly—
or even swimmingly, for that matter—but I thought I'd
held my own. It had more to do with Chris's family. I
know. Who was I to be disappointed in anybody? But as
much as I hated killing Chris, a part of me had hoped to
find a home, join a real family like the ones I'd seen on TV,
even for a little while. Kind of sick, I guess. But the truth
sometimes is.

Problem was, I didn't really like my new family, and
they didn't seem to like me. In fact, I didn't think *any* of
them liked each other. Lying there in bed, I looked out the
window at the half-moon hanging in the sky. *Maybe I
should just leave*, I thought. Why stick around? Part of me
wanted to bolt. *You don't owe them anything. Get back on
the road.* But part of me knew it didn't matter whether I
owed them anything—I owed it to myself to stick it
through, to challenge myself, like my mother would have
wanted. *So the Parkers aren't your dream family*, I could hear
her say. *Big deal. Life is full of disappointments. Suck it up.*

In the end I couldn't bring myself to leave. Not for any

high-minded reason or anything like that. I just didn't have the energy. It was funny—I didn't go anywhere or do much of anything that first day, but for some reason I was exhausted. Maybe it was from more than just today. Maybe it was from everything that had happened the day before, or the week before, or ever since my mother kicked me out. Maybe it was my whole life.

CHAPTER FIVE

Getting to school wasn't too hard. I just stood out on the corner with a bunch of other kids my own age, and pretty soon a bus came by and picked us up. I was a little nervous when I first showed up and some of the kids started talking to me, but after a while I began to relax. It was kind of like a warm-up for the rest of the day.

Some guy asked me where I was yesterday, and I told him I was sick. Another asked with what, and I said it was my stomach. And blahbitty, blahbitty, blah. It's surprising how easy it is to fake it with most people, especially if they think you're who you appear to be and don't know any better. You just sort of keep your mouth shut for the most part, and spend the rest of the time agreeing with whatever the other person says. "You bet!" "You're right!" "Totally!" People like it when you agree with them. And if anybody notices anything different about you, you just say something like, "I'm just really tired," or "I don't feel so hot today," or "I think I'm coming down with something," and people pretty much let it slide. Besides, most of the stuff people talk about is meaningless anyway. Any moron can talk.

Pretty soon the bus dropped us off, and I found myself being ushered along with the crowd into a big brick building with a sign out front that said "Bakersville High School—Home of the Sharks," which I thought was pretty funny since we weren't anywhere near the ocean that I could tell.

I'd seen plenty of high school movies and TV shows before, so the scene inside wasn't too strange. The kids looked pretty much the same, all standing in clusters here and there along the hallways, talking, laughing. Even though it was first thing in the morning, it was a Friday, and people were excited for the weekend.

As I walked down the hall, kids kept saying "Hi!" to me as I passed, patting me on the back, or giving me a little punch on the arm. The girls were especially friendly. They kept giving me these smiles and saying "Hi, Chris," in this weird singsongy voice that made me feel a little prickly in a good sort of way. When Chris told me everybody liked him, I hadn't believed him, but it seemed now that he'd been right, and for the first time it felt good to be Chris Parker. So good that by the time I found Josh and Steve with a bunch of other jocks, I was brimming with confidence.

"What's up," Steve said, grinning and holding out his hand. I held out my hand too, and he grabbed it and did some weird little move that involved clapping and snapping and something else that I couldn't catch in time.

"What's up," I replied. That's another little trick I figured out—if someone says something to you and you're not sure how to respond, just repeat it back to them. Half the time they don't even notice.

"Missed you yesterday, Parker," Josh said. "Coach was mad. You better lay low at practice."

"Planning on it," I said.

"Hey, where's your jersey?" Steve said, giving me a little shove. One of the things I've noticed about human males, especially the jocks, is that they're always touching each other. They make a big deal about not being "queer," but between the shoving and punching and slapping, not to mention the headlocks and butt smacks, it's like they can't keep their hands off each other.

I quickly realized the rest of the guys were all wearing their football jerseys.

"In the wash," I said, hoping it would stick.

Steve shook his head. "I do *not* want to be you at practice today."

Great. The last thing I needed was to call attention to myself.

I stood around with the other guys for a while and half listened to them talk about football. From what I could gather, they were wearing their jerseys because of the game against Waterbury tomorrow, but I was more interested in finding Amber. Shouldn't she have met me by my locker? Isn't that what high school girlfriends are supposed to do?

By the time the bell rang for first period, any confidence I'd gained had vanished. I suddenly realized I had no idea where I was supposed to go. Fortunately good old Josh saved the day.

"Let's go, Parker. We got history."

"You're right," I said, and followed him down the hall.

After about a dozen steps he stopped, then I stopped, and we both just sort of looked at each other.

"Aren't you going to get your books?" he asked, gesturing toward the bank of lockers behind me.

Oops, I thought, following his gesture. This could be bad.

"Um," I tried to stall. "Ah, screw it," I suddenly said, and sort of shrugged my shoulders like I was tough and all, and to hell with school.

Josh just sort of shook his head and snorted. He pushed by me, went up to a locker, and banged twice. It opened to reveal a pile of books.

"Come on," he said. "You know how Johnson can be. Not that it matters—we're just going to be watching a video like we do every other day."

"All right," I said. I went up to the locker and peered in. There was a picture of some girl taped to the inside door that looked like it had been taken out of one of the magazines in Chris's closet. I looked over Chris's books as students continued to rush by on their way to class.

"Hurry up," Josh barked, "we're going to be late."

Finally I just grabbed the whole stack and followed Josh down the hall. We made it to class just in time, taking the last pair of seats as the bell rang. Mr. Johnson called the class to order, and I was off—my first day of school had officially begun.

Fortunately history turned out to be U.S. history, something I'd learned about already. Of course, it wasn't a high school book I'd studied back at the cabin, but based on the questions Mr. Johnson asked us, it wasn't that much harder. In fact, I don't mean to brag, but I seemed to know more than most of the other kids in the class did. It was early in the year, and we were in the middle of the Revolutionary War. After a bit of discussion, the lights were turned out and we watched a video, while Johnson graded papers at his desk.

The video was a documentary on the Founding Fathers. It turned out I'd seen the whole series three times already on public television, so I used the period to go through Chris's notebook and try to get a sense of what was going on. Fortunately his schedule was taped to the inside. History, study hall, science, phys ed, math, English—it all seemed pretty run of the mill. The only class that really raised a flag was Spanish 2, right before lunch. The only Spanish I knew was what I'd learned watching *Sesame Street*.

The bell rang and everyone headed out. Josh and I parted company, and I followed the door numbers until I found my next class.

The day went on like this. I kept a low profile, and nobody really called on me or anything. Even Spanish turned out not to be too bad. The teacher, Mrs. Olson, spoke mostly in English as we worked on conjugating verbs. At one point, though, she turned to me, rattled something off in Spanish, and waited. I just repeated it back to her and then held my breath as she gave me a sort of funny look and a few kids snickered. There was a long pause. *Uh-oh*, I thought.

"That was excellent, Chris," she said at last. "Really, a good job."

"*Gracias,*" I said, and smiled.

In spite of that, I found the period to be pretty stressful, so when the bell rang and everyone headed off, I went up to speak with her.

"I was wondering if it was too late to drop the class," I asked.

She frowned a little and shook her head. "It's still early enough in the year," she said, "but I wouldn't advise it. Remember, most colleges require at least two years of a language."

"Well," I said, "somehow I don't think I'll be going to college."

"Now, Chris," she said, "I know you've had your struggles in school, especially in my class, but you shouldn't give up. I hear a lot of talk about how you're due for a big football scholarship. Just stick with it. You've got a bright future ahead of you."

Yeah, really bright, I thought. "Thanks," I murmured. I suddenly wanted to disappear, to shrivel up and blow away or crawl into some dark hole. I wondered if that culvert Chris was in had room enough for two.

"Besides," she said, "I've never heard you speak so fluidly as you did today. It was beautiful—I think you may be turning a corner."

"Maybe," I said.

I turned and left the room, resisting the urge to break into a dead run and keep on going right out the front door. Instead, I ducked into the boy's bathroom and splashed some water on my face. All of a sudden, I wasn't feeling so good.

"Keep it together," I said, looking in the mirror, watching the water drip off my face.

That was when I saw it.

It started with just a little twitch in the corner of my right eye. As I leaned in to check it out, both eyes swelled to watery, yellow bulbs, both pupils drew into slits, and there I was, staring into doppelganger eyes. I jumped back and gasped.

It only lasted a moment before fading with no more than a ripple.

A toilet flushed, sending my heart into my throat. I dried my face with my shirt as one of the stall doors opened and a tall boy with a shaved head came out.

"Come on, Parker," he said, barely looking at me as he headed for the door. "You're going to miss lunch."

I followed him to the cafeteria and went to the end of the lunch line. It was pretty straightforward—get your tray, get your food, swipe your card, find a seat. I fumbled a little before finding the right card in Chris's wallet, but pretty soon I was through the line, looking desperately for a seat amid the sea of students. Steve flagged me as I drifted by.

I sat down, nodded to everyone at the table, and began picking at my food. It wasn't that I didn't have an appetite. I did. I hadn't had that much to eat these last few weeks and it was all starting to catch up with me. But suddenly I didn't feel like eating. It's like I couldn't swallow right or something. Meanwhile, Steve started going off on all the kids around us, making nasty comments about this guy's face or that girl's tits or which freshman he'd like to bang. Really gross stuff. I tried to ignore it for a while, but toward the end of lunch I just sort of lost it.

"Dude, will you shut up?" I said. I was practically yelling. I knew I shouldn't have said it, but I was still feeling pretty lousy from my talk with Mrs. Olson, not to mention freaked out by what I'd seen in the bathroom. A few heads turned.

Steve seemed pretty taken aback. He kind of shrank for a second.

"What's your problem?" he snipped. Then he looked up over my shoulder. "Oh, I get it," he said. He picked up his tray and left. So did everyone else.

"Feeling better?" a girl's voice said behind me.

Even before I turned, I knew it was her. I'd never heard her speak, but it was like I just knew. I looked up and saw her standing there in a cheerleading outfit, looking down at me. Her red hair was pulled partway back and hung around her like a fiery halo, and she was smiling, but in a weird sort of way. Her lips were tight, like she was trying to hold in a secret.

"Hi," I said, a bit hoarsely. I moved over and she sat down. As soon as she did, the smile dropped. I reached forward to take her hand and saw her flinch. It was almost imperceptible—I don't think anyone else noticed—but it made me pull back.

"I was looking for you this morning," I said.

"Funny," she said. Ouch. I could almost feel the ice crystals creeping up my legs from the bench we shared. I decided to just shut up.

"Where's your jersey?" she asked after a bit.

"Forgot it," I said. That goddam jersey.

"Great. At least we would have been matching. Now I look like even more of a dork in this thing," she said, giving a tug at her uniform. "And I swear just about every guy in school has checked out my ass today with this stupid skirt as short as it is."

"Can't say as I blame them," I said, trying to smile. I figured it was the kind of thing that Chris might say. I must have been right, because she gave me a nasty snort and rolled her eyes.

"So," she said, after a little bit, "we still going out tonight or what?"

I froze as soon as she said it.

She sensed my hesitation. "If you don't want to, that's fine with me. I'd just as soon not go. But Cheryl's been bugging me all week. Says she even got a DJ. I think it's that jerk who graduated last year. Oh, what's his name?"

"I don't remember," I said.

"Well, who cares, anyway."

"I do," I said. "I mean, I wouldn't mind going." I should have taken her up on her offer to bail, but for some reason, I didn't.

She looked at me and rolled her eyes again. "All right, whatever," she said. "Just pick me up at nine. You know how I hate getting there early."

"How about you pick me up?" I suggested. I didn't know how to drive, let alone where she lived. "My father needs the car," I explained.

"You mean I get to drive?" she said. "How enlightened of you."

The bell rang. Everybody around us started moving. She leaned in and fixed me with a glare.

"All I can say is, it better not be like last time."

"You mean last time wasn't good?" I asked. Big mistake on my part. As soon as I said it, she recoiled in disgust. I think if she'd had a knife, she would have stabbed me.

"You're a bastard," she said. She got up and left.

Way to go, Chris, I thought as I watched her walk away.

The last class of the day was English. The teacher, Ms. Simpson, was young and pretty, and you could feel the energy rise in the room the moment she walked in.

"All right, everybody, get out your *Macbeth*s and turn to act two. We're going to pick up where we left off yesterday."

I pulled out the paperback and checked the cover.

Shakespeare. I'd heard of the guy, but my mother never brought any of his stuff home for me to read.

"When we started this play at the beginning of the week, what was our take on Macbeth?" Ms. Simpson asked. "Susie?"

"Well, like, he was a hero, right?"

"Yeah, he was the good guy," a boy added.

"That's right," Ms. Simpson agreed. "Before we even saw him, we heard about his exploits. And, like you said, he was the hero. But what made him a hero? I mean, what was he doing, Richard?"

"Killing," Richard said. "The bleeding sergeant describes him slicing that rebel dude in half and sticking his head on a pole."

"That's right. And how does Duncan, the king, react to the description?"

"He gets all excited," a girl said.

"He does. And who can blame him? After all, Macbeth has just saved his royal rearend. But the point here is that, right away, Shakespeare's showing us that the world of the play is a violent one, and that everyone is complicit in that violence, from the king on down. Most of all our hero— Macbeth is knee-deep in it from the start."

"But even so, why does he turn around and suddenly go after the king?" a boy asked.

"It's his wife, man," Richard said. "You saw what she did to him. She totally manipulated him."

"So what?" the kid replied. "He's still responsible, isn't he?"

"You both raise interesting points," Ms. Simpson said. "What is it that leads Macbeth to do what he does? I want you all to think about that as we make our way through the scenes surrounding the murder. So let's get started."

I shrank in my seat as she went around handing out parts. Her eyes fell on me for a second, but she gave me a pass. I was glad—the last thing I wanted was to have to read in front of everyone on the first day. Not to mention the fact that all this talk about killing had me a little freaked out.

Of course, as soon as we started reading, things only got worse. Don't get me wrong, the play itself was great. I mean, I didn't understand half of what the characters were saying, but somehow it didn't matter. I understood enough, and Ms. Simpson explained the tougher parts. The trouble was that the play was almost too good. It was really creepy—all that darkness in the old castle and the weird hallucinations with the dagger and the blood. Shakespeare didn't depict the actual murder, but I wish he had. All I could see were my hands around Chris's throat, and that look of confused terror in his eyes. I can only imagine what he must have been thinking when that old man strangling him suddenly turned into a slimy monster. What a way to go.

At one point I almost bolted from the classroom. It was the part where Macbeth has just come back from Duncan's room, fresh from the murder, and there's this weird moment of confusion with his wife—they're both jumpy as hell, big surprise. And then Macbeth looks at his hands, and they're all covered with blood. "This is a sorry sight," he says. It's like I could feel the panic in him, the instant regret, and it made *me* feel all panicky. Once again I got that weird rush, that sick sort of full feeling, and I thought I might throw up. I looked around at the other kids. A few were looking at the ceiling or writing notes, the rest were reading along, but none of them seemed particularly bothered by any of it. None of them had done what I'd done.

The scene after that was better. That bit with the gatekeeper was pretty funny. Ms. Simpson called it comic relief, which I guess is a good name for it because it made me feel relieved. Then there was the discovery of the body. Pretty soon you've got the characters running around upset, and in the middle of it all you've got Macbeth trying to act like he's all outraged by the killing, but doing an awful job of it, to the point where Lady Macbeth has to step in and pretend to faint to distract everyone from his guilt. Listening to that I suddenly hoped I was doing a better job pretending than he was. Macbeth just wasn't good at it. He talked too much.

When we finished, Ms. Simpson asked us what we thought, and a few kids talked about it for a while. I looked at the clock—only a minute to go. At that point I was more than ready to get out of there. Then somebody asked Ms. Simpson a question.

"But I still don't get it," the girl next to me said. "Everybody loved him. He was, like, the big hero. Why did he feel he had to go and kill like that?"

Ms. Simpson nodded. "Good question," she said. She looked around the room for a second and then her eyes fell on me again. This time she didn't let me go. "So why does Macbeth do it? What do you think, Chris?"

Everyone turned and looked at me.

I shrugged. "Maybe that's just who he is," I said. "Even if a part of him doesn't want to do it, it's just what's in him."

She raised her eyebrows. "Interesting. I think that's what Shakespeare might be suggesting. That's the horror of it. Even more horrible is the thought that, in the right circumstances, any one of us could wind up in the same position. It's easy to sit there and say, 'Oh, isn't it awful what Macbeth did,' but maybe Shakespeare's trying to tell us we all have a little bit of Macbeth in us. We just have to hope it never comes out."

The room was quiet for a moment. Then the bell rang. Everyone jumped to their feet.

"Have a great weekend, everybody," Ms. Simpson chirped.

I was stumbling numbly toward the buses lined up in front of the school, looking forward to going home and collapsing in front of the TV, when Josh grabbed my arm and spun me around.

"Wrong way, pal," he said.

"What do you mean?"

He laughed. "Yeah, I can see why you'd say that, but if we head over now, maybe we can get you changed up before Coach sees you're not wearing your jersey."

He laughed again, but he seemed all nervous and scared. At that point I was too tired to share the sentiment.

"Good thing I got you to watch my back," I said.

"Screw you," he said, "I just don't want him to get pissed off and take it out on all of us."

I sighed. The last thing I felt like right now was going to practice, but I figured I had to. From the way everyone acted, it seemed that Chris was some big-time player and sooner or later I'd have to face it. To be honest, it wasn't just that I was tired. I was nervous, too. After watching the game yesterday afternoon on TV, I thought I understood the basics pretty well, but how could I be sure? All those positions, and everyone moving every which way at once, like they all knew where they were supposed to go—it looked confusing.

I decided to probe Josh a bit as we headed for the locker room. From what Barry had said, I knew that I was a linebacker, but I didn't have a clue what that meant.

"So what do you think of our positions, anyway?"

"What do you mean?" Josh asked, screwing up his face.

"I mean, do you like them? Do you wish you were somewhere else?"

He shrugged. "I can't speak for you, since I'm not a linebacker. As for tight end, I don't mind it. Get to catch a pass now and then—or drop one, more like it."

"Have you ever thought of being a linebacker?"

He looked at me. "What the hell's gotten into you?"

"Just answer my question. I mean, boiled right down to its simplest form, what does being a linebacker mean to you?"

"Well, it's pretty simple, really. Whoever's got the ball,

you go after them and take them out. That's your job."

I nodded. "Good answer," I said, and slapped him on the back.

He glanced at me with kind of an odd look. "What are you, kidding me?"

"What?"

"You sound like you're still drunk from the other night or something."

"Yeah, I'm just kidding. Just messing with you," I said as we turned into the locker room.

I found the locker with my name on it and got changed. The pads were a little tricky, but after a bit of fiddling, I managed to get suited up. I just copied what Josh, Steve, and everyone else was doing. Of course, I had to be careful—a boys' locker room's not the kind of place you can stare too much. The only bad part was the smell. Doppelgangers have real sensitive noses, and that place stunk even before practice. As soon as I opened Chris's locker, his smell swept over me, that odor of sweat, aggression, and fear—just like the other night—and for a moment I had to turn away.

At one point the coach—whom everyone called "Coach!"—poked his head in.

"Hurry up, you Sallies! We haven't got all day!" he barked, then disappeared.

Coach Ballard, one of the assistants, seemed a little more laid back. He came in clapping his hands and actually smiling.

"Let's go, guys," he said as everyone scrambled for the door. "Big game tomorrow. Got to get ready!" He stopped me as I passed by. "Good to see you back, Parker."

"Thanks," I replied.

"You missed a big practice yesterday. Went over a lot of stuff. Get ready for Coach to ride you pretty hard."

"But I was sick," I said. Jesus, these football people were uptight.

"Just giving you a heads-up, that's all."

"Thanks," I said, and followed everyone out onto the field.

Practice wasn't too bad, at least at first. Coach gave me a scowl as I came out of the locker room, but he didn't say anything. We formed up and ran around the field a bunch of times, then did warm-ups and grunted like gorillas. It was actually sort of fun. I felt like one of the guys. I just fell in line and moved when everyone else moved, like in those aerobics infomercials I'd seen on TV. And I guess all that walking I'd done over the last few weeks paid off, because I didn't really get that tired.

The second part of practice was tougher. We had to do all these different kinds of drills with weird names like "bull in the ring" and "monkey rolls." I mean, who comes up with this stuff? I did the best I could, but I didn't have a clue what was going on—there are limits to faking it. Coach was on me every second for one stretch, standing over me and screaming every time I made a mistake. It was like he was waiting for me to screw up so he'd have an excuse to blow out my eardrums. He seemed like an even bigger jerk than Chris's father. It pissed me off at first, and I had to bite my tongue to keep from screaming right back at him, but after a while I just tuned him out. I think he wanted me to get mad. He kept telling me I needed to be "more aggressive!" over and over. More, more, more, more, more! *Screw him,* I thought.

In the end missing practice the day before turned out to be the best thing I could have done. It gave me an excuse for being clueless. Every time I screwed up, Coach would scream, "If you'd been here yesterday, you'd know what the hell was going on!" and I'd just nod and try it again. After a while he got tired of hassling me and moved on to someone else. Not long after that, practice ended.

What really got me through the whole thing, oddly enough, was Amber. I just kept thinking about her, and every time I did, I forgot about all the other crap. While the autumn sun cast long shadows on the field and we all huffed and hollered and banged each other around, her face kept popping up in my mind.

After a while it kind of annoyed me. I mean, sure I found her attractive—anyone would. But with Amber, it seemed to be more than just the fact that she was hot. There was something else. I just didn't get it. Why was I thinking about her at all? I mean, I didn't even know her. Why did I pull that stupid card out from under Chris's bed and read it again this morning, just like I'd done last night before going to sleep? Worst of all, why was I still feeling this way after our encounter at lunch? She hadn't been particularly upbeat or nice. In fact, from what I could tell, she seemed to hate my guts—or Chris's guts, at least—and I had no idea how to dig myself out of that hole. Not that it really mattered, since who knew how many more days Chris Parker would be around, anyway. I'd have to take off eventually, and right now, between Barry and Coach, I imagined that day would be sooner rather than later.

The point is I was all screwed up, and I knew it. But that didn't stop me from thinking about her as I walked off the field, as I showered and changed, and as I headed home to wait for her to pick me up.

That's one of the weird things about doppelgangers. Just because we're not human doesn't mean we're not attracted to them. From the way my mother talked, it's like we're all supposed to look down on human beings—they're weak, after all, and we're superior. But the truth is, we're drawn to them. We have to live among them, we have to be them, just as much as we have to kill them. They're equal urges. Maybe that's why doppelgangers despise human beings so much—we hate the fact that we're so obsessed with, so dependent on, what we desire. That's our weakness.

CHAPTER SIX

"Chris!" Echo called. "Amber's here!"

"Thanks," I hollered back, but I was already halfway down the hall. I'd been watching from my bedroom window, and the second I saw her headlights in the driveway, I was headed for the door. The last thing I wanted was for her to come inside and get into a conversation with Barry and Sheila. Not that that was likely. Barry was sacked out in front of the TV on his fifth beer, and Sheila was on the phone, murmuring in desperate tones to whomever. As for Echo, I still wasn't sure what she was all about. She just seemed to wander around the house doing nothing in particular.

"Are you gonna kiss?" she asked me with a devilish grin as I threw my jacket on and reached for the front door.

I paused. The possibility of something like that happening hadn't even occurred to me until she asked.

"I don't know," I said.

"Oh." She seemed somewhat taken aback. "Well, have fun."

"Thanks," I said, and headed out into the dark.

Amber didn't really look at me as I went around the front of the car and got in on the passenger's side. Her car was nice—a lot nicer than Barry's or Sheila's, and ten times better than Steve's.

"Hi," I said.

She glanced at me for a second, then backed out of the driveway, and we took off.

"So you still want to go to this stupid party, huh?" she said.

"Sure," I said, gripping the handle above the window to steady myself as we took a corner. Amber was driving really fast. At every curve I could feel my stomach nuzzle up against one side of my rib cage or the other and hang there for a few seconds even after we'd straightened out. I could hardly keep track of where we were going. I glanced over at her for a second. In the glow of the dashboard, her face seemed softer, sort of muted and almost sad, as if she were letting go, drawn into the speed. When she looked at me, the sharpness came back.

"What's the matter, Chris?" she said, sort of smirking.

"Nothing," I said, my other hand squeezing at the plush of the seat as the engine revved up on the straight-away. "You're going a little fast there, aren't you?"

"Isn't that how you like it?"

"Okay," I said. I didn't care—I just wanted her to get her eyes back on the road.

"Are you scared?" she asked.

"Yes," I said.

She slowed down. I breathed a sigh of relief.

"Who would've thought?" she said.

We pulled up to a big house with lots of cars in front of it and got out. I remember thinking the ground had never felt so good. I also remember thinking that Amber was crazy. In fact, all of them were—Barry, Sheila, Echo, Chris, Coach—human beings were just plain nuts.

I followed Amber up to the house. Even before we got to the front steps I could hear the music. It reminded me of Steve's car—*thump, thump, thump*, like the house was some kind of big machine, grinding away. On top of all that was the buzz of voices, of people yelling and laughing, a sound that exploded as the door burst open and some kid ran past us, falling onto the lawn and puking.

Amber was unfazed. "Gross," was all she said before continuing up the steps.

The party itself was nothing special. In fact, I hated it. As soon as we went in, some girl wearing heavy black eyeliner and way too much lipstick pushed through the crowd, ran up to us, and started babbling in excited tones and kind of jumping up and down. I guessed it was Cheryl, the girl whose party it was. The girl whose house was in the process of being ransacked. She disappeared for a second, then came back with two plastic cups, one blue, one red. She handed them to us and started talking again. I had no clue what she was saying—the music was so loud, I couldn't hear anything. While she blathered on, I took a sniff of the drink and recoiled. It was some kind of booze. It wasn't whiskey like the old man and Chris had been drinking, but it reminded me of them. I tried not to think about it and concentrated instead on pretending to understand whatever Cheryl was saying. I nodded and smiled and, when it seemed like the right time, said things I couldn't even hear myself say. Amber did the same in between sips, and every once in a while she'd laugh and so would I, and then so would Cheryl. Somebody was saying something hilarious, and I'm pretty sure it wasn't me.

The whole time we were there, it was like that. If it wasn't Cheryl, then it was someone else stepping up to yammer at us as we threaded our way through the house. It was really hot in there, and the place reeked of alcohol and perfume and sweat. Everyone else seemed to be having a great time, dancing and swaying, swimming in a current of sound as one song blended into the next. Not me. I was drowning. In the dim light, everyone's faces took on a sinister tone, their smiles twisting into snarls, and for a second I thought I was going crazy. It's like they were doppelgangers too, slipping in and out of form, unable to hold on. And at any moment they would drop it entirely and so would I, and we would all be left staring at one another, all echoes of our own horrible selves.

The only exception was Amber, who remained composed from the moment she walked in. I kept close to her as we went along, amazed at how the sea of kids seemed to part before her, leaving her untouched by their slog. Even the ones who accosted us with their tipsy party talk held back slightly, as if a force field surrounded us. She had this coolness about her as she downed one drink and somehow ended up with another, and I managed to catch my breath here and there in her wake.

An hour later we were through. I just remember the cool air on my face and the feeling of relief as we exited through the front door and headed back to the car.

"What a lame party," she said as we climbed in and she

71

started the engine. She didn't seem to like much of anything, but in this case I couldn't argue with her.

"Totally," I said.

"I should get you home," she said as we pulled back onto the road. She was driving slower now. "You probably want to get to bed early, what with the game tomorrow and all."

The clock on the dash said 10:15, but I didn't really feel like rushing back to Barry and Sheila. Besides, I wanted to know more about Amber. We hadn't exactly had a chance to talk at the party.

"I'm not tired," I said. "Let's go to your house."

She sighed. "Right."

She didn't live far away, just a mile or so down the road. Looking out the window, I could tell this neighborhood was pretty different from the Parkers'. The houses were farther apart, not all scrunched together, and they were a lot bigger. Amber's house was even bigger than Cheryl's.

As we pulled into the garage, Amber reached over and took a bottle out of the glove compartment. At first I thought she was going for another drink. But it was something else.

"Mouthwash?" she offered, holding out the bottle. I shook my head. "Don't look so surprised," she said. "This is your trick, after all." She took a swig and started swishing like crazy, then she sort of grimaced for a second and swallowed.

"I hate that part," she said, coughing.

We got out and went into the house. Coming around the corner, I nearly jumped at the sight of Amber's parents waiting in the bright kitchen, grinning like a pair of hyenas.

"There he is," her father shouted, coming over and clapping me on the back. "Hope you went easy tonight," he said, laughing. "Wouldn't do for the best damn linebacker in the state to be hung over tomorrow, now would it?"

Listening to him talk, all loud and sort of slurry, I got the feeling someone else should have gone easy that night.

"Jim," Amber's mother scolded, never losing her grin. "It's great to see you again, Chris."

"Thanks," I said. "Don't worry, I didn't have anything to drink tonight."

"God," Amber said, "cut it out, Chris. You made the good impression months ago. I mean, Jesus, my parents like you better than they do me."

"Now sweetie, you know that's not true," Amber's mother said, cocking her head.

"Well, maybe a little bit," her father said. Her parents looked at each other and burst out laughing, as if it was the most hilarious thing they'd ever heard. No wonder Amber rolled her eyes so much.

After they'd recovered, Amber's father wrapped his arm around me again. At this point I was almost starting to miss Barry.

"So when are you turning pro, Sport?"

Was this guy for real? "Uh . . . ," I figured I was supposed to say something clever here. Then again, maybe not.

"Dad," Amber cut in, "shut up, okay? Just shut up."

"Hey, just asking. Kid's got it written all over him. Everybody says so. And you better start being a little nicer to him, or someday you'll regret it. He just might trade up.

Right, Chris?" He slapped me on the back and started laughing again. Then he kind of looked at me and raised his eyebrows like I was supposed to start laughing too. But after the long day, and then that party, all I could muster was a smile.

"Look, Connie—kid's already got his game face on for tomorrow. That says it all right there. Well, good for you, Chris."

"Come on, let's go," Amber said. She grabbed my arm and started dragging me toward the staircase. I looked back at them as we left.

"Good luck tomorrow," Amber's mother said, waving good-bye. "We'll be watching."

"Give them a good beating," Jim added, raising his fists and jabbing the air a few times. They both started laughing again.

"What a jerk," Amber said as we reached the top of the stairs.

"Your dad really seems to like football," I said.

"Yeah. He's a real fan."

We went into her bedroom and closed the door. Unlike Chris's bedroom, the walls of Amber's room were loaded with pictures, posters, postcards, and collages. It seemed like every square foot of space was covered with something. And then there was the nightstand, the dresser, the desk, the makeup table, even the bed—everything was loaded with stuff. Candles, dolls, coffee cups, bottles of hair products and moisturizers, papers, books, CDs, ceramic figurines—you name it, she had it. The only thing missing was a TV. It reminded me more of Echo's room. I don't know, maybe it's a girl thing.

While I looked around, Amber went to her computer.

"What are you doing?" I asked. I'd never used a computer before, and Chris didn't have one. None of the Parkers did.

"Checking e-mail," she murmured, staring at the screen. She was typing furiously.

"That's right." I'd heard of that. "You've got mail!" I said.

She looked at me sort of funny, then went back to typing. When she finished, she got up and started walking around the room, taking off her earrings, picking up clothes, stuff like that. I just sat on the bed watching her. We didn't talk. It was like I wasn't even there, like she'd forgotten all about me. I tried to think of something to say, but nothing came to mind. I was happy enough just watching her, remembering how she'd been at the party, drifting and smiling through the crowd like she was a queen among peasants or something. And here I was, in the queen's own chamber, in the inner sanctum. But this queen didn't smile, at least not at me.

For some reason I suddenly remembered the scene from Macbeth today. That strange moment after the murder with the two of them, Macbeth and Lady Macbeth, fumbling around in the dark, Macbeth utterly paralyzed by horror at his deed, and Lady Macbeth seeming cool and annoyed by her husband's weakness, but really just as scared. I could tell they weren't a happy couple. And after today I got the feeling we weren't, either. At least the Macbeths were bonded by their crime. What did Amber and Chris have?

I looked up and realized she was gone. Light shone around the partially closed door of the bathroom. Then the light clicked off. The door opened and out came Amber in her bra and panties.

When she looked at me, her face was blank. Or maybe just resigned. Either way, she looked nothing like the picture I had of her at home.

For a moment I didn't say anything. I just sat frozen at the edge of the bed, trying not to stare.

"Not the usual reaction," she said. She didn't sound disappointed. Her eyes narrowed slightly. "I mean, it's what you came here for isn't it?"

I jumped up and almost lost my balance. My heart was pounding so hard, for a moment I felt like I was back in Cheryl's house.

"What about your parents?" I sputtered.

She frowned. "What do you mean? They'll have another cocktail and go to bed."

"What if they came in?"

"They know better." She crossed her arms in front of her chest and shifted into a slouch. "And so do you. What's the problem?"

"Nothing," I said. I sat down on the edge of the bed again. I could hardly look at her, and the fact that I wanted to made me look away even more. None of it made sense. Suddenly I didn't like being in the queen's chamber—the whole thing was too complicated. I was in way over my head.

"Not as exciting when it's given to you, is that it?" she sneered. "Takes all the fun out of it?"

I didn't know what she meant by that, but I knew it wasn't good. I looked up at her. Before I knew it, I'd just sort of blurted it out.

"You don't like me, do you," I said.

She frowned again. "We're a perfect couple. Isn't that what everybody says?"

I didn't say anything. I just wanted her to go back in the bathroom and put some clothes on.

"You're a miserable son of a bitch," she said finally. "How's that?"

"Okay," I said, "then why are you still with me?"

"Since when do you care?"

"Just answer the question," I said. I don't know why, but I was starting to get irritated.

She didn't say anything for a moment, but her face kept changing, passing from confusion to anger, before settling into loathing. It was the same kind of look I'd seen on Chris's face before he attacked me that night—loathing not for me, but for himself.

"Are we going to do it or not?" she said at last.

"No!" I said, jumping up. "Jesus Christ!"

She shrugged, then picked her bathrobe up off the floor and put it on. She went and sat back at her desk, taking the barrette out of her hair and giving her head a shake. She looked sad all of a sudden. Even after everything she'd said, I wanted to make her feel better. I couldn't leave without trying.

"Maybe we could start over," I suggested.

Big mistake. I saw her stiffen. Then she turned and looked at me and laughed in this way that made me wish I could just sort of disappear.

"Are you kidding me?" she said. "After all the shit you've pulled, you think we can just 'start over?'" She shuddered. "You're so clueless, it makes me sick."

77

Well, she was right about that.

"Sorry," I said.

She got up from the chair and came over to me. "Sorry doesn't even begin to cover it, so don't even try. It won't work, Chris."

"Okay," I said.

"Okay, okay," she said, mocking me. "Come on, Chris. You may fool everybody else, but you can't fool me."

"What do you mean?" I said. She was in my face now and starting to freak me out with all her talk. I could feel my heart pounding, even harder than when she'd walked out in her underwear.

"I know who you are. Who you really are," she hissed. "You're a fucking monster!"

"Shut up!" I hollered. Before I knew it, I'd reached out and grabbed her by the shoulders. She pulled away from me and shrank back against the bathroom door, covering her head with both her hands like she knew what was coming. I just kind of froze over her. I could hear myself breathing, huffing in that same weird sort of way Chris had done by the fire.

She sank to the floor and started crying.

"Go ahead," she said. "Do it. I don't care."

I turned and rushed from the room, down the stairs, through the empty kitchen, still bright with lights, and out of the house. Before I'd even left the driveway, I broke into a run.

I didn't know where the hell I was going, and I didn't care. I just kept running. And the whole time, I kept seeing Amber crouching at my feet, shielding herself, and thinking, *She's right. She's right. I am a monster.* I couldn't tell who I hated more—Chris, for whatever he'd done to Amber to make her act that way, or myself. *Forget Chris,* I thought. *I'm just as bad. I'm worse. At least he was real. At least he never killed anyone.*

As the hours passed, I forgot about the words echoing in my brain and just felt lonely. It was cold and the stars were out as I drifted through town with everyone asleep. I'd never felt so alone, not even when I'd left the cabin or when I'd walked in the train yard thinking about my mother.

Just as the eastern sky began to lighten and turn the world blue, I found my street. I crossed the tall, frost-coated lawn and let myself in, went straight to my room, threw off my clothes and collapsed onto Chris's bed. But as exhausted as I was, I couldn't sleep. I just started replaying the night's drama in my head.

So much for my first date.

CHAPTER SEVEN

It was a beautiful day. One of those fall days when everything is crisp and the leaves are changing and the sky is
blue and there's that great smell in the air. It was that kind
of day when things really started to go to hell.

It began with Steve coming by at around ten thirty. I
had just fallen asleep after lying in bed all morning, staring
up at the water stains on the ceiling, trying to forget about
Amber. Next thing I knew, there was this banging on my
bedroom door and in came Steve, all pissed off and yelling
about how we were going to be late. It was game day—I'd
forgotten all about it.

"Late night with the woman, huh?" Steve said, throwing clothes at me while I scrambled around in my boxers.
"Was it wild?"

"It was wild, all right," I muttered.

I could tell he wanted more, but I wasn't talking—not
to him, anyway. Not after all the horrible stuff he'd said in
the cafeteria yesterday. Besides, I don't think I could have
gotten it out anyway. I mean, I was barely standing. I had

a terrible headache, and everything looked as fuzzy as my brain felt.

"Well, you better forget about that and start getting ready for today. You're going to need to be wild for Waterbury in a few hours."

"Right," I said.

It turned out I didn't need to be wild after all. Just before game time, Coach called out the assignments, and my name didn't come up. I didn't say anything, but some others did.

"What about Parker, Coach?" one kid asked. Everyone looked at me.

"Parker's warming the bench today," Coach growled. "Any other goddam questions?"

No one said a word, but you could tell they were all kind of shocked. I just sort of shrugged and sat down while the others did their warm-ups on the field. I was relieved, to tell the truth. I almost asked Coach if that meant I could go home, but seeing that scowl on his face whenever he looked at me, I decided it wasn't a good idea. So I just waited, listening to the school's marching band bang out their crooked-sounding songs, the bass drum beating in time to my headache, and watching the cheerleaders do their cheers, jumping up and down in their little uniforms and smiling so that even the ugly ones looked sort of pretty. Of course, none of them looked as good as Amber. Even from where I sat, it was obvious. She looked at me only once, doing kind of a double take when she saw me sitting on the bench by myself. There were a few times when I thought I caught her watching me out of the corner of her eye, but from a distance, it was hard to tell.

The thing I didn't like was the crowd behind me. By the time the game started, the stands were packed with people. It seemed like half the town had showed up—including Barry, and Amber's parents—and I could only imagine what they were thinking seeing me on the bench all by my lonesome, my helmet in my lap.

Screw them, I thought. I closed my eyes and tried to focus on how warm the sun felt on my face and arms.

"Parker."

I opened my eyes and saw Ballard, the assistant coach, standing over me. He reached down and squeezed my shoulder a little bit.

"What's up?" I said.

"Don't take it too hard, kid," he said. "Coach is still a little mad you missed Thursday's practice. But he mostly wants to send a message to the other guys about the importance of commitment. Don't take it personally."

"Okay," I said. I wasn't about to tell him I didn't care, since he was being nice to me and all.

"Besides, we want to save you for Springfield. That's the game that really matters, you know. Coach figures if he keeps you out today, you'll be even hungrier next week."

"Right," I said. "Sounds like a good idea."

He sort of grimaced and shook his head. "You're a brave kid, Parker. Real brave."

"Thanks," I said. I wasn't sure what I was being brave about, but if that's what he wanted to believe, it was fine by me.

No one else talked to me for the entire game. All the other kids kept their distance, even on the bench. I caught a few of them giving me forlorn looks now and then, but no one would look me in the eye. Like last night in Amber's room before our fight, I was invisible. Today, it was just what I wanted.

The game dragged on forever. I tried paying attention so that I would know what to do next time, but between being tired, my head pounding, and Coach running back and forth screaming at this person or that after every other play, I got a little lost. I just remember that pretty soon everyone was huffing and puffing and sweaty and tired. In fact, they probably looked worse than me.

Finally it ended. In spite of all the cheers of the cheerleaders and the hollering of the crowd and the honking of the band, we lost. Back in the locker room, I kept catching the other guys giving me dirty looks, like it was my fault or something.

Don't blame me, I wanted to tell them. *I didn't even play.*

It was only later that I realized that that was why they were mad. I figured it out as I was walking home alone from the game after everyone took off without me. The stupidest part of the whole thing was that I actually started to feel guilty. I mean, I wasn't feeling particularly good to begin with, but even though I knew I hadn't done anything wrong, I still felt like I'd let the team down. Ridiculous, I know. But there it is.

"Pass the potatoes, please," I said.

Sheila handed me the bowl from across the table without even looking up, then went back to her food. Dinner had started out okay, what with the bustle of plates and bowls as everyone loaded up, but that soon ended, and the four of us had settled into quiet. I was pretty nervous. Barry was cutting his steak with a sloppy sort of viciousness—hacking off chunks that seemed way too big for any normal-size mouth—and sucking down beer. As for Echo, she kept screeching her knife on the plate every time she tried to cut her meat, drawing nasty looks from Barry. Sheila remained oblivious, engrossed in spearing her peas with rapid, futile jabs.

What made me so nervous was that under the silence I knew something was lurking, something ugly. I knew it the second I got home and saw Poppy, the Parkers' dog, take one look at me, crawl under the desk as far as she possibly could, and curl up into a ball. Heck, I knew it even before that, when Barry sped by me on his way home from the game without stopping to pick me up. For the rest of the afternoon, I felt it settle over the house, like the storms that used to roll down off the mountain and break over the cabin, soaking everything in sight. Every time I came out to the kitchen, I'd look into the backyard and see Barry out there scraping furiously at the leaves with a plastic rake missing half its teeth, then stuffing the gathered piles of brilliant yellows and oranges into plastic bags with a vengeance.

"Don't go out there," Sheila said the third time I looked out. I glanced over to where she sat at the table, puffing on one ultralight after another. I hadn't seen her smoke until today, but she seemed to be making up for it pretty good.

"What's his problem?" I asked.

She just sort of frowned and shook her head as if I should know better than to ask, stabbing out one butt before lighting up another. After that I went back to my room and didn't come out until dinner.

And now here we were. One big happy family.

"Goddam it, Echo, would you stop it already!" Barry hollered, reaching over and snatching her knife away. He slammed it down beside him on the table and went back to his steak.

"But how can I cut my meat?" Echo said, her voice practically a whisper.

"You can't," Barry said. "That's the idea."

"Here, I'll do it," I said, reaching over to Echo's plate.

"Don't you dare touch that," Barry snapped, pointing his knife at me.

The hackles rose on the back of my neck. Looking across the table, I could see Sheila staring at me in confusion.

"What's the big deal?" I said, and reached over again.

"That's it!" Barry said. He jumped up and grabbed my plate and Echo's, lurched over to the sink, and threw them in. At the sound of breaking ceramic, Sheila put her fork down and buried her head in her hands. I looked over at Echo. She just sat there with a blank look on her face, but I could see her shoulders droop a little. In fact, her whole body looked like it was shrinking.

"I was still eating," I said as Barry plopped back down into his chair. Sheila looked up sharply in alarm. Echo shrank another inch.

"I don't give a damn about that," Barry snapped, going back to his steak. "If you can't listen to me, you don't get to eat. Either of you." He looked over at me. "Besides," he sneered, "I can't imagine that you're hungry—it's not like you did anything to work up an appetite today."

"I had to walk all the way home from the game," I retorted.

"You deserved to walk home. Give you a chance to think about your screwup."

"It's not my fault they wouldn't let me play," I shouted. "Just because I miss one stupid day of practice—"

"Yeah, because you were too much of pussy to suck it up and go to school." He was really starting to yell now. I could see his face getting all red and puffy.

Might as well get it over with, I thought. Better than just sitting there with all that quiet, waiting.

Barry kept going. "Do you know how goddam embarrassing that was to sit there and see everyone staring at you on that bench while your team went out there and lost? Do you have any idea?"

"No," I muttered.

"And that's not all. Who knows if there were any scouts out there today. What do you think that's going to do to your chances?"

I didn't have a clue what he was talking about.

"Barry," Sheila broke in, "he's only a junior."

"So what?" he said, turning on her. "You think they're not already looking? Especially with the way he's played this year? And what would they have thought today? I'll tell you what they would have thought—that he's a screwup. That's right, Sheila. A screwup with a piss-poor attitude."

Like father, like son, I thought as Barry kept going.

"If you're sitting on a pile of dough that I don't know about, Sheila, please tell me, because there's no other friggin' way he's going to college without a scholarship. That's just the sad fact of the matter."

"All right, all right," she said. She stood up and began clearing the table. I looked over to see that Echo had slipped away. Barry was the only one still eating. He didn't look at me or even seem to notice that Echo was gone. The only time he even really moved was to grab his beer when Sheila tried to take it along with the mashed potatoes.

I got up to leave, but as soon as I started to move, he banged his hand down so hard that the silverware on the table rattled. I guess he had been watching me after all.

"You stay there until I say so," he said. "You like to sit—you can sit *there* for a while."

I got up anyway. I was too tired to deal with this kind of crap, and I couldn't stay at that table for another second watching him eat. I pushed my chair back and headed for my room.

"Get back here!" he shouted.

I could hear the fury in his voice, but I just kept right on going into my room, slamming the door behind me. I waited, half expecting him to burst in at any second, but he didn't. Instead, I heard shouting in the kitchen as Barry and Sheila began arguing. Their voices were muffled coming through the door, so I couldn't hear what they were saying exactly. But I could tell it was about me.

This went on for about ten minutes.

Then things got really ugly.

I heard a loud crash and ran out to see Barry sprawled on the living room floor with the coffee table collapsed under him, the ashtray broken, the newspapers scattered. Sheila stood in the kitchen doorway, frozen with one hand over her mouth.

Barry stirred, pulled himself to his hands and knees, and shook his head.

"Echo!" he screamed.

I saw a bit of movement out of the corner of my eye. It was Echo. The noise had drawn her out of her room as well.

"What the hell are these doing here?" he hollered, reaching behind him and grabbing a pair of pink Rollerblades off the floor. Echo's face had lost all its color. She had that same look I'd seen on Amber's face when I grabbed her the night before.

Barry kept going. "How many times have I told you not to leave these goddam things on the floor? You come here."

Echo yelped and turned to run.

"No you don't," he cried, and grabbed at her.

She slipped out of his grip and bolted for her room with Barry in hot pursuit. The door slammed shut, and he began banging on it, hollering for her to unlock it or she was going to be sorry. The latch clicked. Barry yanked the door open, dashed inside, and shut it behind him. I just stood there, frozen, listening to him scream all this horrible stuff at her while she cried. Then there was a sound of banging and other noises too, and I could hear her begging him to stop.

A screaming noise erupted, sending chills along my back, as Poppy burst out from under the desk and began running back and forth between the living room and the kitchen, yelping the entire time as if she'd been kicked in the stomach, as if she were the one in that room with Barry.

I looked over to where Sheila now knelt on the living

room floor, sweeping ashes into a dustpan. She glanced up at me for a moment, then began picking up pieces of the broken ashtray while Barry screamed and Echo cried, and Poppy ran frantic circles around us. Watching her go about it in the middle of all that noise was almost worse than whatever Barry was doing in the next room. It made me *sick.*

Suddenly I couldn't take it anymore. I ran back down the hall to my room, flipped on the TV, and turned up the volume until I couldn't hear anything else. And even then, I still covered my ears with my pillow.

Not long after that I saw headlights flash over the walls of my room. I glanced out the window. Barry was backing out in a real hurry, practically screeching his tires as he tore off down the street.

I muted the TV. The house was quiet, but when I put my ear up to the wall, I could hear Echo next door whimpering. I almost went in there to see how she was, but I couldn't bring myself to face her. I was the one he was really mad at, not her.

So instead, I just lay on the bed with the remote in my hand and drifted through the channels, emerging an hour later when I headed to the bathroom for some aspirin. My headache had come back.

The house was quiet. Barry hadn't returned yet, and Sheila had gone to bed early. Echo's door was open, her room empty. I looked for her in the living room, but she wasn't there, either. Then, on my way into the kitchen, I saw the basement door was open. Going over to it, I could hear Echo's voice coming from below and crept down a few steps to see what she was up to.

"Be careful, Mrs. Weatherby," I heard her say. "You don't want to spill, now."

I peeked down to see a glow in the corner of the cellar. It was coming from the lamp behind the hanging sheets. Echo was in that little room. I could see her silhouette play across the sheet as she poured imaginary tea for the animals seated at her table. For the next fifteen minutes, I watched that curtain, listening to Echo as she spoke in this funny little voice to her stuffed rabbits and bears. It was kind of weird to hear a ten-year-old talking that way. It was like watching one of those kids' shows that take place in a far-away land where everything is sunny and green. I know they're just make-believe places, but Echo acted like she was really there, as if everything that had happened earlier was forgotten.

I went back to my room and shut the door. I turned to the mirror and saw Chris looking back at me, his face dark and mournful. I'd never realized how much he looked like Barry until now. For a second I almost expected to see the doppelganger eyes pop out. I almost wished they would have.

"You were right," I said to the reflection. "The world is a crappy place."

Seeing the look on his face, I couldn't help but think that maybe he was better off in the culvert. It didn't make me feel any better.

There was a knock on the door. I opened my eyes and looked at the clock. It was half past noon. I'd been asleep for over fourteen hours.

"Yeah," I called out.

Barry stuck his head in. "Get dressed," he said. He seemed excited about something.

"What's going on?" I said, sitting up.

"It's Sunday. What do you think?"

"Church?" I said.

"Funny. Just get your ass out of bed. The game's going to start pretty soon."

He left and I fell back onto Chris's bed. The game. This whole thing was a game. A sick one.

I took my time getting up. Now and then I could hear Barry holler to me. He sounded all chipper. When I finally stumbled out to the living room, I noticed Echo's door was closed and Sheila had gone to work. Barry was on the couch, smoking a cigarette, watching TV with the volume turned up insanely loud.

More football.

Seeing me, he moved over to make a spot on the couch. I glanced around, trying to think of a way to get out of this, but he seemed pretty intent on my joining him, so I sat down. He opened a can of beer and handed it to me. I just sort of looked at him.

"Come on, take it," he said.

"No thanks."

"What's the matter? Too good to have a beer with your old man now?"

"You really think I should?"

"What the hell's gotten into you? It's Sunday."

"Right," I said, "Sunday."

I took the can, had a sip, and tried not to look too disgusted.

And that's how I spent my afternoon—sitting next to

that psycho on the couch, watching football, listening to him shout at the TV, his voice louder with every beer. The worst part about the whole thing was that—this is so bad, I can hardly say it—at first all I could think about was the night before, imagining him slapping Echo around in her room, but then I started to forget about it. Barry would jump up every time there was a big play, a smile on his face. And then he'd turn to me and clap me on the shoulder or sort of punch me in the arm like Steve and the other guys did. And pretty soon I was jumping up and down too, laughing and punching him back. There we were, side by side, drinking beer, father and son, just a couple of guys. The whole scene was too weird for words.

Then Echo came out of her room.

As soon as I heard her door open, I shrank down into the couch. For me the party was over.

"Echo, sweetie, get me a beer," Barry called out, seeing her go into the kitchen. She came back a minute later with two.

"Here, Daddy," she said, but she didn't smile.

Neither did I.

CHAPTER EIGHT

"Okay, people, listen up," Ms. Simpson said. The bell was about to ring and our seventh-period class was getting fidgety. "Don't forget to read the rest of act three tonight, starting with the banquet scene—the climax of the play. This is where Macbeth comes face-to-face with his crimes. Literally."

The bell rang and everyone sprang up. Everyone except me.

I'd stayed in my room after supper reading *Macbeth*, starting from the beginning right through to the end of act three. As depressing and horrible as the story was, it beat watching yet another football game with Barry. Only problem was, I'd been thinking about the play ever since. I even dreamed about it last night. I dreamed that I was Macbeth following that glowing dagger down the hall, and I was the one stealing into Duncan's chamber. Only it wasn't Duncan I stabbed to death, it was Chris, and there was Amber next to me, watching, both of us splattered in blood.

It made me sad to think about what Macbeth had done to himself. All that killing—the poor guy just wasn't cut out for it. Not when it came to offing the people close to him, at least. On the battlefield up against random soldiers—that was a different story. There he could handle it. There it was okay.

I wondered which area I fell under. On the one hand, Chris had attacked me first, and the old man was pretty much a goner already. Besides, I hadn't known either one of them. On the other hand, I couldn't help feeling a little bit like Macbeth, as if somehow I'd lost a part of myself in the killing. And even though I didn't know Chris at the time, I felt like I did now. Too well.

But that wasn't the only thing bothering me now. There was another question on my mind. It occurred to me in class as we read through act three, but it had been in the back of my mind ever since Saturday night when Barry had lost it and I'd watched Sheila stand by and do nothing.

"What is it, Chris?"

I looked up to see Ms. Simpson standing over me.

"Nothing," I said. I started gathering my books, then stopped. "Well," I said. "We were talking today about Macbeth killing his best friend, and why he did it, and his soliloquy and all, but there's one thing I still don't understand."

"Go ahead," she said. She sat down in the desk next to me and crossed her legs. I could smell her perfume from where I was sitting.

"Lady Macbeth is supposed to have all this power over her husband. So why didn't she stop him?" I asked.

"From killing Banquo? She didn't know. Remember we talked about how Macbeth struck off on his own, kept her out of the loop."

"Yeah, but she did know. Before the scene with Banquo and the murderers, Macbeth more or less comes right out and tells her. You know, 'there shall be done a deed of dreadful note,' and that whole thing. And she never says a word."

"Okay, fair enough. And you think she should have?"

"Well, I don't know. Her husband's about to hurt someone close to him, kill him even, and she just stands back and lets it happen. Shouldn't she have at least tried to tell him it was a bad idea?"

"Maybe the fact that she doesn't says something about her. Maybe that's her weakness."

"I guess. But what are you supposed to do with someone like that?"

"I'm not sure I follow you," she said.

"Well, say you know someone who isn't stopping a person close to them from hurting other people. What are you supposed to do?"

She paused and stared at me sort of intently, like she was searching for something. It made me nervous.

"Chris," she said, "is there something you want to talk about?"

"Not really," I said.

" 'Cause you can if you want." She smiled.

I smiled back. "I'm good."

"Okay. Well, in that case, to answer your question, I'd have to say that you have a few options. You could do nothing, of course. Or you could confront the person, encourage them to step up and stop whatever's going on from continuing."

"What if they won't?"

"There's always that chance. Maybe they can't. Or maybe they've tried and the other person keeps on hurting people anyway."

"So in other words, forget about it."

"Of course not. Just don't be disappointed if things don't work out. People can be weak."

They sure can, I thought.

"There's another option, you know. You could always try confronting the other person yourself. Maybe you can stop what's going on."

"Right," I said. I stood up. She stayed sitting at the desk, a smile, on her face. It was a nice smile, but it had an edge of worry to it. I wasn't used to a smile like that.

"Thanks," I said.

"Well, I'm just glad to see you're taking Shakespeare to heart. You didn't seem that interested in what we studied before, to be honest."

"What can I say. It's Shakespeare, right?"

"Right." She laughed.

"See you tomorrow," I said. I left and headed for practice.

Things with the team were better than they'd been on Saturday after the game. Josh, Steve, and a few of the other guys joked around with me in the locker room, but everyone still acted a little cold toward me, like they were pulling away somehow. I figured it was probably for the best, all things considered.

I went through practice sort of numb. Coach spent the

whole first part lecturing us about our loss, rambling on about commitment and effort and all that crap. I barely paid attention. This time I wasn't thinking about Amber. I'd seen her at lunch, but only in passing. As far as I could tell, things were pretty much over.

I had other things on my mind too. My conversation with Ms. Simpson had gotten me thinking more about Barry and Sheila and Echo. I just didn't understand why Sheila would stand by and let Barry hurt Echo any more than I could understand why Barry would hurt Echo to begin with. In fact, I understood it less. In some ways Sheila reminded me of my own mother—a cold fish. But there was a toughness to my mother that Sheila didn't have. My mother had an edge that could cut sharper than any knife. Sheila may have had an edge once upon a time, but it was blunt now. I suppose living with Barry would be enough to dull anyone. Maybe that's why she stood by and did nothing—Sheila was just too weak, like Ms. Simpson said.

And what about me? Why didn't I just take Barry on myself, like Ms. Simpson had suggested? While we did laps around the practice field and ran drills, I kept asking myself the very question. At first I figured I was just scared. After all, I was a coward—at least as far as I could tell. But that wasn't it. Not completely. Underneath it all, I felt like it wasn't my place. I was just a visitor, a stranger in their midst, no matter who I might look like. I mean, what made me think I could come along and try to change anything about the Parkers? Doppelgangers aren't supposed to change the world; we're just supposed to live in it. That's what my mother always told me, anyway. And that's what

I tried to tell myself as I took the bus home from practice.

Along the way, the bus paused before a railroad crossing to listen for oncoming trains. I looked through the window and saw the tracks stretching into the distance on their way out of town. Not too far down those tracks was the culvert. I wondered how Chris was doing in there. I shivered imagining what he must look like by now.

Poor kid. I'd told him that night when I stuck him in there that I'd try not to screw things up. Now, five days later, I couldn't tell if I was keeping my promise. Then again, things were so screwed up already, I wasn't sure if I could really make them any worse. All I could do was make them bad in a different way.

Which was probably what I'd do if I confronted Barry. Who knew—maybe what had happened to Echo was an isolated incident. Maybe Barry felt guilty enough to make sure what had happened on Saturday would never happen again. But somehow the look on Sheila's face had told me that wasn't true. As the bus crossed over the tracks and headed on, I figured I'd just have to wait and see.

I didn't have to wait long. Only three days.

It was Thursday. I'd just gotten home after a grueling practice. The game against Springfield was on Saturday and everyone was freaking out, especially the coaches. Bakersville and Springfield had this big rivalry going way back, and practically the entire population of both towns turned out for "the big game" every year. It was even more important than making the play-offs. By the time Steve dropped me off, I was pretty beat and looking forward to a hot meal, a shower, and then bed, but as soon as I walked in the door, I could tell something was wrong.

Things had been pretty quiet all week. Barry had been subdued, even going out of his way to be nice, particularly to Echo, and after a couple days I started to think that things were better. I was ready to forget about it. I mean, I'd almost allowed myself to forget about Chris, about what I'd done to him. It's like I *was* Chris. Mother would have been proud.

The only time I faltered was when I'd see his face in the mirror. It wasn't so much the fear of seeing those monster eyes again. Though it gnawed at me a little, I had enough trouble worrying about the things I could control. It had more to do with seeing Chris. It never failed to catch me off guard—to see him staring back at me like that, with an accusing look, even though it was my face now. So I took the mirror off the wall in my room and stuck it in the closet next to the pornos.

Things were even starting to get better with Amber. By Tuesday I'd managed to get her to talk to me a few times, and on Wednesday she even smiled at lunch when I made a joke. Of course, there were kids around, so who knows if she was faking it, but it was a start. She was still pretty cold, but I was going out of my way to be as nice as possible. Just like Barry.

But that Thursday when I walked in the door, the first thing I noticed was the smell of booze. It wasn't beer—it was whiskey. That goddam smell was haunting me. I poked my head in the living room. Sure enough, there was Barry, wreathed in cigarette smoke, lying back on the sofa watching TV with a butt in one hand and a glass in the other. I looked at my watch—it wasn't even five. He was home early.

I slipped into my room, dropped off my books and clothes, and headed back out to the kitchen. Echo's door was open when I went by, and I could see her sitting on her bed, reading. She glanced up and gave me a quick, nervous look when I paused in the doorway, then went back to her book.

"What's Dad doing home?" I asked, coming into the kitchen.

Sheila was at the sink, peeling potatoes. As soon as I opened my mouth, I could see her stiffen.

"He was here when I got home a half hour ago. Trouble at work. Trouble with Mitch."

"The boss?" I said. *Uh-oh.* "Did he get fired?"

"No," she muttered. "But that's about all I know."

I could tell she didn't want to talk about it, and she wanted me to talk about it even less.

"Just let me know when it's time for supper," I said, and headed back to my room. The next hour dragged by.

I tried reading *Macbeth* for a while, but it made me even more anxious. First Macbeth goes to the three witches to find out about his future. They conjure up three apparitions who each give him a prophecy. The prophecies make Macbeth feel safe, but any idiot can see he's headed for trouble, especially when he orders that Macduff's entire family be massacred. The whole thing is creepy and bizarre. But the next scene is even worse. Lady Macduff is all upset about her husband taking off to escape Macbeth, and so Ross, one of the lords, tries to calm her down. Then he leaves, and she jokes around with her son. Even in the middle of all this trouble, she still keeps her sense of humor. Then Macbeth's goons show up. At that point, I closed the book—I knew what they were there for.

I watched the news instead. Big pick-me-up there. The police were still trying to figure out who was behind the killing of that woman from Springfield. They hadn't found her Subaru yet and didn't really have any leads. *Good luck with that*, I thought. I knew how those things worked. The rest was more of the same—terrorist attacks, bank robberies, a factory explosion, just a typical day. Oh yeah, and some dog that had gotten itself stranded in a flood got saved. Big deal. Like that made everything else better.

There was a knock on my door.

"It's time," Echo said, looking in.

"Right," I said. I got up and followed her to the table.

Barry was in prime form. As we all sat down for a meal of mashed potatoes (apparently the Parkers had mashed potatoes every night) and frozen fried chicken, he didn't waste any time launching into a sloppy rant against Mitch, who he pretty much just referred to as "that bastard."

Apparently Barry had gotten into a fight with "that bastard" and had been sent home early—not before, of course, making a pit stop at the liquor store. None of us really said much throughout all this, though Sheila made feeble attempts to tone him down now and then.

Listening to the whole thing, I felt more embarrassed for Barry than afraid. At one point he practically broke down. Desperation flowed from him, tainting everything.

"I tell you, Sheila, he just doesn't understand," he said.

"Mmm," Sheila agreed.

"I'm just trying to make things better there. That's all I've ever tried to do."

"I know, dear."

"I have a system, goddamit!"

"I remember you telling me. It's a good system."

"Damn right it is. Only that bastard is too much of a numbskull to realize it. And then he gets pissed off at me because he's too stupid to understand."

"He certainly is."

"That's what I tried telling him today."

"Oh dear," Sheila murmured.

"And what does he do?" Barry went on, oblivious. "He sends me home. Says he's going to dock my pay. Says I'm on thin ice. Like I give a shit."

But I could tell he did. And he was worried. And that's what he was really pissed off about.

Echo could tell too. "May I be excused?" she whispered while Barry paused to take a breath and another swig of his drink. He'd barely touched his food. Neither had she.

"Sure, Echo," Sheila jumped in.

"Wait," Barry barked.

Echo, who had just started to stand up, froze.

Oh God, here we go, I thought. Looking at the faces of Sheila and Echo, I could see they were thinking the same thing.

"You didn't hardly eat a goddam bite," he said, looking at Echo's plate

"I'm not hungry," she said. From the looks of things, none of us were.

Barry frowned. I could see the little drunken wheels turning in his head, trying to decide where or how to direct his anger. Sheila seized the opportunity to step in.

"Go ahead, sweetie," she said. She turned to Barry. "Echo's got a lot of homework for tomorrow. A big project. I told her before dinner started she could be excused early."

Good one, Sheila, I thought.

"Fine," Barry growled, and the rest of us sort of breathed a sigh of relief.

"Thanks, Mom," Echo said, and finished standing up, bumping her plate in the process. The plate jumped forward and collided with her full glass of milk. I watched the whole thing unfold, a little chain reaction of disaster. It was as if everything immediately went into slow motion, just like on TV, with the glass tumbling over and a cascade of milk washing across the table and spilling into Barry's lap. For a second after it happened, we all stopped and stared.

Then, the explosion.

Barry jumped up, dripping milk from the waist down.

"You little brat," he yelled, "you did that on purpose!"

"No!" Echo cried, stepping back as both Sheila and I froze at the table.

"Goddamit!" Barry cried, wiping at his pants with a napkin. It was a futile gesture—he was already soaked through—and he was just sober enough to realize it. He threw the napkin aside, picked up his plate, and slammed it down on the table, where it shattered into a dozen pieces.

Echo, meanwhile, had slipped around the table and was almost out of the kitchen when Barry spotted her. Before I could do anything to distract him, he jumped toward her.

"Get back here and clean this up," he shouted as she darted away.

Suddenly it was Saturday night all over again. There was Barry, banging on her door, threatening. Then, from the other room, I could hear the door opening and slamming, and muffled shouts and Echo crying. Once again Poppy began tearing around the house, yelping. And there was Sheila, at the table with that deadened look, picking up the pieces of a broken plate.

"Go in there," I hissed.

She looked up at me with a sort of dazed expression.

"What do you mean?" she said.

"Do something."

She sort of shook her head a little, like she was waking up from a dream. She glanced toward the hallway, toward Echo's room.

"Oh," she said. "Oh."

Then she went back to gathering pieces of plate, her eyes down at the table.

"Mom!" I shouted. She started and finally looked up at me. I could see resentment in her eyes. I had always thought Chris looked like Barry, but suddenly I could see a little bit of her in him too.

"He's just in one of his phases. It'll pass," she said. "You should know," she added, and looked away.

A slow, silent minute passed. I didn't know what to say. All I could do was sit there and stare.

"What do you want me to do?" she suddenly shouted, even though I hadn't said anything. Her eyes began to well up. "Echo's tough. Just like you."

"Listen to her," I said. Echo was still crying.

Sheila was shaking now. I could hear the pieces of ceramics rattle as she carried them to the sink. She came back to the table with a washcloth. She started wiping up the milk and picked up the tipped glass. It broke in two as she lifted it. She held the bottom piece up before her, looking at it in amazement.

"Everything breaks around here," she said, choking back a sob. "I can't have anything nice."

She dropped the glass back onto the table. I watched as it rolled across and come to a stop in front of me.

Echo had stopped crying, but Barry was still yelling like crazy. I looked up at Sheila. Her eyes were closed. She was squeezing the washcloth, and milk was dripping between her fingers and onto the floor. Finally she threw the washcloth down and left the kitchen. A moment later I heard her bedroom door slam.

That's it, I thought. *If she doesn't care, then neither do I.* I jumped up from the table, grabbed my jacket, and took off.

The days were getting shorter, and it was already starting to get dark. The streetlights were humming to life in the dusk, and the air was sharp with cold and the smell of fallen leaves. It felt good to breathe it in, to be out of that house, that cramped, suffocating box.

It had been nearly a month since my mother kicked me out into the human world. But I felt like I understood them less now than I ever had before in my cabin on the mountain, watching the world from a distance. Things were messier the closer you got. All that emotion, all that intensity. And it wasn't just the Parkers—Amber, her parents, Coach, all the kids at school, everybody. It made me dizzy just thinking about it. Worst of all, I still had the whole rest of my life to have to deal with this kind of stuff. Today in Bakersville, tomorrow somewhere else. Somehow I had the feeling that I'd never get it right, never figure out how to make it. My mother was right—I was an embarrassment. A loser.

Anyway, I just started walking, and before I knew it, I was walking toward the edge of town. I figured I'd keep going. I really didn't see how I could go back to the Parkers'. Besides, I couldn't be Chris forever. I'd have to leave at some point. It had been over a week now, and I hadn't felt any problems with the form, but who knew how long that would last?

But then I tried imagining what my leaving would do to the family. I mean, in the middle of everything else, to have their son disappear, only to turn up dead? They were already falling apart. Wouldn't this just be the final blow? I didn't care so much about Barry or Sheila, but what would happen to Echo? On the other hand, maybe a death in the family was just the thing they needed—something to sort of pull them together. They would all stop and realize what was really important, just like in all those shows on TV. They would be a whole new family. Right?

Either way, I won't be around to find out, I thought as I neared the far side of town.

A pair of headlights came up from behind, casting my shadow out in front of me. I watched it as I walked along, all stretched and thin like a doppelganger. *There I am*, I thought, seeing the shadow weave and shift as the headlights drew nearer.

The car slowed down as it came closer. A moment later, just before it passed me, it sped up again. I looked up as it drove away.

It was Amber. Or her car, at least.

I froze and watched her disappear around the corner.

Guess I won't get to say good-bye, I thought. Then again, considering she'd seen me and hadn't stopped, it probably didn't matter much. I felt kind of sad anyway, which was stupid—she wasn't even really my girlfriend. She only thought she was. And even that was up in the air.

No sooner had I started walking again than another pair of lights appeared, this time heading toward me. She'd come back.

She pulled over, and I went around to the driver's side. She looked at me for a moment before rolling down the window.

"What are you doing?" she asked.

"Walking," I said.

"Duh," she said. "I mean, what for?"

"Just wanted to," I replied. "It's a nice night."

Stupid, I know, but what was I supposed to say? *"I didn't feel like listening to my kid sister who's not really my kid sister get the crap beat out of her by her drunken father while her brain-dead mother stood by and did the dishes. Oh, and by the way, I'm disappearing for good. My body will probably turn up in the spring when some jerk takes his dog for a walk on the railroad tracks outside of town."*

"Since when do you do that kind of thing?" she said, her brow crinkling.

I shrugged. "First time for everything," I said.

"Right," she said. I think she could tell I didn't want to talk about it. She turned off the engine. A long silence passed. She seemed to be waiting for something, but I wasn't sure what.

"So what are you doing?" I asked.

"I just took Christine home from practice."

"You guys went even later than we did," I said.

She snorted. "Got to get ready for the 'big game,'" she said. "Half-time show and all that. Remember, we're hosting this year."

"Oh yeah," I said.

"I hate cheerleading." She sighed. "I've always hated it."

"Then why don't you quit?" I said without really thinking.

Her head jerked up, and she gave me a kind of funny look.

"What are you on?" she asked.

"Nothing," I said. "What do you mean?"

"Oh, come on," she said. "Something's going on. For the last week, it's like . . ." She paused, and my heart started pounding. "You're just different, that's all."

"Is that a good thing or a bad thing?" I asked.

She didn't say anything for a moment.

"You need a ride?" she said at last.

"No thanks," I said. I looked down to where the road disappeared around the corner. In the distance I could hear the blare of a horn as a freight train made its way through town.

"Come on, get in," she said. "I'll take you home."

She glanced up at me. It was just for a second, but it was enough. The coldness, the anger, all of it was gone, and for the briefest moment she looked like she did in that photograph, the one I'd found tucked in Chris's birthday card, maybe even more welcoming. My heart started pounding again and I felt funny, sort of dizzy.

"Okay," I said.

She nodded. The warmth had faded now, the wall was back.

I went around the front and got in, and we drove off.

"So you ready for Saturday?" she asked.

"I guess," I said. Really I was dreading it. I'd made it through a week of practices, but I had no idea what would happen to me when the real thing came. And the fact that it was the "big game" only made matters worse.

"It's all you've been talking about since school started."

"I know," I said.

"Didn't like getting benched, huh?"

"Who does?" I replied.

A few minutes went by. She seemed sort of squirmy as we drove along. At least she wasn't driving a hundred miles an hour like last time.

"So you really think I should quit cheerleading?" she asked.

"If that's what you want. I mean, if you don't really like it, why not?"

She gave a nervous laugh. "God, my parents would kill me. Not to mention my friends."

"No they wouldn't."

"Yes, they would." She laughed again. "Besides, people would talk. About us."

"What do you mean?"

"Star linebacker, head cheerleader—the dynamic duo. You know, all that Ken and Barbie stuff. God, I hate that crap."

"Well, maybe you shouldn't, then," I said. I was starting to feel confused, like I couldn't tell what I was supposed to say.

"Yeah, you're probably right," she said, nodding. But she still seemed pretty wound up.

We pulled into the driveway. Barry's car was gone. I breathed a sigh of relief. She turned off the lights, and we sat for a moment in the dark.

"Want me to come in?" she said.

That was the last thing I wanted. Not that I didn't want to spend more time with her, but I had no idea what the scene would be like in there.

"Now's not the best time," I said. "I've got a big test tomorrow. Need to study." I could tell my voice sounded funny.

So could she. "Right," she said. She looked over at me. "See you tomorrow."

"Okay," I said. I started to open the door, then stopped. "So you want to do something tomorrow night?" I said.

"Sleepover at Tammy's," she said.

"Oh."

"Besides, you're going out with the guys. The usual pregame bash, right?"

"That's right," I said, "I forgot."

She smiled. For the first time, a real smile just for me. "Just stay out of trouble, okay?"

"I'll try," I said. I closed the door and stood back. I watched her drive away and didn't turn until she was out of sight. And that's when I knew that I was in love. To this day, it's the best and worst thing that's ever happened to me.

CHAPTER NINE

Everything was quiet when I walked in the door. And dark—the kitchen light was on, but that was it.

"Echo?" I called out, but there was no answer. I went around the corner and looked into her room. Empty.

"Chris."

I turned to see Sheila standing at the edge of the living room. She sounded relieved to see me. As I switched on the hallway light, she picked up the suitcase by her side and stepped toward me. She was wearing a coat and had a backpack slung over her shoulder.

"What's going on?" I asked.

"I'm going to Aunt Marion's."

"What?" I cried. I suppose I shouldn't have acted so pissed off. After all, I'd been planning on taking off myself not twenty minutes ago. But I was just a visitor. She was the mother. She wasn't supposed to leave.

"I can't take it anymore, Chris. I need a break. It's just for a few days."

"Right," I said. Judging by the size of her suitcase, it

looked like it would be more than a few days.

"I left a note for your father on the table. For when he comes back."

"Great, can't wait," I snapped. "And what about Echo?" I asked. "You're not taking her with you?"

"Echo has school. I can't just pull her out," she murmured. "She'll be fine. You'll take good care of her. I know you will."

That's your responsibility, not mine, I wanted to say to her. Then again, it's not like she'd been doing a bang-up job to begin with. "Where is Echo?" I asked.

Sheila glanced around. "She's downstairs, I think. In the basement," she said. She looked away for a second. "You know, in her corner."

"Right," I said. I still couldn't believe it.

"I'm sorry, sweetie. I just need some time. I've got to get it together, and your father . . ." Her eyes began to fill up with tears.

"When I said 'do something,' this wasn't what I meant."

She didn't answer for a moment. "I'll call you tomorrow," she said at last. She stepped up close to me. "Good luck with your game on Saturday", she said. "I'll be thinking about you."

"Who cares about a stupid game," I whispered.

She stepped back. I could tell she was a little taken aback, but she didn't say anything.

"I'll call tomorrow," she said, and headed out the door. Then she was gone.

I guess human mothers aren't so different from doppelganger mothers after all, I thought, watching as her headlights backed out of the driveway.

"Echo?" I called out from the top of the stairs.

"Down here."

I headed down the stairs and looked in between the sheets. There they all were, just like last time—Echo, the bunnies, and the bears, all seated around the table in their little chairs. Except Echo, of course. She was too big. Teacups and saucers were neatly placed before every member of the party. A plate of real cookies occupied the center of the table.

"There you are," she said, as if she'd been expecting me. "I was wondering when you were going to arrive. Look, everyone, Chris is back."

She got up slowly and moved a few of the animals aside, adjusting their place settings, and went back to her seat at the other end of the table. I sat down at the spot she'd cleared.

"See, Mr. Wimple," she said to the bear at her right, "I told you he'd be here." She looked up at me. "Everyone was worried when you didn't show up last time," she explained. "Would you like some tea?" She offered the kettle.

"Um, sure. Why not," I said. I took the extra cup near me on the table and held it up. She pretended to pour, then put the kettle back down.

"Mom's left," I said.

Echo nodded. "I know. I looked in and saw her packing."

"You don't seem too concerned," I said.

Her brow furrowed for a moment. Then she shrugged again. "She'll be back," she whispered. "She always comes back."

So this isn't the first time, I thought. Whether that was good or bad, I really couldn't say.

"Would you like a cookie?" she asked. She reached forward and started to pick up the plate, then stiffened. I could see a wave of pain flash across her face. It was only for a second, but it cut right through me. Then she straightened up and handed me the plate. She must have seen me wince.

"I shouldn't have spilled that milk," she said.

"Just bad luck, that's all," I said, taking a cookie.

She nodded and went back to sipping from her cup.

"I'm sorry, Echo," I said.

"It's okay," she said. "He's just angry."

It seemed like she didn't even care. "Why would you say something like that?" I demanded.

"'Cause it's just the way he gets sometimes. He can't help it. He isn't always like that, you know."

I couldn't understand why she would stick up for him. "I just wish it was me instead," I murmured.

"I don't," she said. "I remember when I was little, when he used to hit you. Listening is worse."

I don't know why the revelation startled me so much. I mean, after all, why would Echo have been the only one? Still, I had to look away when she said it. Suddenly I felt worse than ever for what I'd done to Chris. To have a guy like Barry in your life, and then have someone like me come along. Awful. I didn't know if she was right about the listening part, but after two nights of it, I had a hard time believing she was wrong.

"Don't you hate him?" I said. "I know I do."

She closed her eyes. "Don't say that, Chris. Please."

"Well, it won't happen again. I won't let it. I promise," I said.

As soon as I said it, I knew it was a mistake. Not just because of the whole involvement thing—though my mother, no doubt, would have been horrified at what I'd said—but also because I couldn't back it up. I couldn't be around forever. At some point Echo would be on her own. And because of me. Because I'd taken Chris—the one person in her life who might have been willing to protect her—out of the picture. On the other hand, it didn't seem like he'd ever done anything to stop it. Maybe he couldn't because it had happened to him, too. Maybe all he could do was escape with her into the basement, into this tidy little corner of the world where they could both forget about it.

So why *did* I say it? I guess because I meant it. Even someone like me, a killer, knew that what was going on was wrong. Yeah, I know my mother always said good and evil and right and wrong were just human fictions, but none of that mattered to me anymore. What was happening to Echo wasn't a fiction. That, of course, was why I was a failure, but at that moment I didn't care.

"You haven't eaten your cookie yet," Echo said. It was like she hadn't even heard me. Maybe that was for the best.

I munched down one cookie and had another. I hadn't finished my dinner and was feeling pretty hungry. For the next twenty minutes, I listened to Echo as she chatted with the animals. I piped in from time to time, like when she asked me a question on behalf of Mrs. Weatherby or something. But mostly I hung back, finishing the plate of cookies and admiring all of Echo's drawings on the wall of the dancing bears and frogs and green hills. Finally I got up to go. I actually did have to study for a test on Macbeth tomorrow. "See you later, Echo," I said. "Don't worry, I'll handle Dad in the morning."

"Wait," she said, struggling to her feet. She went over to the toy box, reached under it, and pulled out a pad of paper and a small box. She came back to the table and set everything in front of me. I opened the box. It was full of markers and crayons and colored pencils.

"You can't go yet. You almost forgot," she said.

"What?" I asked. A shiver ran down my back. She pointed to the pictures on the wall.

"You always make me one. After every time."

So the pictures weren't Echo's. It was like the race car sheets all over again. Only worse. For a second my voice caught in the back of my throat.

"I think it's time you drew one, Echo," I finally managed to say. I didn't want to be insensitive, but I'd never drawn anything in my life—nothing decent, anyway.

Echo paused for a second, then shrugged. "Okay," she said. "But you have to tell me what to draw, just like I do with you."

"Sounds like a good idea," I said, going over to the pictures hanging on the wall. "How about a picture of Mr. Wimple and Mrs. Weatherby building a snowman," I said. It was the first thing that popped into my mind. Besides, I'd always wanted to build a snowman.

"Okay," she said. "But I'm going to put us in the picture too."

"Good. We'll all build one. A big one," I said, looking over Chris's pictures. I tried to imagine him sitting at the table where Echo was now, making those suns with a big yellow crayon for his kid sister. To be honest, they were pretty good drawings. Better than I could do, I'm sure.

A few minutes later, I looked over to see how Echo was coming along. She was an even better artist than Chris. There we were with the rabbit and the bear. The page was mostly white, what with the snow and all, but there were mountains in the background with little people skiing on them. And then there was something else.

"What are they doing here?" I asked, pointing to the two other people helping us with the snowman.

"That's Mom and Dad," she said. "I decided to have us on vacation. Daddy always said he wanted to go skiing in the mountains. So maybe we'll go someday, right?"

"Sure," I said.

When she finished, I hung the drawing up next to Chris's. There were a lot of pictures on that wall. Too many.

We turned out the light and slowly went upstairs in the dark.

CHAPTER TEN

"Come on, guys. Hurry up!" Steve shouted.

We all followed him deeper into the woods, stumbling down the dark road.

It was Friday night, the night before the "big game," and I was out with the guys. My first time, unless you counted the night I killed Chris, which I didn't.

I wasn't going to go at first. Amber was with her friends, so I didn't see any point in it. But I also didn't want to leave Echo home alone. I mean, I wasn't too worried—Barry hadn't seemed particularly distraught when he stumbled into the kitchen this morning and read Sheila's note. He just crumpled it up and pitched it toward the garbage bin like it was a losing lottery ticket or something. At first I thought that maybe he was too ashamed after what had happened last night to get upset, but it was probably that he was just too hungover to care.

No, I wasn't as worried about Echo as I had been last night, but I didn't want to take a chance, either. It was Friday, after all, and who knew what he'd come home like.

So I decided to stay behind. You know, to keep an eye on things. But when I got home from practice, there was a message on the machine from Echo—she was going over to her friend Zoë Simon's house for a sleepover. Said she might be there all weekend. *Just as well*, I thought. That's when I decided to go out. Maybe some time alone in the house was what Barry needed.

Steve and Josh picked me up before Barry got home, and the three of us went out for pizza. After dinner we went to the park in the center of town, where a few hundred kids had gathered for the pep rally. People cheered for us, and everyone gave speeches. You'd think we'd already won the game.

"Going out with the guys" basically meant piling into a couple cars afterward and just driving around, drinking a few beers. Actually, it was kind of fun. Everyone was all pumped up for the game with Springfield, and there was a nervous sort of excitement in the air. Even I felt it. It wasn't like the party I'd been to the weekend before. Sure, we had beers with us, but nobody got stupid—everyone looked out for one another, and even if they hadn't been, guys knew better than to get too wasted and risk letting everyone down. Still, there was a lot of energy hanging around, and even before we headed into the woods, I knew it had to go somewhere.

At first a few guys suggested we go down the tracks, which was the last place I wanted to go. It wasn't so much that I had bad memories of the place—even though I did—I just didn't know what kind of shape Chris would be in. I'd wrapped him up pretty tight in that plastic the night I killed him, but I still didn't know what to expect. I mean, what if we went out there and he was stinking the whole place up? I'd started to feel a little uneasy about the whole body situation in general these last couple days, but there was so much other stuff going on, it wasn't at the forefront of my mind. Until now.

"We just went there last week—there's nothing down there. Let's go somewhere else," I said.

They all kind of looked at one another for a minute before Steve piped up.

"How about Parson Woods?" he said. Even though I was supposed to be sort of the ringleader, he was the quarterback and was used to making decisions.

"Sounds good," I shouted. I didn't know where Parson Woods was, but it beat the tracks.

Some of us jumped into Steve's crappy Ford Escort, a few others into a Pontiac that belonged to another guy's father, and we headed off.

We took our time driving around, weaving in and around town, honking when we saw someone we knew, even yelling stuff out the windows once or twice and squealing our tires. Steve and the other kid took turns in the lead, passing each other back and forth. Apparently there weren't any police in this town. Either that or they decided not to bother us the night before the Springfield game. I just sat in the backseat plugging my ears as discreetly as I could against the blasting music and wishing I were with Amber.

I'd caught a glimpse of her an hour ago at the pep rally. She and her pals were all dressed up in their outfits, shaking their pom-poms and short skirts around and getting everyone in the "spirit." That was the big word of the night, after all.

"We've got spirit, yes we do. We've got spirit, how 'bout you? SPIRIT!"

I don't think she saw me, but I didn't care. It was enough to watch her twirl in the middle of her pack. Just like at the party last weekend, she stood alone in the crowd. It's like she was on fire or something. It's funny how when you realize you're in love with someone, they seem totally different all of a sudden, like they even look different. And all you want to do is just be around them and stare and notice how strange and wonderful they are even though they're just the same person they always were and it's really you who is different.

"Where's the flashlight?" Josh asked as the trees rose on both sides.

"Forget it," another kid said. "We don't need it."

It was sort of true. The moon wasn't quite full yet, but it was getting close. From its spot above us, enough light came down so that the road shone, and all the white stripes and numbers on our jerseys made us glow like a pack of dancing skeletons.

A bunch of guys started running, hooting and hollering down the road, disembodied voices chasing shapes in the moonlight. Pretty soon everyone had joined them, including me. It was kind of liberating in a weird sort of way, like we were all together, but still each one alone. In fact, I got so caught up in it, I practically ran right into Josh, who had stopped along with everybody else. Then I saw it too.

"What's that doing all the way out here?" Steve asked.

The station wagon gleamed where it sat off to one side of the road. It was a white Subaru Legacy, an older model. Everyone sort of walked around it for a minute, wondering where it had come from, wondering what it was doing out here, wondering if the owner was coming back anytime soon.

Everyone but me. I'd seen that car before—they'd shown a picture of it on TV, or one just like it. Apparently none of the other guys watched the news. Seeing it shining there under the moon, I felt all prickly. Suddenly I wanted to get out of there, and fast.

"Come on, guys, let's head back," I said.

No one seemed to hear me. They were all pumped up from the night and started walking around it, looking in the windows, kicking the tires and laughing, then kicking the doors, then things really started to get out of hand.

Crash!

One of kids had taken his beer bottle and thrown it at the passenger's side window. The window cracked but didn't break. Everyone laughed, as if the sound of smashing glass was hilarious.

Then *crash!* And *crash, crash!* Three more bottles hit the window, and this time it broke to cheers from all the guys. Then:

Boom!

Steve had taken a rock almost the size of a football and managed to heave it through the windshield. This brought even bigger cheers, and before you knew it, they were all going crazy, scratching the door panels with stones and pieces of glass, slashing the tires, snapping off the antenna. I just stood back and watched in awe as they transformed the wagon into a broken-down husk. I wondered what the police were going to think when they finally found the car. If they ever found it.

When they'd finally exhausted themselves on the car, they all stepped back, still giggling. Then Josh turned to me.

"What's the matter, Parker, a little property damage too much for you?"

Actually, I didn't really see the point in the whole thing, but I wasn't about to tell them that.

"I was just having too much fun watching you guys," I said.

They all hooted at that one, and before long we were heading down the road back to the cars. Before we left, I took one last look back at the station wagon. I didn't know why it had been left there of all places, but I didn't like it. All I knew was that the one who'd left it there probably wasn't coming back for it. The only question was—where was that person now?

"All right, you Sallies, get your asses out there!"

That was Coach in his usual lovable game-time persona, which didn't actually differ much from his off-the-field persona.

The air had changed. It was a cold day, and clouds had moved in over the early morning hours, turning the sky into a single dark, angry bruise. I knew that because I hadn't really slept much last night after the guys brought me home. When I came in, Barry was passed out in front of the blaring TV. I turned it off and left him snoring on the couch. I was pretty tired myself, but after I got into bed, I suddenly started thinking about the game, and pretty soon I was wide awake again. I was nervous as hell, which pissed me off. Why should I care about this game, just because everyone else seemed to?

As the hours drifted by, I just looked out the window, watching the moon sink farther into the sky before the clouds rolled in and ate it up. And pretty soon the sky lightened a little and it was dawn, and there I was, still awake.

The funny thing was, I wasn't tired now as I ran out onto the field with the other guys. I don't know if it was the cold air or the nervousness twitching through me or the shouting and cheering coming from the packed stands, but I was pumped. Who knows, maybe it was that partially incoherent speech Coach had given before game time—the one where he sounded like a cartoon bulldog who'd swallowed an air horn—that had me revved. I'd understood only about half of it, but he'd yowled with such conviction I had to believe he meant every word.

The game had just started. Springfield, the visiting team, had won the coin toss and had gotten the ball first. They'd run it up to their thirty-yard line on the kickoff, and our defense, of which I was supposedly the starring member, was out there to stop them. I knew enough by now to know where I was supposed to line up, and I also knew what my job as linebacker was—I was there to take out whoever had the ball. If the running back or some other back got it, my job was to tackle him. Otherwise, I went after the quarterback.

The first play was terrible. It's one thing to tackle in practice; it's another thing altogether to do it for real. The noise was what got me the most—all those helmets and pads cracking together and everyone yelling and grunting and crying out. I pretty much froze up and barely managed to get a hand out to brush the running back as he took off by me down the field for twenty yards before a safety brought him down.

The next play wasn't much better. As the quarterback dropped back to pass, the left tackle moved up to block me. I sort of slapped at him a few times, but I didn't go anywhere. The pass was caught. Touchdown.

Coach had an earful ready for me as I came off the field.

"What the hell was that out there?" he screamed as I headed for the bench. I was already pretty tired and just wanted to sit down, and here this guy was yelling so loud I could feel my eardrums rattle.

"I don't know," I snapped. "They just got by us, I guess."

"I'll say they did," he screamed. Then he launched into a tirade about how I was this miserable failure and he'd been wrong to think I was ever going to be a big star someday and how I was an embarrassment to the team. It was like my mother and Barry rolled into one, and listening to him, I could feel myself getting madder and madder.

He finished chewing me out just in time to turn and see our halfback fumble the ball near the fifty.

"Goddamit!" he cried, and threw his hat down on the ground. He turned back to me and grabbed me by the face mask. "All right, you useless piece of crap—get back out there and try it again."

He hurled me in the direction of the ball. As I ran out there, I just kept thinking, *I'll show that creep. He wants a tackle, I'll give him a tackle. I'll prove him wrong.*

Of course, in the back of my mind I knew that's exactly what he wanted me to think, but I didn't care. I was so pissed off at this point that I just wanted someone to pay.

"Hut, hut, hike!"

The quarterback took the snap and handed off to the running back. This time I had it picked up from the start. Before the runner had a chance to get back to the line of scrimmage, I'd flipped the right guard aside and was into the backfield, flying through the air.

Crack!

I could feel the poor kid collapse under me as we hit the ground, like he was hollow or something. I'd nailed him so hard he never even had time to make a sound other than a little grunt as all the air blew out of him. I'm sure he never saw the ball go flying out of his arms and start skittering across the field into the hands of one of our players, who picked it up and ran it down the field into the end zone. I barely saw it, I was so distracted by what had just happened.

The next thing I knew, there were like five guys lifting me up off the ground and jumping up and down and hollering for joy and slapping me on the butt while in the background a steady roar rose from the people in the stands.

As for the running back, he was still on the ground. I guess I'd knocked the poor kid for a loop. It didn't take long for him to come to, but he had to be carried off the field. We all knew he'd be out for the remainder of the game.

The rest of the half went like that. With every play, I got bolder, more aggressive, getting closer and closer to the quarterback, knocking down the ball as it left his hands, knocking down the players. After a while I could see it in their eyes as we lined up across from each other—that fear that I was coming after them. I forgot about everything else and just focused on how good it felt to push everyone around. It wasn't that hard—doppelgangers are strong, stronger than we look. In fact, if you ever tangle with one, don't ever try to wrestle it or anything. The best thing to do is to go for the eyes, then run like hell. It's probably your only chance.

Anyway, I ended the half with a big sack, nailing the quarterback from behind. I could hear his arm snap as we came down. The next thing I knew, he was pleading for me to get off him. I jumped up, and a second later he started crying. I felt pretty bad—he looked like he was in a lot of pain—but before I could say anything to him, the horn sounded to mark the end of the first half. My teammates grabbed me and ushered me toward the sideline to a chorus of cheers. Coach was waiting for me with a big smile on his face. He gave me a big slap on the helmet as I went by.

"That's the stuff!" he said, and we all turned and headed to the locker room for halftime.

We gathered around the benches, all of us sweating, some bleeding, a few limping, forming a circle around Coach. He blew his whistle and everyone went silent.

"All right, ladies, we're up by seven. Not bad. But we need to step it up. Offense, you need to get serious and stop wasting time. Most of all, I need all of you to be more like this guy right here. . . ."

He reached out and grabbed me by the shoulder pads and hauled me into the center. Suddenly all eyes were on me.

"You see this guy right here?" he said, shaking me.

"This guy is a goddam killer. That's what he is. Did you see him out there? It was like someone unleashed an animal in this kid—a predator taking down his prey with no mercy. That's what I want all of you girls to do out there. Be the killer!"

The guys all started cheering and shaking their fists in the air, but I didn't join them. All I could think about was what the coach had just said, about how he'd called me out, revealing me to everyone, mostly to myself. The adrenaline still running through me now mingled with the feeling of that running back crumpling under me, the sound of the quarterback's arm breaking and him crying, crying for me to get off him, to have mercy. It was that same sort of giddy sickness I'd felt after killing Chris, and I hated it. Worst of all, I was the big hero because of it.

Coach went on blabbing for a few minutes, talking about strategy and plays, but I didn't really hear what he was saying. To be honest, I didn't really care anymore, about any of it. All I knew was that I'd lost control out there on the field, just like at the fire with Chris, and people had gotten hurt. I'd been reduced to nothing more than an animal, and I hated that feeling more than anything.

As the adrenaline faded and the sick sweetness filtered away, and everyone starting scuttling out of the locker room, I suddenly realized what I had to do.

"Parker, get up," Coach barked from the doorway as the last of the players headed out to the field.

I got up, went over to my locker, opened it, and started taking off my jersey.

"What the hell are you doing?" he hollered, and strode over to me.

I didn't say anything. I just kept taking off my shirt.

Coach shook his head. "I don't have time for this crap. Now come on, we got a whole second half to play."

"Not me," I said. "I'm finished." I threw my helmet in the locker and tossed my jersey on the floor.

Coach made a kind of choked noise that sounded halfway between a groan and a growl. I could tell he was about to lose it, but at that point I didn't care anymore.

"I don't know what's gotten into you these last couple of weeks. I sure as hell don't like it, but we'll deal with it later. Now, for the last time, let's go."

"Sorry, Coach," I said, continuing to undress. "I said I'm finished. Done. As in, I quit."

He grabbed me by the shoulder pads, slammed me back against a locker, and held me there.

"You can't quit," he shouted, stabbing a finger toward my face. He was so close I could see every white whisker on his chin. More than anything I wanted to grab him right back. I wanted to do to him what I'd done to those Springfield players.

But I didn't. I just looked him straight in the eyes, looked through his eyes, into his brain, and right on out the back, and after a few seconds, he let go. He seemed tired all of a sudden.

"Chris, think about what you're about to do to everyone. Forget about me. Think about your teammates, think about the town, think about your father," he said. As soon as he mentioned Barry, I made a face. I couldn't help it. "Then think about yourself," he said. "Think about your future, how you're hurting it."

"I don't have a future," I murmured.

He took off his baseball cap and sighed. "Chris, you're an angry young man. I can see it in your eyes—for whatever reason you're pissed off at the world. I know what it's like. I was there, too, once. But that's why you can't quit. Because you know you can go out there and let it all out. You need this, Chris. Just like I needed it when I was your age."

"That's not who I want to be," I said. "Not anymore."

Before he could respond, Coach Ballard poked his head in the door.

"Coach?" he said. "We're starting."

"Dammit," Coach muttered. He gave me one last look and walked away.

"We'll win it without you, then," he hollered back as he marched out the door. Ballard looked at me for a moment in surprise, then turned and followed Coach.

"Good," I said. I actually hoped they would win. For their sake as well as mine.

Just as I turned back to the locker, I felt the twitch in my eye. It had been a while. I glanced into the little mirror hanging in the locker and, sure enough, there they were—those doppelganger orbs, swollen against Chris's face, leering at me as if they had a mind of their own.

"Go away," I said.

The slitted pupils—cold, reptilian—narrowed for a moment before fading away. Soon Chris's eyes were back, looking as dark and forlorn as ever.

"And don't come back."

I changed, emptied out my locker, and walked out.

"Echo?" I called from the doorway.

The house was empty. She was still at her friend's.

I went into the kitchen and checked the answering machine. Sheila still hadn't called. Big surprise. Then I flipped through the numbers on the phone's caller ID, like I'd seen Sheila do, until I found the number Echo had called from yesterday. I dialed it, and a woman answered.

"Hi . . . Mrs. Simon?" I said. I was a little nervous. I'd never used a phone before.

"Yes?" she said.

"Is Echo there? This is her brother, Chris."

"Oh, hello, Chris. The girls are upstairs. I'll get her."

There was a clunking noise and then a long pause. A minute later Echo's voice came on.

"Yeah?" she said.

"This is Chris," I said.

"I know," she said.

"Oh, okay. Listen," I said, "I was wondering if you wanted to stay another night. I mean, it might be good for you to stay another night. Think they'll let you?"

"Probably," she said. "What's going on?"

"Nothing, really," I said. I wasn't sure how Barry would deal with my quitting the team, but judging by how he'd reacted when I got benched, I wasn't taking any chances, at least not by having Echo around. "It's just that things might be better if you came back tomorrow."

"Okay," she said. Her voice sounded so small on the phone.

"Good," I said. "See you later, then."

"Bye," she said, and hung up.

I knew Barry was still at the game along with everyone

else—probably wondering why I wasn't out there—and he wouldn't be back for a while, so I took a long shower and washed all the sweat and grime off me, scrubbing until my skin was raw and tingly. It felt good to be clean, to feel clean, if just for a little while. I even shaved afterward, something I hated to do because it meant I had to look at Chris in the mirror for more than a few seconds.

"Sorry, Chris," I said as I finished the last few strokes. Even though I figured he would have been upset about my quitting, I felt a lot better. Like I was doing it for both of us.

Barry got home not long after that. I came out of my room as soon as I heard him walk in. I decided to get it over with now and not wait. Besides, he probably wouldn't have started drinking at this point—not much, anyway.

Seeing me standing down at the end of the hall, he stopped and leaned against the wall near the kitchen doorway. He took a cigarette out of his shirt pocket and lit it.

"I quit," I said.

He snorted. "Yeah, I know. I found out after I chewed the stupid coach out for ten minutes for benching you in the second half." He took another drag. "You made me look like an asshole, Chris."

"Sorry," I said.

"Me too," he said. He shook his head. "That's it, you know. Forget the scholarships, forget college, because we sure as hell can't afford to send you on our own. Not that I'd pay for you anyway. Not now. Not for a quitter."

"That's okay," I said. I didn't mean to sound nonchalant. I mean, *I* knew why it wasn't a big deal whether Chris got a scholarship or not.

But Barry didn't. He turned and slammed the wall with his fist, punching a hole right through the Sheetrock.

"Stupid shit!" he shouted, shaking his hand. I couldn't tell if he was talking to me or to himself. Probably both.

I could see his knuckles were bleeding. He took another drag, tightened his fist again with a grimace, and turned into the kitchen.

A second later the phone rang. I heard Barry pick up.

"Yeah," he snapped. There was a moment of silence. I wondered who it was. Echo, maybe? Sheila, at last?

"Sorry, Amber. He can't come to the phone right now," Barry said, then hung up. He came back out into the hallway and stared over at me for a second. Even from where I was, I could see the look on his face. He looked just like Chris, just like the real Chris had the night I'd killed him.

He shook his head again in disgust and looked at the hole in the wall. "What a perfect week," he said. He went back into the kitchen to make himself a drink.

"So who won?" I called down the hallway.

He didn't answer.

CHAPTER ELEVEN

"Chris, could I speak with you for a minute?" Ms. Simpson said as the bell rang that Thursday.

"Ooooo," the class said as they picked up their books and backpacks and headed for the door. I just stayed in my seat wondering what it was all about.

"Don't worry, you're not in trouble," she said after everyone was gone. She came over with a few papers in her hand and sat down across from me.

"Okay," I said, trying to get a look at the papers.

"I just wanted to see how you were holding up. I'm sure this hasn't been an easy week for you."

By the time I got back to school on Monday, everyone had heard I'd quit the team. For the most part, the kids didn't really seem to know how they were supposed to react. I mean, Mr. Football giving it all up—it was ridiculous. As a result, just about everyone ignored me. My teammates, of course, were the most confused. And I could tell by the way Steve, Josh, and some of the others looked at me when I walked into school that first morning that they were pissed off and even hurt. I didn't blame them. I even felt bad about it. But I didn't bother to try to talk to them or pretend everything was okay. I just kind of kept to myself, and for the most part, aside from a few murmured comments, people left me alone.

The fact that we'd won the game helped. Since I'd taken Springfield's two best players out of commission, Bakerville had had an easy time of it in the second half and won 37–16. Still, the season wasn't over by any means. Play-offs weren't that far away, and now they'd lost their star player. Which was me, of course.

The rejection was good, in a way. As the weekend went on, I'd started to worry that I was acting too much out of character—I knew Chris would never have quit the team—and I was afraid I'd drawn too much attention to myself. People might start asking questions. But now it looked like the opposite was happening—it was like, all of a sudden, I didn't exist. I was a nonperson again, which was fine by me. Don't get me wrong—I sort of enjoyed all the attention at first. All the looks from the girls and the high fives and salutes in the halls between classes. But that stuff gets old fast. Besides, I had other things to focus on.

Like Amber. She was one of the only people who didn't ignore me. In fact, she seemed to pay more attention to me after I'd quit. When everyone else went to a different table at lunch, she sat alone with me. We even went to the movies one night. This time she asked me out. We were going to rent something and go to her house, but at the last minute she changed her mind and we went to a theater instead. It was fine by me—I wasn't crazy about the idea of seeing her whack-job parents again anyway, especially now.

I don't even remember what the movie was about. Some sort of romantic comedy, I guess. I just remember about halfway through brushing Amber's hand, not on purpose, and then her brushing back and then the next thing I knew, we were holding hands. Her hand was warm, and her skin softer than anything I'd ever felt before.

It was more than enough to compensate for the cold shoulder the others were giving me. Still, I didn't want to seem like I didn't care at all.

"It's been a little hard," I said to Ms. Simpson. "But I'm getting used to it, I guess."

She nodded. "Good, Chris. I'm glad to hear it."

"Thanks for asking," I added.

"Just so you know," she said, "if you want someone to talk to, I'd be happy to arrange a meeting with the school's counselor. Mr. Morovitch is very good."

I wasn't sure what she was getting at. Why would I need to talk to anyone? Especially a shrink.

"No, I'm okay. Really. It's just a game. I didn't feel like playing anymore. That's all."

"All right," she said. "I just didn't know if there was something else. If your quitting was a part of something bigger. I don't mean to pry, but I can't help worrying."

She seemed genuinely concerned. As nice as it was, I suddenly felt very nervous.

"You know," she said, "when a person goes through a lot of changes all at once, they don't always realize what's going on, how it's affecting them."

"There aren't any changes," I said. "I mean, just football."

"Perhaps. But I have to wonder about this." She handed

me the paper. It was my test from last Friday. The final test on *Macbeth*, the one I'd studied for.

"But I got an A," I said. "That's good, isn't it?"

"It is good. It's very good. This is better than anything you've done this year, by quite a bit. There's something different about it, in the way you write. Even your handwriting is more legible."

"I didn't cheat," I said.

"I know," she said, "I watched you take the test with my own eyes."

"I'm just trying to get better," I said.

"There's nothing wrong with that," she said, nodding. "I just haven't seen anything like this before. So much improvement. And now that you've quit the team, and then the conversation we had last week—I just want to make sure things are okay."

"Well, they are," I said.

"Good then," she said. She didn't seem too convinced, but I could tell she wasn't going to push it any further. "You know, I found your essay really interesting. You were the only one who said Macbeth wasn't a tragic hero."

"Well, I was reading over that handout you gave us, you know the one about Aristotle, and he was talking about how the tragic hero can't be too evil, otherwise we're just happy when he goes down at the end."

"And I could see in your essay you think Shakespeare goes too far with Macbeth."

"I don't know—I just felt sort of relieved to see him die. He seemed relieved too."

"Perhaps. But to say that he wasn't a tragic hero is to say he lost his humanity for good. That he became a monster and never recovered from it. But that isn't the case."

"So my essay was wrong?"

"I think it was."

I glanced over my paper. "But you gave me almost full credit on this section."

"Because you made a good argument. I like to see students go out on a limb, even if I don't agree with their conclusions. And I think there's a case to be made for what you said." She paused. "But I also see a man in act five who's come full circle, who's come to realize what's happened to him, what he's lost, and is utterly shaken, and more human than he ever was to begin with."

I suppose she was right. But I couldn't get over what he'd done. Maybe because it reminded me so much of what I'd done to Chris, to the old man, even to those guys on the Springfield team. I still remembered what Coach had said about me in front of everyone at halftime. It had been on my mind ever since.

"So you think that someone who loses themselves in all that rage can still come out okay in the end?"

"Careful now," she said. "I'm not trying to say that Macbeth comes out okay in the end. And neither is he. You're right, by the way. A part of Macbeth does long for it all to be over. I'm just trying to say he reclaims a part of that noble man he used to be."

"I just wonder if it's possible for people who've done awful things to ever redeem themselves at all."

"Of course it is," she said. "It's not easy, though, and it doesn't happen often. And it depends on two things—someone really has to want to change, and the other people in their life have to be willing to let them."

I nodded.

"But that's not what *Macbeth* is about," she added. "Shakespeare's not writing about redemption. He's writing a tragedy, which is only a part of life, not the whole story."

"Good thing," I said, and stood up to leave.

"So did you figure it out yet?" she asked.

"Figure what out?"

"You know, what we talked about before, about Banquo being killed and Lady Macbeth not stopping it? You wanted to know what someone should do in a situation where, well, someone was being hurt."

"Oh yeah," I said. I still wasn't really sure about the situation in *Macbeth*, but I remembered what I'd told Echo in the basement last week.

"I guess sometimes you have to take matters into your own hands," I said.

There was a knock. I looked over my shoulder to see Amber standing in the doorway.

"Hi, Ms. Simpson," Amber said, smiling. Amber had Ms. Simpson for English too. Only she had her third period instead.

"Come in, Amber," Ms. Simpson said.

Amber took a few steps into the classroom. "Sorry to interrupt."

"That's okay," Ms. Simpson said, getting up from the desk. "We were just finishing anyway. Right, Chris?"

"Right," I said, standing up and grabbing my books.

"What do you need?" Ms. Simpson asked.

"Nothing," Amber said. "I was just looking for Chris. Stacy said he was here."

"Well, he's all yours now."

I headed for the door. "Thanks, Ms. Simpson," I said, looking over my shoulder. "I'll see you tomorrow."

"'Tomorrow and tomorrow and tomorrow,'" she replied, and winked at both of us. Amber laughed and we turned to leave together.

"Oh, and by the way," Ms. Simpson said. Both of us stopped. "Better watch out, Amber—your boyfriend got a higher grade on a test than you did."

Amber looked at me and raised her eyebrows. I just shrugged as we left the room together.

"Got lucky, I guess," I said.

"Damn right you did," she replied.

"So where are we going?" I asked, lifting my head to try and catch something through the speck of light showing along the bottom of the blindfold.

"It's a surprise. Don't worry; we'll be there pretty soon. And no peeking."

"Right," I said. I had been distracted enough by my talk with Ms. Simpson that I hadn't really noticed Amber was acting funny until we reached her car and she pulled out the blindfold. That's when I realized how quiet she'd been as we left the school, just walking beside me with a sort of odd expression on her face that was almost a smile, but not quite.

We'd been driving now for quite some time, maybe twenty minutes. And fast, too. I kept feeling myself being tossed from one side to the other, just like that first time I'd ridden with her on the way to the party. Only this time, with the blindfold on, I had no chance to brace myself.

"You scared?" she asked at one point. Same as last time. But one thing was different.

"No," I said, "just a little sick, that's all."

She laughed. "Do you trust me?"

"I guess I have to."

"You don't have to," she replied.

"Then I will anyway," I said.

"Good."

A few minutes later we stopped. Amber helped me out of the car and removed the blindfold. We were at a lake. It was a nice day, and though many of the leaves had fallen, there was enough gold in the trees to make everything glow. And it was warm, warmer than it had been for a couple weeks, as if the sun had been holding on to one last day of summer and decided that today was the day to let it go.

There was only one other car in the parking lot—it belonged to some old couple at a picnic table down near the shore—so we had the place pretty much to ourselves. We got out of the car and started walking down through the pines toward the water. The trees were far enough apart to be able to see all around. I could make out some hills on the other side of the lake and picnic tables scattered here and there, and everything was quiet as we stepped across the pine needles.

"It's nice here," I said. "I like this place."

"I know," she said, taking my hand.

As we walked down onto the sand, I suddenly stopped.

"Wait a second," I said. "Aren't you supposed to be at cheerleading?"

"I quit," she said, looking down with a smile. "I figured if you could do it, then so could I."

"Great," I said. "Now we can both be losers."

She laughed. "That's right. And why not?"

"Why not," I agreed. It made me feel kind of strange. I had never *caused* anyone to do anything in my entire life—unless you wanted to count Barry punching his fist through the wall—or at least never gotten anyone to change something about themselves. It wasn't the only reason why I loved Amber, but at that moment, it was the most important one.

We kept walking across the beach toward the far end. I was getting all kinds of sand in my sneakers, but I didn't care—it just felt good to be holding Amber's hand again. Even though we more or less walked side by side, I let her sort of lead the way. She seemed to know where we were going, and I didn't have a clue. There was something familiar about this place, but I couldn't figure out what it was.

Pretty soon we reached the end of the sand and entered a path that disappeared into the woods. Now I was really confused.

"Where are we going?" I blurted out.

She glanced over and gave me a look. "Funny," she said.

I tried not to wince. I had to be more careful about stuff like that. I never got in trouble for things I didn't say, only the things I did.

I kept catching glimpses of the water through the trees to my right and realized the path we were on basically skirted the edge of the lake. Pretty soon we came out into a clearing right by the water. I could see the curve of the beach across the way. I started toward the far side, where the path continued.

"Where are you going?" she asked.

I turned to see her standing by a rock on the shore.

"Nowhere," I said, coming back. "Just wanted to see if

there was anyone else on the path." I knew right away it was a stupid thing to say. But I was totally out of it. I'd never felt so happy and so nervous at the same time before.

"Yeah, like there's any chance of that," she said.

She sat down on the rock, and as I walked over to her, I suddenly realized where we were—this was the picture, the one I'd found in the card. I sat down next to her.

"Well, this is the place," she intimated.

"It's even better in real life," I said.

"What do you mean?" she asked, glancing at me.

"Better than the picture. You know, the one you gave me for my birthday."

"Oh," she said, looking down. "That's right. I almost forgot."

I started to ask her what she'd meant, but suddenly I knew that would be a big mistake. Something had happened here before. Something important.

"It feels like so long ago," she said. "You know, when we came here."

"It does," I said. "Like forever."

She wrapped her arm through mine and looked up at me. I closed my eyes for a second and just inhaled. The scent of perfume and oranges wreathed about her, and as I breathed in deeply through my nose, it felt like I was pulling her toward me, like I was almost drawing in her essence. And when I opened my eyes, I saw that it had worked—she was actually leaning in. All of a sudden, I knew what I was supposed to do. I was supposed to kiss her. Only I couldn't. For some reason, I froze. I mean, I'd killed two people, and now here I was, too chicken to kiss a girl.

The moment passed. To her credit, she didn't seem to hold it against me. I could see a glimmer of surprise in her eyes before she looked away, but it wasn't an angry kind of surprise. If anything, it was the good kind. Like when you suddenly realize something about another person, but it really makes you discover something about yourself. Kind of like how I'd felt a week ago when Amber dropped me off and I realized I was in love with her.

For the next hour we just sat on the rock and talked. We talked about school and parents and friends and all kinds of stuff. Actually, she did most of the talking. I didn't have much to say about my own life, nothing good, anyway. So I asked her questions instead, about what she wanted her future to be, about the stuff that bothered her, that sort of thing. And it wasn't just because I didn't want to talk about me.

After a while the sun started heading toward the far hills. The last bit of light was on us.

"I'm glad you came back," I said as we stood up to leave.

"What do you mean?" she asked.

"That night, a week ago. You drove by me as I was walking. But then you came back."

She snorted a little and nodded.

"So why did you do it?"

She shrugged. "Something in the way you were walking, I guess. I'm really not sure."

"I suppose it doesn't matter," I said.

She shook her head. "I think it does. Everything matters. Everything happens for a reason. That night when I drove you back to your house, I felt something. All the way

144

home, I couldn't stop thinking about it."

"Is that why we're here?"

She nodded. "I thought about what you said to me that night a few weeks ago after the party."

"About things being like they were before?" I asked.

"No," she said, looking away. I felt a sinking feeling in my stomach as I watched her shake her head. "I don't ever want things to be like they were before, not even in the beginning. Not even when we came here. But that's not what you said. You asked if we could start over."

"Is that what we're doing?" I asked. I could feel my heart pounding now.

"I guess it is," she said. "I never thought it would happen. All week I've been wondering about it, trying to decide if you should get a second chance. To be honest, I'm still not sure if you deserve one."

"Neither am I," I said.

She stepped up to me, put her arms around my waist, and before I knew what was happening, she was kissing me, slowly at first, with little kisses, then with long, deep ones. Her mouth was soft and warm and her tongue felt strange and wonderful against my own. It was the most bizarre sensation of my life. For that moment I forgot about being a doppelganger, I even forgot about being Chris. The universe had been reduced to the point where our lips joined together. Nothing else existed.

Then she pulled back, and we smiled at each other. It was only when she turned away that I saw her smile fade, and in its place that look of confusion. She glanced at me for a moment, then took my hand and started down the path back to the beach. I didn't know what to make of her bewilderment. I was feeling pretty bewildered myself, and too happy on top of it all to really care too much about it.

She was warm to me on the drive home but quiet, and I could tell she was thinking. Something had happened in the moment of our kiss, and in spite of the giddiness still coursing through me, deep down I couldn't help but feel that there was trouble ahead.

CHAPTER TWELVE

It's funny how being in love makes you forget just about everything else that's going on in your life. Especially the crappy stuff. I'm sure most of the time that's a good thing. But it wasn't when Amber dropped me off later after our drive to the lake. I was still so lost in the memory of that afternoon that I didn't see the trouble until it reared up and bit me right in the butt.

In the week since Sheila had left, things had settled into a routine. Barry was still pissed off about my quitting the team and wasn't really speaking to me—which was a nice change, to tell you the truth. He barely spoke to Echo, either. He didn't mention Sheila, but I could tell he was starting to get worried. The last few days, he went right to the answering machine as soon as he got home from work, then checked the caller ID, but there were never any calls.

The task of making dinner had fallen to Echo. I thought about helping her a few times, but I could barely get a bowl of cereal together in the morning. At least I set the table, which is more than I could say for Barry. The most he seemed to be able to manage when he got home was to crack a beer and hit the couch.

I have to give Echo a lot of credit—the poor kid did the best she could, especially for a ten-year-old. She played it safe the first couple nights. We had hot dogs, which she heated up in the microwave, and baked beans. I wasn't too crazy about the beans, to be honest. They brought back too many memories of my mother and the cabin, but I wasn't about to complain. Then on Wednesday she got a little fancier and made yellow meal. Even Barry didn't raise a stink over that. That went over so well that when I walked in the house now, she was busy putting together some kind of new creation.

"What's up?" I said, coming into the kitchen.

She was standing on a chair over the stove wearing Sheila's apron, which hung practically down to her toes. I leaned over her shoulder and looked into the pot of boiling water.

"Noodles?" I said. "Is that what we're having for dinner?"

"Sort of," she said. "I'm making a casserole, the kind with tuna. We made it in school once." She paused and leaned in toward my neck. "You smell funny," she said, sniffing.

She broke into a smile. "You've been kissing Amber," she said. She began repeating it in a sort of singsongy voice.

"Shut up," I said, but I couldn't help smiling. Pretty soon we were both laughing.

I went back to my room, still laughing, and lay back on the bed. I didn't bother with the TV. I didn't need it—I had the afternoon to relive instead. I looped it over and over again in my head, remembering what she had said, and what I had said, and how her lips had tasted like peppermint. I was so distracted I didn't even hear Barry get home early, and I barely paid attention when he went muttering into his bedroom to change, or when I heard the clink of ice cubes tumbling into his favorite glass as he mixed himself a drink in the kitchen, and then later another.

In fact, I was so out of it I barely noticed how terrible Echo's casserole tasted—how the undercooked noodles crunched amid the curdled cream sauce heavy with salt. I just filled up my plate and munched happily away until the sound of Barry slamming his hand down on the table jolted me from my daydreams.

"Goddam it, Echo, what the hell is this?" he said after struggling to swallow his first bite and washing it down with a gulp of his drink.

Echo shrank in her chair. It was as if, by making herself smaller, she thought Barry's anger would somehow slide over her. By now it was a familiar gesture, but I still winced seeing it.

"Tuna casserole," she squeaked.

"Shit casserole, more like it," Barry muttered, but amazingly he took another bite.

"I like it, Echo," I said, and smiled at her.

Barry looked at me and made a face. Then he turned back to Echo. "If you hadn't driven your mother off to your goddam aunt's, then you wouldn't be stuck making dinner every night this week."

What a jerk, I thought. I didn't care if he was half in the bag or not, it was a rotten thing to say. Not least of all because it wasn't true.

"I don't mind," she whispered, picking at her food. She hadn't eaten more than a bite herself.

"Well, I do," he grunted. "This is just awful," he said.

He kept saying it, even as he kept eating it. I couldn't figure it out, but I wasn't going to let him get away with being mean to Echo for the rest of the meal. Before I knew it, the words just fell out of my mouth.

"So, I noticed you got home early today. More trouble with Mitch, huh?"

He dropped his fork and leveled a glare in my direction.

"I don't want that bastard's name mentioned in my house again. Understand?"

"Sure. But this is the second time in two weeks. Can't imagine he'll take much more of it."

I knew I was picking a fight with him, but I didn't care. The excitement I still felt from earlier had made me reckless. *Besides*, I figured, *better me than Echo*.

To my surprise, Barry wouldn't take the bait.

"You don't know anything about the real world," was all he murmured, glancing over at me. "All you know is how to quit."

I looked down at my plate.

"Where are you going?" Barry barked. I looked up to see Echo frozen at the edge of the table.

Not again, I thought. On the other hand, why should it be any different? The whole evening had been coming to this point ever since Barry stormed home early from work. Only I'd been too gaga to realize it. And now, there was Echo, hanging out there on the other side of the table.

"I'm all done," she said.

"No, you're not. You didn't even touch your food," he

snapped. "I was watching. Now sit back down in your chair and eat your dinner. You're not leaving until you do."

Echo plopped back down in her chair and picked up her fork. She poked at the pile on her plate but didn't eat any of it. Barry, meanwhile, had finished shoveling all of his down. He lit a cigarette, leaned back in his chair, and watched her twitch silently in her seat.

"What's the matter?" he asked. "Not hungry?"

"I just don't want to eat it," she whispered, without looking up. "It isn't very good."

"Damn right it isn't. But you're going to eat it anyway—after all, you made it. We don't waste food in this house."

Echo frowned but didn't say anything more. She didn't eat anything more either, and I could see Barry getting more and more irritated as the minutes ticked by in silence.

"You can leave, Chris," Barry said to me at one point, though he never took his eyes off Echo. I'd finished my plate not long after Barry had, but I stayed at the table right along with the two of them—I wasn't going anywhere, not without Echo anyway.

"Suit yourself," he said when I didn't respond.

Another minute passed, then another, then five, then ten, and still no one moved except when Barry pulled his glare away from Echo long enough to light up another cigarette. Finally Echo stuck her fork into the pile and lifted what had to be by now a cold bite. She started chewing quickly, her face twisting into a look of pure disgust. She chewed and chewed, her face continuing to contort. I started laughing. Seeing that look on her face,

I just couldn't help it. Hearing me, Echo started to smile as she chewed, and I could see she was trying not to laugh like I was.

Barry, big surprise, didn't find it too funny.

"Cut it out!" he hollered, and banged a hand down on the table for the second time that night. Ash from the cigarette in his other hand floated down onto his plate like dirty snowflakes.

I guess you could say that Barry had a way with words—both of us stopped laughing, and Echo went back to chewing, her jaw moving around like a little goat's, though there couldn't have been anything solid left in her mouth.

"For chrissake, swallow," Barry said.

Screwing her face back to its former disgust, Echo started to swallow and everything went downhill from there. I watched her squeeze her eyes shut and then sort of convulse a little. It was as if she were trying to gulp down a tennis ball. The next thing I knew, she was gagging, and the mouthful and then some spilled back onto her plate.

I thought it was kind of funny myself, but before I could start laughing again, Barry leaped up from the table, furious.

"Scoop that back up," he shouted.

"I can't," Echo wailed, and started to cry.

Barry tore around the edge of the table.

"You eat that," he shouted. "Eat it!"

She put her arms up to cover herself, but he swatted them away and cuffed her alongside the head. Then he grabbed her by the neck and pushed her face down closer and closer to the plate as she squirmed and cried. The more she fought him, the darker his face grew. I could see his cheeks start to quiver.

"Stop it!" I shouted, jumping up.

Barry didn't seem to hear me, he just kept pushing Echo's face down farther. Now her nose was in it.

I stepped right up to Barry and shouted in his face. "I said cut it out!"

He turned and looked at me, his eyes narrowing as he pushed Echo's face the rest of the way into the plate of food.

All of a sudden, I was flying through the air, taking Barry down with me. It was like the Springfield game all over again, only this time there were no pads to cushion the blow.

I heard Barry grunt beneath me as we hit the ground.

Then I started hitting him.

"Don't. Ever. Touch. Her. Again!" I screamed, coupling every word with a punch to the face. Before long, blood was welling from his nose and his mouth, and his eyes started rolling in his head.

But as good as it felt, it wasn't enough. My hands went to his throat. I squeezed and his eyes widened as they looked into mine, just like Chris's had. I could see that same look, the one of sheer terror, and a part of me wondered if I was losing my form, if those big monster eyes had returned. The other part of me, the bigger part, didn't care. I could feel him kicking underneath me, trying to pull me off him, but I was stronger. Suddenly it was two weeks ago and I was back at the fire. Suddenly I was killing Chris all over again.

Echo saved us both. Through everything—through the

blood pounding in my ears, through the strange gurgling coming from Barry's throat, through the sound of chairs being kicked around us—her voice sounded in my ear, small and scared.

"Stop it, Chris," she said. "Please, stop. You're hurting him."

She said it again. And then again. I wanted to let go the first time, but I just couldn't. It took her four tries to get through. The fourth time, I felt her hand on my shoulder, pulling me away.

I let go of Barry and fell backward. Barry's hands went to his throat, and he started gasping for air, pushing himself across the floor with both feet until he had his back to the wall. He looked up at me—the anger was gone. Only fear remained.

I turned to Echo. She had tears running down her face. She'd wiped most of the casserole away, but there were still white streaks along the edges of her jaw and forehead. A limp noodle clung to her hair.

"Are you okay?" I said, trying to get my breath back.

She nodded.

"Go pack a bag," I said. "Make sure you have clothes for school tomorrow."

She looked over at Barry. He was wheezing and making these weird gurgly noises. All in all, he looked pretty messed up, and I could tell she wanted to go over to him.

"Echo," I said, "did you hear me?"

She nodded again and ran to her room.

"Now, you listen to me," I said after she'd left. As soon as I stepped toward Barry, he cringed. All of a sudden, I felt awful—even worse than I'd felt at halftime last weekend. But this had to be done.

"I don't care about what you did to me, what you used to do," I said. "But you won't do the same thing to her. Not anymore. Not ever again. Understand?"

He didn't say anything. I took a step toward him, and he began nodding like crazy.

"Otherwise," I said, leaning in, "next time I'll make sure Echo isn't around to stop me."

I fixed him with a glare. He looked away. He was starting to shake now. I looked down at my hands and realized I was shaking too. The whole scene was pathetic all the way around.

I left him on the floor and went into Echo's room. She was finishing up stuffing clothes into a backpack.

"Ready?" I said.

"Where are we going?" she asked.

"You're going somewhere else for tonight. I don't want you here. Who's that friend of yours you sometimes stay with down the street?"

I wasn't sure if there even was such a girl, but I had to find someplace for her to stay tonight, and I still didn't know how to drive.

"Tina," she said. "The Denbys. You know."

"That's right, the Denbys," I said. "I forgot."

I grabbed her hand and led her out into the hall. We both paused in the doorway to listen, but everything was quiet in the kitchen. Then we grabbed our coats and headed out into the night.

We didn't say anything as we marched down the sidewalk, but Echo held tight to my hand. The stars out were bright, and our breath billowed around us in the glow of the street lamps, lighting up the cold. I suddenly remembered that first really chilly night more than a month ago when I'd drifted through the train yard on my way to meeting the old man. Back then I was alone. Not anymore.

Echo led me across the street. We went a little farther, then turned into the driveway of a house—a ranch that looked almost like ours, only with newer paint. Echo rang the doorbell.

A plain-looking woman with dark hair peeked through the window at us, then opened the door.

"Chris. Echo," she said in a surprised kind of way.

I had no idea what the rules were in this kind of a situation, but I was too freaked out over everything that had happened to really care.

"Hi, Mrs. Denby," I said. "Sorry to just show up like this, but I was wondering if Echo could maybe stay over tonight. It would just be one night."

She looked a little confused. I could tell she was trying to figure out what was going on.

"Everything's all right," I added. "We just had something come up, that's all."

"Oh dear," she said. "What happened?"

"Dad's really sick," Echo broke in. "And Mom's away visiting my aunt."

"Yeah," I said, "I'm taking care of him, and we all thought it would be better if Echo stayed with a friend tonight. You know, one less thing to worry about."

"Sure," Mrs. Denby said. "Tina would love to have Echo for the night."

For a second we all kind of stood there. I could see Mrs. Denby working our story out in her mind. Then

Echo's teeth started to chatter.

"Okay, thanks," I said. Mrs. Denby sort of started a little.

"Oh. Now you're sure your father's all right? Maybe you should take him to the hospital."

"He's just got a sore throat, that's all. He can hardly talk. But I think he'll be better tomorrow."

"I hope so," she said. She looked down at Echo and, for the first time, smiled. "Come on in, Echo. It's cold out."

Echo started to go, but I took her hand.

"Could I just talk to her for a second?" I said to Mrs. Denby.

She nodded and closed the door. I kneeled down in front of Echo.

"You're okay with all this?"

She nodded. She looked just like she had that first morning I saw her—with that sort of far-off expression on her face, like she was somewhere else.

"It would probably be a good idea if you didn't talk about what happened tonight," I said.

"I know that," she said.

"Good," I said. "Just go to school tomorrow, and I'll see you when you get back."

"What about you?" she asked.

"Don't worry about me. I'll be fine."

"Don't hurt him any more," she said.

"I won't. I promise."

She nodded and walked into the house. I watched the door close, then left.

I walked back down the street, but when I reached our yard, I suddenly picked up speed again. I couldn't go back into that house, not with him in there. I'd promised Echo I wouldn't hurt him again, and I didn't think I would, but I wasn't sure I trusted myself. Not now.

And so I kept on going, down the street, farther into the cold.

I tried waving someone down for a ride a few times, but no one stopped. Still, it was so freezing that I walked fast, and soon I was crossing the wide lawn and going around behind the house, where I could see Amber's bedroom light was still on.

I flicked a pebble up, then another. She appeared at the window for a brief moment, then disappeared. *Maybe she didn't see me*, I thought. I wondered if I should throw another rock up. Then another thought occurred to me as I stood there in the freezing cold. I remembered the look that had crossed her face after we kissed. Maybe she did see me. Maybe she'd changed her mind. I blew into my hands to try to warm them up and waited a minute, but when she didn't come back, I started to walk away.

"Chris."

I turned to see her standing in the back doorway in sweatpants and a T-shirt, her arms wrapped around herself against the chill. She beckoned with one hand, then turned back inside, leaving the door open, and I hurried to follow her in.

CHAPTER THIRTEEN

Amber shut the door of her bedroom behind me as I stumbled in. I pulled off my jacket and collapsed onto the bed. For a minute I just lay there, feeling my nose and cheeks begin to thaw. The burning felt good.

Amber, meanwhile, sat at her desk, watching me.

"What's going on, Chris?" she finally asked.

"Not much," I said, sitting up. "Just thought I'd pop in for little visit. So how you doing?"

She laughed. "Right," she said. She fixed me with a look. She'd let me slide before; she wasn't going to now.

I shrugged. "There's some stuff going on at home," I said. "I just needed to get out of there for a little while, that's all."

What was I supposed to say? That the family was falling apart piece by piece? I tried to think of what was left of the Parkers. After tonight, it seemed like nothing.

"Okay," she said.

"Barry's such a creep," I muttered, seeing him shove Echo's face into the food all over again in my head. I knew he'd done far worse—to her and to Chris—but for some reason the gesture really bothered me.

"Who?" Amber asked, her eyes narrowing.

Whoops. "I mean Dad," I said, looking down.

She got up from her chair and came over to sit beside me on the bed, and took my hand.

"I'm sorry," she said.

"Thanks," I said. "And thanks for letting me in. I wasn't sure if you saw me out there."

"I saw you," she said.

"Good thing. I was just about frozen. After I dropped Echo off, I walked all the way over here. No one would stop to pick me up."

"People don't stop anymore. It's too dangerous—you never know who you're going pick up."

"Well, they're right about that," I murmured.

"Why didn't you just drive?" she asked suddenly.

I hesitated. "I couldn't," I said at last. "It's a long story."

"Is Echo okay?"

"She'll be fine. Things will be fine," I said. "I think so, anyway. I hope so. I mean, I did what I could to put an end to it, an end to all of . . . well, you know what I mean."

"No, I don't," she said. "I don't know anything about it. You've never told me."

"Oh," I said. *Idiot.* Why would I have ever thought that Chris would tell her about Barry, about Echo and Sheila and everything that was going on between them? Then I remembered that night of our first date, how Amber had cringed when I stepped toward her, just like Echo had with Barry, and suddenly I knew why. I guess, deep down, I'd known all along.

"I'm sorry," I said, turning toward her. "I'm sorry for everything."

She reached up and drew me toward her like she had at the lake and kissed me again, just once, a long, slow kiss.

After it was done, she pulled back and looked up into my eyes. I felt like she was looking right into me, right through Chris and deep inside, into my ugly old screwed-up self. It was too much. I had to turn away.

From the corner of my eye, I watched her stand up and walk back toward the desk. But halfway across the floor she slowed, then stopped and looked up. She turned toward me and paused for a moment.

Before she even said it, I knew it was coming. Looking back, I think she was even giving me a chance to stop it, to step in and distract her from what she didn't want to say, and then we could have both gone on pretending.

"Who are you?" she whispered.

I tried to act like I hadn't heard her, but she said it again, louder.

"What do you mean?" I said, standing up. I tried laughing, but it stuck in my throat.

She didn't move from where she stood. She looked beautiful, like a statue with her hair pulled back and her arms wrapped tight around her just as she had appeared standing outside earlier in the open doorway. She even seemed to shiver a little, though the room was warm.

"I don't know who you are. But you're not Chris."

"That's ridiculous," I said.

"I know," she said. "But it's true."

We were both silent for a minute. Every second that went by, every second I sat there saying nothing, confirmed it.

But all of a sudden, I realized I wanted her to know. What's the point of loving someone if they don't even know who you are or that you exist? Or worse, if they think you're somebody you're not? But Amber didn't think that anymore. She deserved to know the truth.

"How'd you know?" I said at last.

She shifted from one foot to the other and shrugged.

"Lots of things," she said. "The way you've been acting lately—it's not Chris. Trust me. And then this afternoon at the lake. It was like you'd never been there before. You had no idea what happened there. The first time or the second. Right away I could tell."

I looked down at the carpet. I couldn't help wondering if that's what our surprise trip had been about.

"So you were testing me?" I asked.

"No," she said. "Not on purpose, anyway. Not in that sense. I guess if I was testing anyone, it was myself, trying to see if everything I'd been feeling about you these last few days was real, or if it was all some crazy mistake." She paused. "But when I kissed you, that's when I knew for sure."

"How?"

She shrugged again. "You didn't kiss like Chris did. You just . . . it's hard to explain."

I nodded and tried to smile.

"Where's Chris?" she asked suddenly.

The question took me off guard, though it shouldn't have. I took a deep breath.

"He's dead," I said at last.

For a second she didn't say anything. I watched her eyes fill with tears.

"Oh God," she gasped, and closed her eyes. She covered her face with her hands and turned away. All of a sudden, my heart began pounding. I started to reach out for her, then stopped. Something told me it wasn't a good idea just then. So instead I hung back and waited and tried to stop my chest from beating so loud.

Finally she turned back to me. "So who *are* you?" she asked. "Don't tell me you're some long-lost twin brother or something like that."

Actually, that wasn't a bad explanation. I used to see stuff like that all the time on the soap operas. For a brief moment, I was tempted to go with it.

"No," I whispered. "Nothing like that."

She hesitated. "Then *what* are you?"

I thought back to the old man in the boxcar. He'd asked me the same question.

"I'm an angel," I said, remembering what the old man had said. I shook my head and started to laugh, but it came out all bitter sounding.

"Just tell me the truth," Amber said, disregarding my laugh.

"You want to know the truth, huh?" I sat back down on the bed. "Okay. The truth is, I'm a monster."

"Don't say that," she said, shaking her head. She came over and sat back down beside me.

"No, really, I am."

I started explaining to her what a doppelganger was. I told her about the shape changing, the stalking, all that stuff. Except for the mating part. I didn't feel like bringing it up. Instead, I told her about my mother and where I'd grown up. I even told her what had happened with

Chris—how I came to meet him and how he ended up dead. She was quiet through the whole thing with this funny kind of look on her face, like she was taking me seriously, but at the same time trying to decide whether I was crazy or she was crazy or both of us were.

She didn't stop me until I got to the part about Chris.

"So it was an accident," she said, like she was explaining it to me instead of the other way around. "You know, like self-defense."

"Well, not exactly," I said, hesitating.

"Yeah, but he attacked you first, right?"

"I guess."

"And you didn't really want to kill him," she went on.

"No. I just wanted to be left alone."

She nodded. We were both quiet for a minute.

"How many other people have you killed?" she finally asked.

"Just the old man, that's the only other one."

"That's not so bad," she said. She stood up and came over to me. It's like she was sticking up for me. I should've been happy—I mean, it was the last thing I would've expected. To tell a girl that you're a killer—that you killed her boyfriend, no less—you'd think she'd be screaming for her parents and bolting for the door. Not Amber.

"I mean, you said you don't really like it, right? You don't really want to kill people, do you?" she said.

That's when I knew Amber loved me, at least on some level. When you love somebody, you make excuses for them. You rationalize all kinds of things. Echo had done it for Barry, Amber was doing it for me now.

"No," I said. "And yes. It's hard to explain. It's like an

urge inside you. You end up giving in. I felt it before. I know I'll feel it again. It's only a matter of time."

"But I don't understand," she said. "I mean, you said before that doppelgangers can eat just about anything, that they're tough creatures. Why don't all of you just go live out in the woods and eat bugs or something? Why do you have to come after us?"

It was a good question, the same one I'd asked my mother. *Because that's just the way we are*, she'd told me. But I'd never liked that answer. It wasn't even really an answer.

"I don't know," I said.

She turned and walked away from me toward the door. I had a sudden fear that she was about to take off, make an escape. But then she stopped and turned around.

"I want to see you," she said. "You know, underneath. What you really look like."

"No, you don't," I said.

"Yes, I do," she replied. "Otherwise I don't really know. I want you to prove it to me. Prove who you really are."

"I can't, Amber. I wish I could. But if I let go of Chris, he's not coming back."

It wasn't completely true—I could've shown her a glimmer, like the ones I'd seen in the mirror. My mother used to do that, especially when I was little and she'd come home as someone else and I'd be scared. She'd blur the form for just a second or two, enough for her real, hideous self to show through for a moment. But I'd never done it before on purpose, and I wasn't sure if I'd be able to do it right. Besides, the last thing I wanted was for her to see how monstrous I really was. I mean, if we could hardly stand to see ourselves, how could a human stand to see us?

"You just have to trust me," I said. "Please."

She nodded and came back over to me. The next thing I knew, she was putting her arms around my waist and leaning her head against my chest. I slowly put my arms around her, too, and for a couple minutes we just stood there and didn't speak. It felt good to hold her, to feel her warmth after all that cold.

"I won't tell anyone," she said.

I hadn't even thought about the possibility that she might, but as soon as she said it, I felt a sudden relief.

"So you really do believe me, then?" I asked. I probably shouldn't have pushed my luck, but it seemed strange, her taking the news so well.

She looked up into my eyes. "Yes," she said. "I do."

"Why? I mean, it's ridiculous."

"It is," she said. After a moment she shrugged. "I don't know why. Maybe I just want to."

Finally, we both let go and stood back.

"It's pretty late," she said.

I looked at my watch. It was ten thirty, and we both had school the next day.

"You have a lot of tests tomorrow?" I asked. Tomorrow was Friday. The teachers always gave tests then.

"Yeah," she said. "I've got a big one in geometry," she said.

It felt weird to suddenly be talking about ordinary stuff like school. I didn't like it. I don't think she did either.

"I better go," I said, and headed for the door.

"Wait," she said. She grabbed my arm and stopped me. "Stay here tonight. It's a long walk home. You already froze once."

Hearing her say that was a big relief. I didn't care about the cold so much, but I sure didn't want to run into Barry again, at least not tonight. "As long as you don't mind sleeping with a monster in the room." I smiled, but she shook her head.

"There's more than one way to be a monster," she said.

She went into the bathroom and got ready for bed. I took off my sweater and my jeans but that was it. I was starting to get a little nervous as I listened to her brush her teeth and all that stuff. I'd never slept with another person in the same bed before. And then there was that other thing. You know, the whole sex thing. I got a sudden flashback to the last time I was in her room, and felt even more nervous.

In the end, it wasn't a big deal. She came out in a pair of pajamas, and we crawled into bed, turned out the light, and just sort of snuggled up under the covers. She had a pretty nice bed, and lying there next to her, with the smell of her hair heavy around me, I don't think I'd ever felt more comfortable or safe, and I wondered if she felt the same way.

"We'll have to be careful in the morning," she said. "I'll have to sneak you out."

"I guess your parents wouldn't be too excited about you having a guy sleep over."

"I don't think they'd care too much about that. It has more to do with you. They're not so psyched about you since you left the team. They like the old Chris better," she said, and snorted.

That didn't surprise me too much. "Wait till they find out you quit cheerleading," I said.

"They already did," she said. "I told them tonight at dinner."

"How'd it go?"

"It was bad," she said. "Whatever."

"They probably think it's my fault."

"They tried to blame it on you, that's for sure."

"Sorry."

"Forget it," Amber said. "I should have done it a long time ago."

She squeezed my hand and nuzzled closer. We were both quiet for a while, and pretty soon everything that had happened that day finally caught up with me and I felt myself drifting away. Just before I fell asleep, she whispered to me in the dark.

"What's your name?" she asked.

"I don't have one."

There was a long pause.

"That's not right," I heard her say. Then I was gone.

A sound woke me later in the night, followed by a steady shaking beside me in the bed. My heart leaped into my throat, then I remembered where I was.

Amber was crying. I wanted to comfort her, but something held me back. There was something in the sound of her crying that told me I shouldn't, though I couldn't say what it was. All I could do was stare at the glowing digits of her alarm clock and count the minutes as they crept by. Even after she fell back asleep, I kept counting. Minute after minute, hour after hour, I watched the numbers change until morning.

CHAPTER FOURTEEN

Amber smuggled me out of the house the next morning with no trouble. She got me up early and led me downstairs and out to her car in the garage. I lay down in the backseat and waited for another hour or so before she came out and drove us to school. From there, the rest of the day slipped by in a hazy sort of way. I felt like I was in some kind of movie or TV show where nobody else was real. Except for Amber. When I saw her at lunch, she gave me a shy sort of smile and we sat at one end of a table, away from everyone else. We didn't say much to each other. It was like, now that I wasn't Chris anymore, we were kind of strangers all of a sudden. But not in a bad way. It's like we really were starting over, and it felt good because it was real, because I wasn't alone anymore.

Amber had a dentist appointment after school, but she dropped me off at home on her way there. Barry was still at work, and Echo hadn't gotten back yet. We made plans to get together tomorrow, and then I said good-bye and went inside. It felt strange to be back in the house. I'd only been away since last night, but it felt like forever. I walked past the hole Barry had punched in the wall last weekend—the pieces of cracked drywall around the edges of the circle were still pushed in, like a mouth full of broken teeth—and went into the kitchen. To my surprise, it was clean. The dishes had been washed and put away, the table wiped. The scene had been cleared.

Not long after that, Echo got home.

"Did you have fun last night?" I asked. "With your friend, I mean."

She shrugged. "We watched a video."

"How are you feeling?"

"Fine," she said in a chipper sort of voice, but I could see the memory of last night in her eyes. She was still stuck with it. I guess all of us would be for a while.

We both spent the afternoon in our respective rooms, her reading, me watching TV. Then Barry got home. I watched him through the window as he got out of the car and headed in with a couple of pizza boxes in his arm, a half-smoked cigarette dangling from his mouth. I could tell there was something different about him, even in the way he walked. He sort of shuffled toward the door. He seemed smaller somehow, almost stooped, like the pizza boxes were made of concrete or something.

I peeked out into the hall as he passed through, then left my room and went down the hallway, pausing in the kitchen doorway.

Barry had just put the pizza boxes on the counter and was turning toward the fridge when, seeing me, he stopped. I could see the bruises along his throat, slight but plainly visible, not to mention the cut lip and swollen eye.

I wondered how he'd explained them to the people at work, to his boss. He didn't say anything. He just sort of gazed at me with this hollow look tinged with the remnants of fear, and for a second I panicked, wondering if he'd caught a glimpse of those doppelganger eyes. I didn't think so. If he had, he would've been more afraid.

But there was something else in Barry besides fear. He reached into the refrigerator for a beer, then grabbed one of the pizzas and brushed by me into the living room. As I watched him, I tried to figure out what it was, but I couldn't. It was only later, as Echo and I sat at the kitchen table eating pizza and listening to the TV blaring from the other room, that I realized what I'd seen, not just in his eyes but in every part of his body. It was defeat. Total deflation. You'd think it would've made me happy to see him so broken, but for some reason it didn't. It made me feel a little sick, to tell you the truth, because it was me who'd done that to him.

For the next week Barry and I pretty much avoided each other. That first weekend I spent most of the time out of the house with Amber. Echo stayed with a friend Saturday and Sunday. When I did see Barry, he was on the couch in the living room, drinking beers and watching TV. He didn't watch football—guess I'd turned him off from it. Sure, we spoke a few times, but we really didn't say anything— nothing real, anyway—and whether we hated each other more than ourselves for what had happened, I really couldn't say.

The rest of the week went pretty much the same way, with Echo and me taking care of one another and Barry slinking around the house with his tail between his legs. Amber and I spent more and more time together, going for walks after school to the mall or to the lake, or going to the library to study together, wherever we could go that wasn't home for either of us.

All in all, it was a pretty good situation. Good enough that I'd convinced myself that I could go on being Chris forever. Which was exactly when I ran into trouble.

It started with an itch, right along my back down at the base of the spine. It wasn't too bad at first, just a little itch before bed, but it was the beginning. By the time Thursday came along, I'd developed a bit of a rash across my stomach, and in general my skin started to feel dry and kind of flaky. It had been three weeks, and I knew I was starting to lose the form. Just a little bit, but it was enough to scare me.

As I lay in bed that Thursday night, half watching the TV, I wondered how long I had. I'd gone out to the movies again with Amber earlier that night and had spent most of the time squirming in my seat, trying not to scratch. She didn't say anything, and maybe she didn't even notice, but I knew it would only be a matter of time before she did. I'd have to let her know what was going on eventually. I just didn't want to—not now, not when things were going so well. Not when things were getting started.

But that wasn't even the worst part.

Flicking through the channels, I came across the local eleven o'clock news. I didn't really notice at first what was going on—the backdrop of woods behind the newswoman seemed like it could have been anywhere. Then the camera shifted and I noticed a police officer and then another and then the edge of a familiar white car. I turned up the volume.

". . . police are telling us that the hunters who came across the Subaru wagon said it was in the shape you see it now. And Kip, as I'm standing here looking at it, let me tell you, the thing is trashed. Whoever abandoned it here sure wanted to leave a mess for the authorities."

Goddam hunters, I thought. *They find everything.*

The camera flashed for a moment to the anchor in the studio.

"Sharon, do we know, in fact, that this is Jill Vitelli's car?"

"Yes, Kip. State police confirmed just moments ago that this is the car authorities have been searching for. What's not clear, however, is how long ago the Springfield killer abandoned it here or why it was left in such condition. Certainly one speculation is that the level of rage leading to this sort of destruction could be an important key in understanding what kind of person we're dealing with."

"What else do you have for us, Sharon?"

"Well, Kip, police say they're going to begin an extensive search of Bakersville and the surrounding area over the next few days in the hope that some clue will emerge that might lead them to Jill Vitelli's killer. The authorities are asking anyone who has any information to call the state police. Back to you, Kip."

I flicked the TV off and fell back in bed. All of a sudden, I was wide awake as the adrenaline began pumping through me.

I was pretty sure the police wouldn't find the killer—whoever had abandoned the car in Parson Woods was long gone. But what I wasn't sure about was what else the police might discover in the process of looking.

I'd been nervous already about leaving Chris stuffed in that culvert just waiting for someone to come along and find him, but now I was downright terrified. The idea of dozens of cops combing through the area with dogs and God knows what else made it just about impossible to sleep, and when I did, I dreamed about it, which was even worse.

In my nightmare I was walking up and down the train tracks, and no matter where I went, I could hear Chris calling out. As he did, a crowd gathered, coming out of the woods in bunches.

"Here I am!" he kept shouting as Barry, Sheila, Echo, Coach, and everyone else I knew kept coming closer and closer to the culvert. I tried to distract them, tried to tell them the noise was coming from the nearby woods, but they wouldn't listen to me, and pretty soon the pack had gathered around the culvert just as the sun was setting. They pulled the roll of plastic out, and the next thing I knew, Chris was ripping his way out of it and standing up. His skin was all rotten and discolored, like the zombies in those old movies on TV, and he turned toward me with everyone else behind him.

He didn't say anything to me. He just lifted his arm and pointed a shriveled, bony finger in my direction, looking at me with his sad, swollen eyes, and began walking toward me. It was just like that banquet scene when Banquo's ghost comes after Macbeth in the middle of his dinner party, only in my dream Chris was no ghost. Everyone could see him. In fact, they began following him, drawing toward me with that same look of recrimination. They kept coming closer and closer, and I knew I had to get away, but I didn't know where to go. I finally stumbled down the far side of the bank and crawled into the culvert from the other side. The culvert was suddenly bigger than in real life. It was pitch-black inside except for a circle of light way in the distance, and as I sat up with my back against the wall, another flicker of light appeared. Chris was sitting right beside me, holding a candle.

"I was wondering when you'd come back," he said.

I screamed and turned to escape, but when I looked back at the hole in the distance, I could see the faces of everyone peeking in. Before I could do anything, they were plugging up the hole, and all the light, but for Chris's candle behind me, had been extinguished. I heard a little puff, and everything went dark.

I woke up from the dream covered in sweat and rolled over to discover it was half past nine in the morning. I'd overslept.

I took my time getting up and getting ready for school. I figured there was no point in rushing since I was already late. I spent a long time in the shower, feeling the water wash over the body I'd worn now for over three weeks, trying to shake the dream. At least my rash was gone.

The walk to school wasn't much better. These police cruisers kept driving by, going real slow. Every time one of them passed me, I had to fight the urge to start running away. I suddenly thought of *COPS*, a show I used to watch on Friday nights. In fact, that stupid theme song started running through my brain, over and over again: "Bad boys, bad boys, whatcha gonna do . . ." It's like I kept expecting a whole pack of cruisers to tear around the corner and surround me, with their sirens blaring and their lights flashing, while an army of cops jumped out with their guns all pointed in my face. I guess that's what happens when you know you're guilty.

One of them did stop. About halfway to school, this cruiser pulled up behind me. I didn't even see it until it was right on top of me and the cop inside let rip one of those siren noises—*boo-bweep!* I practically jumped three feet off the ground.

"Sorry. Didn't mean to startle you," he said, grinning out the rolled-down window. I just sort of stood there and looked at him with as blank a look as I could muster. *Don't let him see you're scared*, I kept telling myself.

"What're you doing?" he asked.

"Going to school."

"Little late, isn't it?"

"I guess," I said. What did he care? I mean, wasn't he supposed to be out looking for the murderer? I almost said that to him, but for once I was smart and kept my mouth shut.

I couldn't figure out if he was done with me or not. I was just about to start walking again, when he called out.

"Seen anything?" he asked, still looking straight ahead through the windshield in front of him.

"Like what?" I asked.

"Anything suspicious? Anything unusual?" he said, turning to look back at me.

"Not really," I said.

He took off his glasses and leaned out the window a little to squint at me. My heart started pounding.

"I've seen you before, haven't I?" he said.

"I don't know," I said. "I don't think so."

He snapped his fingers. "Chris Parker," he said. "You're that football player, right? The one who quit."

"That's me," I said.

"Why'd you quit?"

I shrugged.

He sort of shook his head. "Keep your eyes open. There's a killer walking around out there," he said.

"Right," I said as I watched him drive away.

With so many cops around, the kids in school were wound up even more than they usually were on a Friday. Everyone was talking about the investigation, speculating like crazy. As far as I could tell, none of the guys had come forward and admitted to trashing the car. I sure wasn't going to say anything.

I had to do something about Chris. And soon. Sitting in history class while the video droned on, I thought about it some and decided to bury him that night. I hated to wait that long, but I figured it would be easier to do it in the dark, when there wouldn't be so many police around.

The rest of the day dragged by. It was excruciating. I was already feeling twitchy in my deteriorating form as it was, and having to sit in school, watching the seconds tick by, worrying that the search had made its way from Parson Woods to the tracks on the other side of town, was sheer torture.

At lunch I canceled plans with Amber for after school, making up some dumb excuse, and took the bus home. Then I got everything together—shovel, gloves, flashlight, rope in case I needed it, and waited. I knew it would look suspicious walking along the roads with a shovel over my shoulder, but I had to risk it—no way I was going to try to dig a grave with my hands.

Around six thirty, Echo and I made dinner. I'd started helping her this week with meals. I figured after the casserole fiasco, I owed it to her to help. We made grilled cheese sandwiches and heated up some tomato soup.

We talked about school and stuff for a while as we ate. I let Echo do most of the talking. I liked to listen to her funny stories about school. She was a pretty smart kid and knew how to tell a good story, better than I could, anyway. Then, halfway through a story, she suddenly stopped.

"Where's Dad?" she asked.

"I don't know," I said. I'd been so distracted thinking about the job ahead of me that I hadn't noticed Barry had never come home. "It's Friday. He's probably at Twisty's," I said. Twisty's was his favorite bar.

"Maybe we should call," she murmured.

"He'll be home in a while," I said. "Besides, it's nicer without him here. Don't you think?"

She shrugged and nibbled at the corner of her sandwich. I could tell she didn't like me talking that way.

"I'm going out tonight," I told her, to change the subject. "I don't know when I'll be home."

"Are you going on a date?" she asked, brightening.

"Sort of," I said. "You going to be okay here? You got a movie or something to watch?"

"I have a book. The new Lemony Snicket came in at the library. I got to sign it out first."

"What's Lemony Snicket?"

"He's a writer. He writes these books. They're called 'A Series of Unfortunate Events.' They're really funny."

"'A Series of Unfortunate Events,' huh?" *I could write a book like that*, I thought. "Well, good, then," I said, finishing my sandwich. I got up and did the dishes. By the time I finished, it was quarter past seven. Time to go.

I grabbed my jacket, snuck out to the garage for my things, and went to leave. Just as I was coming out of the garage, though, a pair of headlights turned into the driveway, shining right on me, shovel and all.

Blocking the headlights with my hand, I saw Amber sitting behind the steering wheel watching me. She turned off the lights and got out of the car.

"Hey," was all I said.

"Where you going?" she asked.

"Nowhere," I said. "Just picking up around the yard."

"At night? In the dark?"

"Something like that."

"Chris," she said. I started when she said the name. She'd stopped calling me that after learning the truth, and it felt strange to hear her say it now. Then I realized she wasn't calling me that at all.

"You're going to Chris, aren't you?"

I nodded. "I've got to take care of him," I said. "I didn't do the best job before, and now—"

"All the cops looking around," she said. "That Springfield Killer."

I nodded again and started to walk by her. As I did, she grabbed my arm and looked up into my eyes.

"You're not him are you?" she asked.

"Who?"

"You know. The one they're looking for?"

"The Springfield Killer?" I said. I started laughing. Probably not the nicest thing to do, but a look of relief came across her face. "No," I said, "but it doesn't matter. If the police find the body . . . well, you can imagine."

She let me go. But as I reached the end of the driveway, she called out.

"Wait!" she said. I stopped and turned as she approached. "I want to come with you."

"Amber, I don't think that's a great idea. It's bad enough if I get caught, but I don't want you to be involved. Besides, it could be pretty gross. I mean, it's been three weeks. You know what I'm saying?"

"I don't care," she said, shaking her head. "I want to help."

I hesitated.

"Please, let me do this," she said.

I shrugged. "Let's go."

I threw the shovel and pack into the back of her car, and we headed off toward the abandoned lot at the edge of town next to the tracks. We didn't say a word, but as we drove away into the night, I realized I'd never been so happy not to be alone.

"How much farther?" she asked. Even though Amber was right behind me, holding on to my jacket, her voice sounded far away as we walked along the tracks.

"Not much," I said.

There wasn't any moon out, not yet at least, but between the stars and the lights from town, I could see well enough. Amber's human eyes had a tougher time. Still, I didn't want to use the flashlight. Not yet, anyway. I didn't want anyone to see us. Not only that, I had no idea how long the batteries would hold out. The last thing I wanted was for the flashlight to die in the middle of digging.

A couple minutes later, the trees on our right fell back. We were coming to the clearing. It looked different in the dark without the campfire. It seemed bigger.

I smelled Chris twenty yards from the culvert, that odor of decay that's sweet but not sweet. It wasn't strong, but it was enough to make me pull up.

"Sorry," I whispered as Amber bumped into me.

"What's wrong?" she asked.

She was nervous. I could hear it in her voice. I wanted to tell her it was okay, that I was nervous too, but I held back. I figured it would only make her feel worse if I told her the truth. Besides, it actually made me feel better to pretend not to be afraid. Like pretending made it real.

"We're close," I said.

We went a little farther, and then I spotted the culvert. By then we were close enough that Amber could smell him too. I heard her take a sharp breath and groan a little, but she didn't say anything.

We scrambled down the bank and paused by the edge of the culvert.

"Hold these," I said, handing her the pack and shovel.

I reached way into the culvert as far as I could. For a second I couldn't feel the plastic, and I got scared. I had this sudden fear—what if they'd found him? What if they'd taken him away and only the smell had stayed? But then my fingers brushed along the edge of the rolled sheet. It was a weird feeling—both relief and revulsion at the same time.

Planting my feet, I reached in with my other hand, got a good hold, and pulled.

To my surprise, the body slid out pretty easily. In fact, I almost fell over and would have pulled him right on top of me if I hadn't caught myself at the last second. It seemed as if Chris had lost a little weight.

"Ugh," Amber gasped as the smell suddenly grew stronger. I could hear her breaths starting to come quick.

"If it weren't for the cold and the plastic, it would probably be worse," I offered.

"You think?" she murmured.

"Breathe in through your mouth."

"I'm trying," she said.

I leaned over to her, opened the pack, and pulled out the flashlight.

"Wait," she said, grabbing my arm in the dark.

"Amber, we need to see. I have to find a spot. Somewhere to dig."

"Don't shine it on him," she whispered. "Not yet."

"I won't," I said.

I flicked the light on. It was bright. Painfully bright, even with it pointing straight at the ground, and I felt like every cop in the area suddenly knew we were here. Then my eyes adjusted, and it wasn't so bad. I left Chris and headed toward the edge of the clearing. Amber was right beside me. I didn't blame her for not wanting to be left back there alone.

After a little bit of poking around, we found a good spot behind some trees in a little opening where the ground was soft. I planted the spade and turned to go back for Chris, when Amber stopped me.

"Leave him there," she said. "Dig the hole first."

"Good thinking," I said.

And so I did. For the next hour, I dug while Amber stood by holding the flashlight on me, lighting up the dark shower of earth that flew from my shovel with every scoop. It takes a lot longer to dig a grave than you might think, especially when you're trying to make it deep. And I was going for the six-foot standard. It wasn't just about keeping the dogs or whatever else away, not anymore. I wanted him to stay buried for good. So I tried to be careful, to do it right. In fact, I spent almost as much time cutting up the sod into squares and setting them aside to put back later as I did digging the hole.

We didn't say much, though at one point Amber asked if she could help dig for a while, to give me a break. I told her no, that it was my job.

"After all," I said, "I'm the one who killed him."

"Maybe so," she said, gazing down at the hole, "but I'm the one who wanted to."

We looked at each other for a moment, then I went back to digging.

Not long after that I finished. We went and got Chris, pulled him across the grass and up beside the grave. I was about to roll him in when Amber spoke up.

"I want to see him," she said.

"You do?" I said, stepping back from the body.

She glanced up at me and nodded.

I took the jackknife I'd swiped off Barry's workbench from my pocket and opened it up.

"You're sure?" I said, holding the knife over the plastic.

She nodded again, holding the flashlight close to herself so that her breath sent little puffs of steam into the light's beam.

I cut through the layers of plastic, one at a time, until I made it all the way through, then pulled the layers apart so that everything was open from the shoulders up.

Then I stood back. She slowly moved the light until it was shining on his face. Needless to say, he didn't look too good. In fact, he almost didn't even look like Chris, but enough so that there was no mistaking him.

Amber turned the light on my face for a second. I squinted and covered my eyes. When she pulled the flashlight away, I could see she was shaking her head.

"What's wrong?" I asked.

"I'm still trying to get my head around all this. I think a part of me was holding out, believing that you—or him, I guess—had just gone insane. Some bizarre schizophrenic crack-up, you know? And this story of the doppelganger. This crazy, elaborate fable . . ."

"It's no fable," I said. "Sorry to disappoint you."

"No, I'm glad."

"Why?"

"Because now I don't have to feel guilty," she replied.

"For what?"

"For playing along. For letting him be crazy because I liked him better that way."

We were quiet for a minute, staring down at the body, a decayed echo of my own form.

"We'd better get going," I said, pulling the plastic back together to cover him as best I could. "We've got more work to do."

I was going to just roll him in, but at the last second, it

didn't feel right. Like it was the wrong thing to do. So I had Amber grab the legs and I took the top, and we dropped him down in as gently as we could.

We started piling dirt on. Even Amber helped, kicking dirt down in, sometimes scooping it with one hand while she held the flashlight with the other. I shoveled like crazy. It's like we both wanted to get it over with as fast as we could, especially at first when the dirt hit the plastic, making a weird sort of crackling sound. Then it was dirt on dirt and real quiet and not quite so bad. We finished by laying the sod, with its long grass, back in place. It wasn't perfect, but it looked okay.

We stood back, side by side, me holding the shovel, her shining the flashlight on the slightly mounded ground. Our breath, heavy from the exertion, clouded in the cold. We were both dirty, but it was done.

Amber reached over and took my hand. All of a sudden she started to cry, a little bit at first, but pretty soon she was choking back sobs. It was over pretty quick.

"Sorry," she said, sniffing.

"Don't be."

"It's just that I grew to hate him so much, especially these last couple months," she said, wiping her eyes. She kept looking at the ground.

"He used to hit me, you know," she said. "Not much at first. More toward the end."

I didn't know what to say. I'd already figured as much, but to hear her say it was still strange. Maybe it was the way she said it, like it was a confession, an admission of sorts, even though she'd been on the receiving end. Maybe she was saying it for him, because he couldn't.

"I thought at first that it would stop, that it was just a temporary thing, like when you come down with a cold for a few weeks and then it sort of disappears." She shook her head. "I was so stupid, to let him treat me that way, to just sort of block it out like it was happening to somebody else. In the end it only made me feel worse. I felt like I was nothing."

She hesitated. "That's why I hated him so much," she said at last. "Because he made me hate myself."

"But it's over now," I said. "If it makes you feel any better, Chris hated himself too. For the same reason. I know," I said. "I saw it in his eyes that night, right here in this clearing."

We lingered for another minute. I didn't want to leave yet. Not now, not after what she'd said, no matter how true it was. Chris was a messed-up kid, no doubt about it. But there was more. There's always more.

"I didn't know Chris when I killed him," I said. "But I still felt bad. And now after being him, even for just a little while, I feel worse. He didn't deserve it, Amber."

"Maybe he didn't," she said. "But who's to say why things happen the way they do?"

She leaned her head on my shoulder, and I put my arm around her. I felt so good all of a sudden. I shouldn't have, but I did.

"We'd better say good-bye," I said. She nodded.

"Tell me something about him," I said. "Something good. Let's say good-bye that way. There must be something."

"There's lots of things," she said. "He was an asshole most of the time, but every once in a while, he'd let his

guard down. There was this side to him, like a little kid."
She paused for a moment, thinking. "He had these sheets,"
she said suddenly.

"Race cars," I said.

She laughed. "I thought they were cute. I even picked
on him once about them. He got pretty mad, but he never
took them off," she said. "What about you?"

I thought for a second. "He was good to his sister," I
said. "I think he really loved her."

I turned to look down at Amber. Her eyes closed all of
a sudden, but the tears came out anyway. She wiped them
with her sleeve, and we turned away.

We kept the flashlight going until we got up on the
tracks. Then we switched it off and walked the rest of the
way back in the dark. With every step, I felt new relief. I'd
finally buried Chris and didn't have to worry anymore
about either of us being found out. Everything would be
okay. That's what I thought, anyway, as Amber and I headed
down the tracks side by side, still holding hands, close
under the stars.

CHAPTER FIFTEEN

It was around ten o'clock when we got back to Amber's car. She opened the trunk, and I laid the shovel down in it. Clumps of dirt still clung to its blade.

For a minute we just stood there gazing down at the shovel, the trunk's light illuminating our faces from below. Then we looked at each other.

"I don't want to go home," she said. "Not yet."

"Me neither."

There was another long pause.

"I don't know. We could get some coffee, I guess," she said at last.

"That's probably not a good idea," I said. "I mean, look at us."

Even in the dim light of the trunk I could see both of us were filthy, with dirt on our hands and on our pants and shoes.

"Hey," I said, "why don't you teach me how to drive? I mean, Chris knew how. So I should too, right?"

"Sure," she said. "It's not that hard."

She was right. Once I got used to knowing how hard to hit the gas and the brakes, it was actually pretty fun. We spent the next two hours driving the roads around Bakersville, laughing and having a good time. I don't know, maybe we shouldn't have. I mean, I suppose it wasn't too respectful, considering what we'd been doing earlier. But it felt good to laugh and fool around a bit and forget about Chris for a while.

By the time she dropped me off, it was midnight. Barry's car was parked in the driveway. He must have come home and passed out—I couldn't see any lights on in the house.

"We have to go visit my grandmother this weekend," she said. "I won't be back until Sunday night."

"I'll see you Monday, then," I said. She leaned toward me, and I kissed her. "Thanks," I said, "for everything."

She nodded, and I got out and watched her drive away.

I tried to let myself in as quietly as I could, but as soon as I opened the door, Poppy tore past me with a yelp and disappeared around the corner of the house into the back-yard. Standing in the doorway, I knew something was wrong. By now it was a familiar feeling, only this time it was worse than all the other times combined. I mean, I could feel the hairs on the back of my neck stand up straight as I went in and closed the door behind me. The only light came from over the sink in the kitchen, and the odor of fresh cigarette smoke lay heavy in the house, mingled with the smell of booze.

I was about to call out when I heard a sort of choking noise coming from the kitchen, followed by the sound of a glass being smacked onto the table. I'd heard that sound before—Barry was drinking.

I started to head for my room, when all of a sudden I froze.

I still don't know why I stopped or why I turned around and went into the kitchen. Maybe it was anger. I was in kind of a weird mood after having buried Chris. And all of a sudden, I realized I was fed up with Barry doing nothing but sitting around getting a load on. Even if he never touched Echo again, I suddenly felt like it wasn't good enough. I mean, Chris was dead. And now it was like Barry was dying too. Slowly, bit by bit, he was killing himself, and even though I didn't have to stick around and watch, Echo did. It wasn't fair to her.

Maybe I just wanted to see him sitting there at the table, wallowing in his misery, drunk and pathetic.

If that's what I'd wanted, then that's what I got. And then some.

He was at the table, all right, in his usual spot, sitting there in the darkened room with his favorite bottle, his favorite glass, his favorite ashtray with a burning cigarette resting on its edge—all the accessories of his screwed-up life gathered around him. And there was one other thing there besides.

I didn't notice the gun until I'd moved farther into the kitchen, over to the counter. It was the pistol I'd seen in his drawer that first morning. He was resting it in his left hand up against his head, the barrel pointing at the ceiling, like he was holding himself up with it or something. So much for him killing himself slowly.

He didn't notice me at first, but when he did, he started, and for a second I was afraid he might shoot me. But the gun hardly moved.

He didn't say anything. He just looked away, reached down to pick up his cigarette, and took a drag. I could tell he was pretty drunk, more than usual. His arm moved in that herky-jerky sort of way, as if it were some robot arm operated by remote control.

"Hey," I said.

"Go to bed," he growled.

I didn't move. For a minute I just watched him, trying to figure out how to get us all out of this and get him safely to bed, which was kind of twisted, considering I'd tried to kill him a week earlier.

"What are you doing?" I asked.

He shook his head and started laughing.

"What am I doing? That's a good question," he said. He was slurring his words pretty badly. "I don't know. I don't fucking know. I thought I was doing the right things—job, wife, kids." He paused. "But what do I have? That's the real question, after all. And you know what the answer is? I'll tell you what the goddam answer is, Chris. Nothing. I've got nothing, Chris. No wife—she left me. No kids—they hate me. No job—"

"You got fired?" I blurted out.

"That bastard, Mitch," he said.

He splashed some more whiskey into his glass and downed it, smacking the glass back on the table even harder this time. I wondered why it didn't break.

"So you're going to kill yourself—" I started to say.

"Go to bed."

"—is that what you're going to do?"

"I said go to bed!" he hollered.

"Is everything okay?"

I whirled around to see Echo standing in the kitchen doorway all sleepy eyed and husky voiced. I went over to her. I didn't want her to come in and see Barry at the table with the gun. Heck, I didn't want her to be *around* Barry with the gun.

"Go back to sleep," I whispered, crouching down in front of her.

"What's wrong with Daddy?" she asked. It was funny— I'd never heard her call him that before.

"He's just a little drunk, that's all," I said. "Don't worry. Everything will be okay. Just go back to sleep."

"You're all dirty," she said, looking me over.

"A little bit," I said. "Just go back to bed, okay? Please, Echo."

She nodded slowly, then went back into her bedroom and shut the door.

I headed into the kitchen and sat down across from Barry at the table. I don't know why, but all of a sudden I wasn't scared anymore. He glanced up, squinting his eyes at me like I was far away. I could tell he didn't want me there. He started tapping the gun against his head.

"So you're really going to do this?" I said. "Blow your brains out with her in the next room? You really hate her that much?"

"She won't care," he said. "And neither will you, so fuck off." He waved the gun vaguely in my direction for a second. Then he took one last drag from his cigarette and stubbed it out. "You want to talk about hate, talk about yourself," he said.

"I think you should give me the gun."

"I want to hear you say it," he muttered, this time

pointing the gun straight at me. "I want you to tell me you hate me."

"No," I whispered.

"Say it!" he cried. "I know you do. All of you do!"

I didn't say anything. I wasn't going to give him what he wanted. Besides, seeing him there, I suddenly realized I didn't hate him. Not anymore. He was like Chris. Or Chris was like him. Both of them just made me sad.

He put the gun down onto the table but kept his hand on it, and then brought the other hand up to cover his eyes.

"Why wouldn't you," he said.

He kept his hand over his eyes. Then his body began to shake. Not much, just a little bit, rocking up and down. That's when I realized he was crying. A long moan escaped him. It was a terrible sound, even worse than his yelling.

I didn't say anything for a while. I just let him finish. The only thing I did was reach across the table and slowly pull the gun out from under his hand, and he let me.

"It doesn't have to be this way," I said at last.

"It's too late," he croaked.

"They'll forgive you," I said. "Echo, Mom, both of them will. They want to."

"What about you?" he whispered.

"It's over," I said. "Just go to bed. We'll figure it out in the morning."

I got up, went around the table, and helped him up. He started to lean on me, then pulled me close to him and put his arms around me. He squeezed me so tight for a second, I could hardly breathe. He just held on to me for a minute, his feet unsteady, so that we both swayed. I let him hold on. Before he let go, he whispered in my ear.

"I'm sorry."

I didn't say anything. I just guided him down the hallway to his room, helped him take his clothes off, and put him to bed.

I got up early the next morning. Echo and Barry were both still sleeping. I looked out the window. Most of the leaves had fallen from the trees, but the sky was clear and it looked like it was going to be a nice day. It was Saturday, and the street was quiet.

I dressed and went into the kitchen. The first thing I did was take all the booze in the house—all the beer in the fridge, all the bottles in the cabinet—and pour it down the sink. Then I put all the empties in a bag and left it by the sliding glass door. I wanted him to see it before I took it out to the garbage. After that I waited.

Echo got up first. She came into the kitchen in her pajamas and poured each of us a bowl of cereal while I put some coffee on. Then Barry shuffled into the kitchen. He was all hungover and looked like crap, but when he glanced at me, I could tell he remembered last night—well enough, at least. I wondered if he'd ask me about the gun. I'd kept it after putting him to bed and stashed it under my mattress. I wasn't going to give it back, not unless he asked.

He plopped down at the table and for a minute just sat there looking a little lost. I got up and brought him a cup of coffee, then went back to my breakfast. He took a sip, then lit a cigarette. The three of us sat there at the table together, silent.

The rest of the day was just as quiet. Echo and I went about our business. Barry sat at the table most of the morning, drinking coffee and smoking cigarettes. In the afternoon he went out into the backyard and finished raking up the leaves. At one point I went to the sliding glass door to watch, and when I looked down, Echo was next to me. He moved slower this time than the last time I'd watched him work, less furious. Maybe he was still hungover. Maybe it was something else.

"Not all the leaves have fallen," Echo said, pointing to the big tree.

"He'll get the rest later."

"Maybe we should help him," she said, but neither of us went out.

Things that day weren't much different than they'd been for the last week, but there was the slightest change, like a subtle shift in the breeze. I felt it later that afternoon when Barry left for a while and came back with dinner from some chicken place, without any beer. And instead of piling up his plate and heading for the living room, he stayed and ate with us. None of us really said much of anything, but it didn't matter.

He joined us the next morning at breakfast.

"So what do you want to do?" he asked, finishing his cigarette.

Echo and I looked up and then glanced at each other. I didn't know what he meant; neither did Echo.

"Echo," he said, "you decide."

"What do you mean?" she asked.

"What do you want to do?" he repeated. "It's Sunday. There must be something you'd like to do."

She shrugged. "Can we go to the movies?" she said finally.

"All right," he said. "This afternoon. We'll go to a matinee. What do you think, Chris?" He looked over at me. It was weird, like he wanted my approval or something.

"Sounds good," I said.

"Can Mom come too?" Echo whispered.

Barry's face dropped for a second. "If she wants," he said.

"I'll ask her," I offered. I went over and picked up the phone.

"Chris," Barry barked. I looked back at him. "Don't call now. It's early," he said, lowering his voice.

I nodded and put the phone down.

"And don't tell her I got fired. Please."

I called her later that morning at her sister's. To my surprise, she agreed to join us at the mall where the theater was.

It was pretty tense when we first met up, like we were all strangers. It's funny how when you haven't seen somebody for a while—even if it's just been a couple of weeks—they can look so different. Sheila looked better—more like that picture hanging in the hallway—like she was younger or something. She seemed to feel the same way about me.

"You look different, Chris," she said, giving me a hug. "I don't know what it is. There's just something different about you."

It made me kind of nervous when she said it, but I shrugged it off.

"So do you," I said.

Barry and Sheila didn't say much, but I noticed they kept looking at each other, though they pretended not to. Only Echo was at ease, laughing and jabbering away as we stood in line for the movie. It was some kid's movie. All her friends had seen it, and it almost seemed like she'd seen it before too. She told us half the story before we even sat down.

After the movie Sheila went to say good-bye, but Barry convinced her to join us in the food court for ice cream. It was only when we all sat down that I realized today was the most time we'd ever spent together, all of us at once. I also realized that the itching had stopped and that I hadn't felt it since Friday, since laying Chris to rest.

A strange feeling came over me. I didn't know what it was at first, but as we finished up our ice cream and headed for our separate cars, I realized it had to be what people call hope.

CHAPTER SIXTEEN

Don't ever wish you could be happy or even think that you are—that's just when something or someone will come along to make sure that you aren't.

The next day started off well enough. A plan had been brewing in my head all night, and when I left the house that morning with Barry looking as dark and lost as he had on Saturday, I was pretty sure of what I had to do.

Instead of getting on the bus, I headed in the opposite direction, toward the main part of town. Using the address from one of Barry's pay stubs, I found the place less than an hour later—a concrete building at the edge of the industrial park with a big sign in blue letters over the door: MITCH'S HEATING AND PLUMBING SUPPLY.

A little bell chimed as I walked in, and an older guy with thinning hair and glasses came out of the back. He gave a quick smile when he saw me and met me at the counter. The name "Bill" was stitched over the pocket of his blue shirt in red curvy letters.

"Haven't seen you in a while, Chris. How you doing?"

"Okay," I said. "Is Mitch here?"

His smile faded and he nodded, pointing to the room out back.

"How bad was it?" I asked.

"Pretty bad," Bill said. "He and your dad got into it pretty heavy on Friday. Worse than usual. I told your father to keep his mouth shut, but he wouldn't listen. He never does. That's the problem."

"Mind if I go talk to him?"

"Suit yourself," Bill replied, and sort of shrugged. He didn't make me feel too hopeful.

I walked around the counter toward the back, where the offices were, and paused at the edge of the hallway. For a second I almost turned around and left, but when I looked back, Bill was still standing at the counter watching me. I took a deep breath and kept going.

There were four rooms off the hallway—a break room on the left, with a room across from it full of file cabinets and shelves, followed by a pair of offices. A little sign said "Barry Parker" outside one office. The other belonged to Mitch Reynolds. I stepped up to the doorway of Mitch's office and looked in. A big, beefy man sat behind the desk eating a doughnut and reading the newspaper, with his sleeves rolled up past the elbows. He looked older than Barry but younger than Bill, and even sitting there reading the paper and eating a doughnut, he looked pissed off. No wonder he and Barry butted heads.

I gave a little knock on the open door. He glanced up. As soon as he saw me, he sort of groaned and shook his head. *Good way to start,* I thought. He lifted one arm and waved me in.

"Jesus Christ," he muttered, "don't tell me he sent you."

I sat down in a chair across from him, my backpack on my lap. "He doesn't know I'm here," I said.

"Want a doughnut?" he said, holding up the box beside him.

"No thanks."

"Let me guess," he growled, "you want me to give your old man his job back."

"Mr. Reynolds," I said, "Dad's had a tough time lately. All of us have. My mom's not around, and then there's me. I've been kind of a screwup."

"Why the hell did you quit the team, anyways? Jesus Christ, you were a goddam killer."

There it was again. They just wouldn't let it go.

"Anyway," I said, "the point is, there's a lot going on at home."

"Big deal," Mitch snapped. "All of us have problems. But you should hear your father. Acts like he's the goddam boss around here. I mean, it's my business, and here he is calling *me* an asshole and crap like that. And it's not just these last few weeks. It's been all along. If he hadn't made me so much money, I'd have canned him a long time ago." He paused and shook his head. "Everyone has their limit, kid."

"You're right about all that," I said. "But Dad feels really bad. He knows he screwed up. I mean, you should have heard him all weekend. All he talked about was how sorry he was. How stupid he was for what he'd done."

"Yeah, right," Mitch snorted.

"Sure he did," I said. Of course he hadn't, but I couldn't tell Mitch that. Besides, Barry was sorry—in his own sort of way.

"Just give him another shot," I said. "Please, Mr. Reynolds. He needs this job. He needs you."

I was slinging it pretty good, and Mitch bought it. I could see it in his face.

"Go to school, Chris."

"Just think about it," I said. "I know if he comes back, it'll be different."

"It better be," Mitch grumbled as I stood up.

"Who knows," he said just as I started to go, "maybe you'll be working here someday."

I didn't say anything. I just shook his hand and got out of there as fast as I could.

I was feeling pretty good about myself by the time I got to school. I figured Barry would probably screw it up again, but who knew? Maybe he was serious about changing. Fact is, I was doing it more for Echo than for Barry—she had big trouble ahead if things didn't turn around at home. Still, it felt good to do something for somebody else, even for a guy like Barry. I felt like I'd spent the first few weeks making a mess of everything. Maybe life would be different now.

I signed in at the main office and went to math. It was late morning, and I was eager just to get through the next few classes so I could meet Amber at lunch. I hadn't seen her since Friday night, and I'd been missing her all weekend.

For some reason I didn't notice it when I first walked into school. But as I headed out of math class, something stopped me in the middle of the hall, and I just stood there while the swarm of kids flowed around me. I wasn't sure what it was, to tell you the truth. A scent, maybe? Or just the echo of a scent? Something out of place but oddly familiar. Whatever it was, it seemed to hover in the hall, swirled along by students scurrying to their next class.

Someone gave me a sharp push from behind.

"Move it, loser," a voice said.

I turned around to see Josh grinning at me. He was one of the only guys from the team who still talked to me.

"Hey," I said.

"What's the deal? You look lost."

"I was just thinking about something, that's all."

"Chris Parker deep in thought. The world must be coming to an end," he said. "Where were you this morning?"

"I had to run an errand."

"Errand, huh? Sounds better than oversleeping, I guess." He walked by me and headed down the hall. "You'd better hurry, errand boy, or you'll be late for Spanish." He gave me one last grin, then turned into a classroom.

I actually was late for Spanish, but I didn't care. Neither did Mrs. Olson, who let me slink into the back of the room and take a seat. I tried to pay attention, but it was tough. Even in the room I could still feel it, still smell it, subtle but present, like a whiff of smoke from some faraway fire. Whatever it was, it was spreading throughout the building, only nobody seemed aware of it but me.

Lunchtime came, and I found Amber at our usual table. Nobody joined us. It had been that way for a while now. I was just as glad—I didn't really want to talk to anyone else anyway.

She smiled at me as I sat down, which made me feel

pretty good. To tell you the truth, I was a little worried that after Friday night things might be weird between us. After all, not many couples do what we had done. Then again, there probably aren't many girls out there like Amber. If there are, I haven't met them.

"How was your trip?" I asked.

"The usual. My grandmother spoiled me rotten and picked on my mother most of the weekend. Then on Saturday, all the aunts and uncles came over. Everyone had too many cocktails and started arguing at dinner and getting all weepy. As always, it became this big scene. And I was the only person there my age. . . ." She paused. I glanced over to see her staring at me.

"What's wrong?" she said.

"What do you mean?"

"You keep looking away toward the door." She hesitated. "Oh, my God, I'm boring you, aren't I?" She sounded less angry than afraid.

"No," I said, shaking my head. "It's just . . . I don't know. There's something in the air. I keep catching bits of it here and there. Don't you smell something funny?"

She shook her head. "This building's a piece of crap. Air circulators are loaded with bacteria, I'm sure of it. Something probably just died in a duct somewhere."

"Yeah, you're probably right," I said.

But I knew she wasn't. I'd smelled decay before, and this wasn't it. This had a bite to it, a bitter-edged tang with a sweetness underneath that both drew me in and frightened me.

I reached across the table and took her hand.

"By the way," I said, "I pretty much spent my entire life

in a cabin in the middle of nowhere. Don't ever worry about boring me."

She smiled and continued telling me about the weekend, and I did my best to forget about the scent. It was a little easier in the cafeteria—the smell of Tater Tots and chicken fingers mostly drowned it out.

But after lunch, as we headed out of the cafeteria and said good-bye, there it was again, stronger than ever. And it only got stronger as the day went on, until I could barely sense anything else. By the time I walked into English class, I could feel it heavy in the air around me, like a fog enveloping everything, sticking to my skin. What drove me crazy was that everyone else was walking around talking and laughing like normal, as if there was nothing going on at all.

Maybe I'm losing my mind, I thought.

Then the bell rang and Ms. Simpson walked through the door. Only it wasn't Ms. Simpson. And that's how I knew I wasn't crazy—I'd found the source of the smell.

The pit that had been sinking in my stomach ever since I got to school deepened as the doppelganger strode to the front of the room.

"All right, class," the sheganger said, "test time. Clear off your desks. You just need something to write with."

As we followed her instructions, I knew for sure it wasn't her. The real Ms. Simpson would have been nicer. She would have asked us how our weekend was. She would at least have said hello.

The test was handed out and we all got to work, but I could hardly concentrate. I couldn't even think. There was this roar in my ears that kept distracting me. It took me a while before I realized it was the sound of my blood pumping in my ears. I kept looking up to the front of the room where Ms. Simpson sat up on her desk, legs crossed, surveying the room. Every time she glanced in my direction, I looked away in a hurry.

Halfway through the period, she got down and started pacing the room. Again, Ms. Simpson never did this. Whenever we took a test, she always sat behind her desk correcting papers, leaving us alone to work. But this one kept going up and down the aisles real slow, her heels clicking on the linoleum tile like a metronome, a sound that echoed in my brain, booming with every step as she kept coming closer.

I sank down in my seat as she came up beside me. *Please don't notice*, I thought.

I breathed a sigh of relief as she kept on going. But two steps past me she froze, then slowly turned and stared down at me. I lifted my eyes only to glance at her, to see if she was really looking at me the way I felt her looking. It was enough—she caught my gaze and held it for a moment. A brief smile flickered across her face, then she let me go and kept on walking.

She didn't look at me again for the rest of the period as we finished our tests and handed them in, but when the bell rang and I sprang up with everyone else, she called me out.

"Chris Parker," she said, eyeing the name on my test. Everyone froze. "Stay."

Again, the oohs and aahs, but the nervousness I'd felt when the real Ms. Simpson had held me after class was nothing compared with now. I could feel the drops of sweat along my forehead. I almost bolted, but I knew that it would probably just make things worse, so I sat back down.

After everyone left, she went and closed the door, then came over with that same grin she'd fixed me with earlier. She perched on the desk in front of me, crossing her legs like before, pulling up her skirt a little. I looked away.

"So here you are," she said. "I found you at last."

My eyes snapped back. "You've been following me?"

She shrugged. "I came across your trail in Springfield a few weeks ago. It was faint, but not faint enough. I've always had a nose for young blood."

Springfield, I thought. Suddenly it all made sense. Although, remembering the sight of that abandoned car glowing in the moonlight, I realized that, deep down, a part of me had known all along.

"So you're the one," I said. "You're the Springfield Killer."

"Springfield Killer," she scoffed. "The names these humans come up with. So imaginative, aren't they? Still," she said, sighing, "I suppose I deserve it. I got sloppy, you know. Didn't tie the weights on well enough—stupid girl popped right up and floated to shore as soon as I turned my back."

"But why'd you have to pick *her*?"

"The Vitelli girl?"

"No. Ms. Simpson."

"I traced you to the school. Figured you were probably a teacher, but this is just as good," she said, her grin widening. "Maybe even better. It didn't take me long to pick this one. It's easier when they're single. Besides, it's a lovely

206

form, isn't it," she said, leaning in toward me.

"You're not doing a very good job," I told her. "You're nothing like the real Ms. Simpson."

She shrugged. "I'm not really trying. I don't plan on sticking around."

"Then what do you want?"

"You know what I want. Even if your mother never told you, you know inside, don't you."

Trouble was, she was right. I did know. All of a sudden, I could feel it, but it wasn't what I wanted. I didn't say anything. I just looked away again.

She sighed again. "Young ones are so difficult," she said. "They're hardly worth it. Is this your first form?" she said.

"Second."

"Let me guess. Two weeks?"

"Three and a half," I said.

She raised her eyebrows. "Impressive. You don't have much time left, though. I'll bet you've already started to feel it."

I nodded. "But it went away," I said. "The itching stopped."

"It'll come back," she said. "Count on it."

I hated being there. I hated listening to her. I looked back at the door, hoping someone would come along, but there was nobody in the window.

"Ah," she said, "you don't want it to, do you? You like being . . . what's his name? Chris? How sweet."

There it was, that cold, patronizing voice, the kind my mother used when I was at my lowest to chide me for being weak.

She knew she was pissing me off. "Come on, don't be

mad now," she said. "Most of us get attached to a form at some point, usually in the beginning. But all things come to an end. You'll find out."

"But why does it have to come so quickly?" I asked, suddenly forgetting myself. "My mother used to spend months in a form. Once she went over a year."

"You're young," she said. "As time goes on, you'll build up the strength to hold it longer. Some of us can last for years in a form, though I've never met any who really wanted to. A life gets old after a while. Before you know it, it's time to take a new one."

I suddenly thought about what Amber had asked me, about what I'd always wondered. "Why do we have to take any at all? Why don't we just live alone, away from them?"

"Aren't you the philosopher," she murmured. "What can I say? Nature's strange. She made us this way for some reason, maybe one that has yet to be realized. Still, everything has its niche. Humans have theirs, we have ours." She stood up from the desk and took slow steps around me. "Think of us as parasites. Only the most sophisticated, most successful parasites that ever evolved." She waved an arm around the classroom. "I mean, we sit back and let these creatures create a world for us, do all the work, and then we find a cozy little corner to squirm into and enjoy it without them ever knowing. That's why we're the superior species, don't you think?"

"Maybe," I said. "But a parasite is still a parasite."

"Greatness comes in different forms," she said, laughing. "Surely your mother taught you that."

"You're a lot different than she was. You smile, for one thing. And I don't think I ever heard her laugh."

She shrugged. "She was probably young. The young

females are all business. As we get older, we lighten up."

"And you smell different. It's strong. In fact, it's too strong. I don't ever remember her smelling that way."

"Pheromones," she said, her eyes flickering. "We females release them when we're ready to couple. In my case, they're pretty strong. It's been twenty years now since I last coupled," she said, drawing nearer. "As you can imagine, I'm quite eager."

"Twenty years?" I said. "How old are you, anyway?"

"Eighty," she said, then hesitated. "Well, okay—eighty-two. But I don't feel a day over sixty." She started laughing again. "You should feel privileged. This will probably be my last time. My last, your first. It's perfect."

I could feel myself loosening as she came closer to me. It was horrible and strange. I mean, I didn't want to be there, a part of me even hated her, but I found myself not caring. And as she moved in, unbuttoning the top button of her blouse, I felt this sudden sort of hunger. It's like her body was a puppet, moving, gesturing in a way that made my blood burn. Like the girls in those magazines Chris kept in the closet, she wasn't real, which, in a weird sort of way, made her all the more alluring.

"Your teacher has a house," she murmured, standing over me. "Nice little place right on the park in the middle of town. I say we head over there right now."

I didn't want to move. I didn't want to obey her or the part of me that was pushing me to. The knuckles on my fingers turned white as I gripped the edge of the desk.

But my hands weren't strong enough. Before I knew it, I was getting up, moving numbly to my feet as she watched, smiling.

All of a sudden, her smile faded. There was a knock on the door.

I started at the sound and shook my head. It was like coming into the icy air from a room that's too hot.

I turned around in time to see Amber open the door. I'd never been so happy to see her.

"Ms. Simpson?" Amber said, taking a step into the room.

"Yes?" Ms. Simpson snapped.

Amber hesitated. "I was just looking for Chris," she explained. "Chris, are you almost done?"

I looked back at the sheganger. Now it was my turn to smile.

"Got to go," I said.

"Well, we'll just have to finish this later, then," the sheganger said.

"See you tomorrow, Ms. Simpson," Amber called as I headed to the door.

"Right," Ms. Simpson replied.

"And make sure you give me a better grade than Chris on the test this time," Amber joked.

"I'll see what I can do," the teacher murmured, turning back toward her desk.

Amber looked up at me and raised her eyebrows. I just shrugged, and we headed for her locker.

Ten minutes later we were out the door.

"What's up with her, anyway?" Amber said as we crossed the parking lot.

"Who?" I said, even though I knew.

"Ms. Simpson. This morning she hardly said a word. And then just now, she was all bitchy. I mean, you heard her, right?"

"I didn't notice," I said. I didn't really want to talk about it, to be honest. And I definitely didn't want to tell Amber the truth. I'd dragged her into enough already—the last thing I wanted was to get her involved in this new complication. In fact, all I wanted was to get as far the hell away from the school as I could.

"It's just not like her," Amber said. "She usually acts like she gives a shit. You know what I mean?"

"Yeah," I said.

I reached down and took Amber's hand. I had been so shocked at first to discover the doppelganger, and then so relieved to get away from her, that I hadn't even really thought about the fact that Ms. Simpson was dead. Now, listening to Amber, it hit me pretty hard, and suddenly all I could think about was the first time Ms. Simpson had kept me after school. It was probably the first real conversation I'd ever had with anyone in my life. It made me sick, to tell you the truth. I felt like it was me who'd done it. And in some ways, I *was* sort of responsible. After all, Ms. Simpson and the doppelganger would never have crossed paths if I hadn't been around.

"I guess she's just having a bad day," Amber said. "Maybe something happened over the weekend."

"It doesn't matter," I said. "Whatever's going on with her, with anyone, doesn't matter. We have each other now. We care about each other, right?"

"Right," she said. She looked up at me and smiled, and it was even better than the smile in her picture because I knew that it was for me and no one else.

Rrrrrr!

We both jumped at the sound of screeching brakes and

looked over to see Ms. Simpson about six feet away, peering at us through the windshield of her black Volkswagen Jetta.

She rolled down the window as we moved out of the way.

"Careful, kids," she chirped. "Better watch where you're going."

She gave us a little wave, then smiled and drove away.

"Speak of the devil," Amber murmured.

"You said it," I replied as I watched the car turn out of the parking lot and disappear.

CHAPTER SEVENTEEN

I was so caught up thinking about the doppelganger as I came in through the Parkers' front door that when Echo jumped out from around the corner, I practically had a heart attack.

"Mom's home!" she said, hopping up and down in a little dance.

"That's great," I said.

I meant it too. It was going to be good having Sheila around again. And I didn't mean to cook and do all those things we'd been stuck doing—or usually not doing—since she'd left. It was just good to have everyone back together again and, most of all, to see Echo so happy. I don't think I'd ever seen her more excited. It made her seem more like a normal ten-year-old.

"Hi, Mom," I said, coming into the kitchen. She was at the sink washing dishes. All of a sudden, it was like she'd never left.

"Hey, sweetie," she said. She came over and gave me a quick kiss on the cheek—something she'd never done before. It sort of caught me off guard.

"Back for good?" I asked.

She nodded and returned to the sink. "Looks that way." She sighed. "I don't know. After the movie yesterday, I started thinking about things, about how much I missed you. All of you. So I called your father this morning at work."

"Uh-oh," I said.

Her smile faded a little. "Yeah, I know," she said. "Anyway, I came over for lunch, and we had a long talk. And, well, here I am."

"Where's Dad?" I asked.

"He took my car to get some groceries. Should be back soon."

I turned to head for my room.

"And Chris," she said. I stopped and looked back. "Thanks for taking care of Echo the way you did. I knew I could count on you."

She had this weird expression on her face—a look of gratefulness and relief, but mixed with sadness and more than a little shame. I gazed into her eyes and tried to figure out what she knew. Had Barry told her about our fight? It didn't seem like the kind of thing he'd do. Then again, nothing he'd done the last few days seemed like the kind of things he'd do. That's what's so hard about human beings—you can never really figure them out. They always end up surprising you.

"I didn't do much," I said.

She just smiled. "Well, thanks anyway."

Pretty soon Barry came home, and that evening we all had supper together. Don't get me wrong—it wasn't like we were the Brady Bunch all of a sudden or anything like that. In fact, it was a little tense, like we were all trying to figure out how to act toward one another. It was as if a bunch of strangers had been stuck in a room and told to pretend that they were a family all of a sudden. Still, no one argued. Echo didn't spill any milk. And Barry stayed at the table for the whole meal. He even helped clear the dishes at the end.

Best of all, after dinner, Mitch called and gave Barry his job back. I don't think Mitch told him I'd come by that morning. Barry didn't mention it or give any indication that he knew, which was fine by me. Who knows how Barry might have reacted if he'd found out? I mean, he'd already been humiliated by me once—twice, if you wanted to count last Friday night when I'd stopped him from blowing his head off. The last thing he needed was to be told his son had begged his job back for him. Besides, it kind of made me feel good to be the only one in the family who knew. I'd been living with them this whole time holding on to a terrible secret; it was nice to have a good one for a change.

Like I said, things weren't perfect, but the Parkers were coming together faster than I'd ever thought they could. That's the thing about life that I just don't get. It'll go to hell pretty fast—sometimes all it takes is one little thing, and all of a sudden everything's falling apart. But then the opposite is true, too. Just when you think there's no point in even trying, you find out you're not so bad off after all. I don't know, maybe things are changing all around us the whole time and we just don't notice until it's all over.

But just when the Parkers were starting to become a real

family, I could feel myself pulling away from them. I guess it was partly because I realized that no matter what happened or what I'd done to make it happen, in the end I didn't really belong.

There was another reason. When I woke up the next morning, the rash was back, and I itched worse than ever. Scratching didn't help. In fact, it only made it worse, sending lines of pain burning across my skin. I was losing Chris again, this time probably for good, and as I got dressed for school, I felt a whole new hate for the sheganger. She'd jinxed me. I just knew it.

As Tuesday slipped into Wednesday I began to feel more and more agitated, like there were beetles under my skin, crawling from place to place, looking for a way out. It came in waves. One minute I'd feel normal, the next I could hardly concentrate on where I was or what was going on around me. I was focusing all my energies on just being Chris.

It was all too much. But it made me aware of one thing. I'd seen enough *Oprah* and *Dr. Phil* to realize I'd succumbed to a serious case of denial. I mean, I'd gotten so used to being Chris, so content with how things were going with the Parkers and with Amber, that I realized I didn't have any plans for what to do once Chris was gone for good. The whole thing scared me.

The stress of knowing *she* was waiting for me didn't help, either. The best thing for me to do would have been to ditch school entirely, but I knew I'd get in trouble if I did. And now that it looked like Barry and Sheila were getting back together, I didn't want to do anything that might screw it up. So instead I just skipped English. On Tuesday

I went to the infirmary seventh period and pretended to be sick. On Wednesday I just plain cut class and hung out in the bathroom with the smokers.

There I was, secluded in a locked stall, perched on the toilet seat with my arms wrapped around me, sort of rocking back and forth. I was a nervous wreck. If anyone had seen me, they probably would've called for a straitjacket.

I have to say, though, the smokers were actually pretty cool. After offering me a cigarette, they more or less left me alone. I guess having abandoned my jock persona gave me some weird sort of credibility in their eyes.

As I sat there surveying the gems of wit carved into the door of the stall, I tried to sort it all out. The whole thing was totally messed up. You see, a part of me really wanted to go to English, to give in to Ms. Simpson, or rather, to her doppelganger. *What's the harm?* a voice inside me said. *Just do it and get it over with. Then you'll feel better. It doesn't mean you don't love Amber. Besides, she never even has to know.*

I remembered what my mother had told me about the coupling. That it wasn't a matter of choice—it was a matter of proximity, a biological imperative. Survival of the species and all that crap. But that's what made me want to dig in and fight it even more. I had given in already, with what I'd done to the old man and to Chris. I didn't want to be a slave anymore. This was where I'd make my stand—with her. And I wasn't going to be unfaithful to Amber. No matter how much that part of me tried to rationalize it, I knew that giving in to the sheganger would be a betrayal, at the very least of my feelings. Feelings I wasn't supposed to have in the first place.

It all wouldn't have been so bad if I could've been with Amber. But now, when I needed her more than ever, I felt like I had to avoid her. I'd seen her at lunch and in between classes a couple times, but it was horrible. I mean, it was all I could do to act normal, to not tear off my clothes and jump up and down screaming. I just didn't want her to see me like this. So I begged off getting together with her after school on Tuesday and again on Wednesday. I told her I was sick, which was true in a way. I just didn't tell her why.

It all caught up with me on Thursday. I was fidgeting in history class first period, when the principal's voice came over the intercom.

"Mr. Johnson," the voice said.

"Yes?" the teacher replied, looking up from his newspaper while we did worksheets.

"Is Chris Parker in your class right now?"

"He is."

"Would you send him to the office, please."

"Right away."

Everyone suddenly turned and stared at me. There were no oohs or aahs this time, just silence. Even Mr. Johnson didn't say anything, he just sat there and watched right along with the kids as I gathered up my books and left.

A few minutes later, I was sitting before the principal— a slender, balding man with a mustache that seemed way too big for his face, like it was fake or something and he'd just glued it on that morning for a joke. But I quickly realized that that would have required more humor and imagination than he was capable of.

"Do you know why you're here, Chris?" he intoned.

"Not really," I said.

"Well, I received a note this morning from Ms. Simpson complaining that you skipped English two days in a row."

"I was sick."

"Well, you were in the infirmary Tuesday. And yesterday?"

"I was sick," I said again. I knew I wasn't being too helpful, but I wasn't in the mood to banter with the guy. In fact, sitting there in his overheated office, I could feel another wave coming on.

"You're twitching, Chris," he suddenly said.

"I am?" I said, gripping the sides of the chair.

"What's wrong, Chris?" He sort of leaned back in his chair, cocked his head, and gave me this suspicious look. "Are you on crank, son?" he said.

"No!" I exclaimed. "Of course not." I had no idea what crank was. But whatever it was, it couldn't be any worse than what was happening to me.

"Maybe I should call your parents," he murmured, reaching for the phone.

"No!"

His hand froze. He sat back and looked at me.

"I'm sorry I cut class," I said. "I mean, I really wasn't feeling well. But still, I shouldn't have done it. Just tell me what I need to do."

"Well, the first offense for skipping class is an office detention. . . ."

"Fine," I said.

"However," he continued, "Ms. Simpson has requested you serve the detention with her. She wants to get you up to speed on what you missed."

My stomach did a flip-flop. *I'll bet she does,* I thought.

"You'll go to your seventh-period class like you're supposed to do and stay after for the detention. I suggest you do whatever she tells you to. And if I find out that you skipped out again, you'll be suspended. Understood?"

"Yeah," I said.

So she had me. And she knew it too. I could see it in her eyes as I walked into English seventh period and sat down—this sort of triumphant gleam. And that smell—it was still there. If anything, it had grown stronger.

The period seemed to drag on forever. She had us read silently in our books, which, I found out, was what we'd been doing for the last couple days.

I don't think I read a whole page the entire period. I just closed my eyes and tried to think about how I could get out of this. Once in a while, I'd open my eyes and look up, and every time there she was, staring at me.

As the period wound to a close, she gave us our homework and, right in front of everyone, reminded me of my detention. A few kids laughed. The bell rang.

Then we were alone.

She closed the door like last time and came up behind me.

"You've been avoiding me," she said.

"I haven't been feeling good," I said. "Don't take it personally."

"It's slipping, isn't it?"

I nodded.

"I told you it would happen," she said.

"How much time do I have?" I asked.

"How long can you hold on? That's the question. How

220

long has it been now? A month? God, it must be killing you."

"It's not bad," I said, shrugging, trying more than ever not to scratch at my neck and arms.

She laughed. "You really are a funny one. I don't think I've met another quite like you, and I've come across quite a few in my time."

"Gee, thanks," I retorted.

She came up close behind me, until I could feel her breath on the back of my neck. She sniffed a few times then stood back.

"Just as I thought," she said. "I bet your mother never told you you had human blood in you, did she."

"What?" I said, whirling around. "I'm part human?"

She shrugged. "Not much. A quarter, maybe even less. For whatever reason, it only gets passed on to the males. The females stay pure."

"I didn't think we could . . . you know, breed with them," I said. I hated using that word, but talking to her, it seemed appropriate.

"Males can't with human females," she said. "But every once in a great while, one of the girls will stray. She'll randomly go into heat and the next thing you know, she's diluting the gene pool. Not her fault, the poor thing. Fortunately it hardly ever happens. But it looks like your mother ended up with a rare half blood."

"Doesn't sound like her," I said. I remembered how she'd always disdained males, how she'd called the one who'd fathered me weak. Now I knew why.

"She probably didn't have an option. We'll take whoever's at hand."

"Like me?"

"Exactly," she said, coming around to face me. "But you're different," she said. "It's strange—normally I can't stand the mixed ones, but I can hardly resist you. Now where were we the other day?" She unbuttoned the top button of her blouse like she had before.

I'd been preparing myself for this moment. I stood up from my seat and took a deep breath.

"No."

"What?" she said, halting her advance. A look of surprise came over her face.

"It isn't going to happen," I said.

Her surprise turned into a look of amusement. She chuckled. "It's not, is it? What makes you think you even have a choice in the matter? Now let's get out of here."

She held her hand out and beckoned. I could feel myself being pulled toward her, like there was some magnetic field emanating from her outstretched palm. I gritted my teeth and fought it.

"I don't want this," I said, panting. "Let me go."

"What is it, anyway?" she said, lowering her hand. She ran her hands down across her body. "Don't you find me attractive?" she mocked.

"Go to hell," I said, closing my eyes.

"Ah," she said, "I know what it is. It's her, isn't it? That human girl you're with—Amber, right?"

My eyes snapped open. "Leave her out of this," I said. I could hear the blood pounding in my ears.

"That's pathetic," she said, "even for a mixed blood like you. Doppelgangers don't fall in love. It's one of the cardinal rules. One of the *only* rules."

"Besides," she said, drawing up close to me so that

her face was right before mine, "why settle for a girl when you can have a woman?"

She unclasped the barrette holding back her hair and shook her head, letting her hair cascade down around her shoulders. Next thing I knew she was unbuttoning another button so that I could see her bra.

The whole scene was bizarre, almost comical in a sick sort of way. I felt like I was trapped in one of those soap operas I used to watch every day growing up. What made it even worse was that it worked. I found myself weakening again, just like before.

Suddenly her eyes flashed behind me toward the door and a slow smile crept over her face. I turned and looked over my shoulder.

Amber was frozen at the door, gazing in through the tempered glass with her mouth open in shock.

Our eyes met. Before I could do anything, she disappeared.

"Oh, that's too bad," the doppelganger cooed. "Looks like you lost her. Just as well. It was going to have to end sometime."

As nasty as the comment was, it was the best thing the sheganger could have said to me. I was so angry, all desire disappeared. I tore myself away and ran out into the hallway. Amber was gone. I sprinted down the hall and around the corner just in time to see her head through the door that led to the parking lot. I took off after her.

"Amber!" I shouted, throwing the door open and stumbling out into the parking lot.

She paused, looked back at me, and kept walking.

I caught up to her just as she reached her car. She started

to open her door, but I slammed it shut.

"What the hell *was* that back there?" she said. She wouldn't look at me, and I could tell she was trying not to cry. "So that's why you've been blowing me off all week."

"No, of course not," I said. I reached over to take her hand, but she swatted me away. "Like I told you at lunch, I got detention for skipping. I had to be there. I didn't have a choice. But nothing happened, Amber."

I hesitated for a moment, wondering if I should tell her who "Ms. Simpson" really was. It would've solved the immediate problem, but I just couldn't bring myself to do it. I wanted to keep Amber as far away from the situation as I could, and I figured it would be safer if she didn't know.

"That's not what it looked like to me," she said, seeing me hesitate.

"It doesn't matter how it looks, I'm telling the truth. Nothing seems the way it is, you know that. I mean, look at me, for chrissake."

"I don't know *what* I know. The last couple weeks have been so screwed up, I can't even tell what's real anymore."

"That's why we have to trust each other," I said.

She shook her head. "I thought I trusted you," she said. "But the way you've been acting these last couple days, I don't know why I should. I mean, you skip out after school. You hardly talk to me at lunch. And don't give me that bullshit about being sick, either—"

"Amber, I'm losing it!" I shouted. "I'm losing Chris."

She hesitated. "What do you mean?"

"Look," I said. I pulled up my shirt and showed her the rash, a swirling red band that encircled my torso and spread up my back.

She winced when she saw it and looked away. I didn't blame her. It was pretty gross.

"I didn't know that could happen," she whispered.

"It's been really bad the last few days. It's taking everything I've got to hold on. That's why I've been acting this way."

"You never told me it wouldn't last," she said.

"I didn't want to talk about it," I said. "I didn't even want to think about it. It started more than a week ago, but then it stopped. I guess I was hoping that maybe it would go away for good. That I could stay being Chris, stay being with you."

She looked back up at me. Her eyes sharpened.

"You talk about trust," she said, "but you don't even trust me enough to tell me what you're going through, or trust that I can handle it."

I looked away. She had me there.

She shook her head. "I don't know what all this means. I've just got to think about it," she said, getting into her car. "I hope you feel better."

Then she drove off.

As I watched her disappear, I thought about what she'd said. And the more I did, the more I realized she was right. I mean, I'd trusted her with the biggest secret of all by telling her who I was, what I was about, and she hadn't turned me away or tried to hurt me. So why couldn't I have told her that Chris would soon be gone?

I guess when it came right down to it, I just wasn't ready to stop being Chris yet. I wasn't ready to go back to being what I really was.

That's what I would tell her the next time I saw her. She would understand. I mean, when you love someone, that's what you do, right?

CHAPTER EIGHTEEN

When I got to school the next morning, there was a note taped to the inside of my locker, written in Amber's round letters: "I'm sorry about yesterday. Meet me in the parking lot after fourth period."

As soon as I read the note, I felt better. In fact, I went practically the whole morning without feeling like I was going to crack out of my skin—the first time in three days.

Fifth period was when I normally met Amber for lunch, so instead of going to the cafeteria after fourth period ended, I went to the main office to sign out.

"I have a dentist appointment," I said.

"Didn't you just have one last month?" the secretary asked. She was a heavyset woman with dyed hair that matched the color of her skin, making her look like a bronzed statue someone had dressed in frumpy clothes as a joke.

Damn, I thought. *How do you remember that in a school with a thousand kids?*

"Well, I have another one," I replied.

"Do you have a note?"

"My mother forgot to write me one. I'll bring one in tomorrow."

"Tomorrow's Saturday."

"Then I'll bring one in on Monday."

She gave me a sort of frown and glanced back at the principal's office. For a second I thought she was going to bust me, but then she handed me the clipboard.

"Floss," she said as I signed my name on the sheet.

"Excuse me?"

"If you floss, then you won't get cavities."

"Thanks, I'll try to remember that."

"Forget the dentist; you should see a doctor," she said as I started to leave.

I stopped and looked back. "What do you mean?" I asked.

"You don't look so good," she said, and brushed her neck a few times, nodding in my direction.

I reached up and felt the side of my neck. The skin was all bumpy. I didn't even have to look to know the rash had spread. Not only that, I suddenly realized my hands were all blotchy and chaffed. I turned and practically ran out of the building.

Amber was waiting in her car. When I came up beside her and knocked on the window, she jumped. But when I got in, I could tell she was relieved to see me.

"I was starting to worry you might not show."

"Are you kidding?" I said. "It's all I could think about."

As she started the car and drove out of the parking lot, I pulled down the visor in front of me and glanced in its mirror. Sure enough, the right side of my neck was covered in little red welts. I flipped the visor back and turned up the collar of my jacket.

For a long time, we didn't say anything. She just kept driving with this real serious look on her face.

"Where are we going?" I asked her as we headed out of town.

"It's a surprise," she said.

Pretty soon I could tell we were heading toward the lake where she'd taken me a couple weeks ago—the day I'd revealed myself to her. Only, once we got there, instead of going into the parking lot, she kept driving before turning onto a road about a half mile past the park. Soon the road started to climb, twisting back and forth up this steep hill.

"Discovered this place yesterday afternoon when I was driving around," she said. "I was so busy thinking, I went right past the park. Next thing I knew, I was making my way up the hill. Can't believe I never thought to drive up here before."

A minute later the road came out of the trees and ended at a lookout over the lake. I could see Bakersville in the distance. For a second it reminded me of the mountains where I'd grown up, except all I'd been able to see there were trees.

"Wow. Nice view," I said.

I looked over at her and saw she was smiling, and all of a sudden I forgot about my itching, about the sheganger, about the Parkers. I forgot about everything.

"Let's go," she said. "I'm hungry."

We got out of the car, and while Amber rummaged in the trunk, I walked over to the edge of the lookout and glanced down. The cliff dropped almost straight into the water about a hundred feet below. Suddenly I felt a little woozy and stepped back.

"Don't let yourself go."

I turned around and saw Amber standing there with a blanket tucked under one arm, holding a basket.

"Why would I?" I said.

She shrugged. "I read once that the reason people are scared of heights isn't because they're afraid of falling. It's that they're afraid of jumping."

"You think people want to die?"

"Maybe a little part of them."

"What about you?" I asked.

She shook her head. "I'm a teenager," she said, and laughed. "We all think we're going to live forever, right?"

"What's in the basket?" I asked her. I wanted to change the subject.

"I made us a picnic," she answered.

"It's a little cold for a picnic, isn't it?" Even though the sun was out, the air had a bite to it.

She shrugged again. "You've got to take your opportunities where you can," she said, looking down. I knew what she meant—neither of us knew what was going to happen.

I helped her spread the blanket out, and pretty soon we were eating lunch. She'd gone all out—gourmet sandwiches, fresh salad, stuffed olives. Some of the best food I've ever tasted.

"Thanks for bringing me up here," I said after we'd finished eating. "This is really nice—the food, everything. It's great."

"I drove all over the place yesterday afternoon," she

said. "I thought about what you said, about what you were going through, how hard it must be. It made me feel horrible. All of a sudden, I just felt so selfish."

"No, Amber," I said. "You were absolutely right. I should have told you before. I should have trusted you. I just didn't want to think about it myself, let alone worry you about it."

"Well, I do worry," she said. "I want to worry. That's what you're supposed to do when you're with somebody."

"You're right," I replied. "I guess I'm just not used to having someone that I can tell things to. I've been alone my whole life. Even when I was with my mother, there was all this space there between us, in spite of that tiny little cabin. I never knew who she was going to come home as, who she was going to be next. And for the most part, she did her own thing. I just knew enough to stay out of the way."

"See, that's what I mean," she said. "Hearing that makes me sad."

"I never thought so growing up," I said. "It never even occurred to me that I should. That's not how doppelgangers think."

"Then that's even sadder," she said.

"I guess," I said. "I think what it comes down to is all of us hate ourselves. The doppelgangers, I mean. Not just the way we look—we can't help that—but *because* we feel that way about how we look. And because we're dependent on our urge to become something other than what we are."

"Well, that may be true," she said, "but you're not alone. Lots of people want to be someone different than who they really are. I mean, look at half the kids in our school. Same thing with hating yourself. I know I did for the longest time when I was with Chris. And like you said that night when we buried him, so did he. It makes me mad because it didn't have to be that way. It could have been better. It could have been more like . . ."

"More like this," I said. She nodded.

The wind picked up and it was starting to get colder, so we fetched another blanket from the car and wrapped up together. For a long time, we just sat and watched the lake, watched the seagulls as they wheeled over the water, and didn't say anything. She sat in front of me, leaning back a little against my chest, and I could smell her hair like I'd been able to the night I slept in her room. All of a sudden, I wished we never had to move. I wished we could just freeze right there like a single statue that would forever be the same.

A long time passed before she broke the silence.

"So what are we going to do?" she asked, taking my hand under the blanket.

"I don't know," I said. "Pretty soon I'll have to let go of Chris."

"Will you become somebody else?" she said. It was the question I'd hoped she wouldn't ask.

"Maybe," I said. "I mean, probably. At some point."

She leaned forward and turned around to face me.

"We could run away," she said. "I could go with you. You know, help you find people to become. We could find the bad people, people no one would miss."

"You mean like Chris?" I said.

Amber didn't reply. She just glanced at the ground.

"I don't know if there are such people, Amber. That's

what makes human beings different from doppelgangers. If one of us disappears, no one's the wiser. None of the others care. People are different.

"Besides," I added, "you can't leave. You're only sixteen."

"So are you."

"Yeah, but you've got a life. You can't just leave it.'"

"But I have you," she said. "You're a part of my life." She hesitated. "Then, promise me you'll come back. Promise me you'll keep coming back. I won't care who you are."

"Let's just forget about it," I said. "I don't want to think about it right now."

There I was, going right back into denial mode. But talking about the whole thing was starting to make me feel really depressed, and it wasn't the right time or place to feel that way. I figured there'd be more than enough time later.

She frowned but didn't say anything.

"My parents are going away for the weekend," she said after a few minutes. "They're leaving this afternoon." She took my hand again. "I was thinking you could come over. Spend the weekend with me, you know?"

My heart started pounding. Suddenly I felt all nervous.

"Okay," I said.

"What's that?" she said, reaching for my neck. I drew back for a second and put my hand up, thinking she meant my rash, but she pushed my hand aside and pulled the chain out from under my shirt.

"Just a necklace."

"I don't remember seeing it before. Where'd you get it?"

I hesitated, remembering how it sparkled around the

old man's neck in the moonlight. "I found it a while ago," I said. "A long ways from here. It's the only thing I have that's really mine."

She turned the medallion over and examined it up close.

"St. Jude," she said, reading the back. She looked up at me. "The patron saint of lost souls."

"Figures," I said, and tried to laugh. She let go of the necklace and looked down at the lake.

A few minutes went by and we didn't say anything. Then she turned back to me.

"You know you could stay around, stay with me and not be Chris. Not be anybody. Just yourself."

"How's that?"

"Let me see you," she said. "The real you. I want you to show me."

I shook my head and looked away.

"I don't care what you look like," she said. "I'm not shallow, you know."

"It's not even a matter of that. You've never seen a doppelganger before. Trust me, we're repulsive."

"How bad can it be?"

"Just imagine the ugliest thing you can think of in the whole world," I said. "Whatever it is, it isn't even close. I can't explain it any better than that."

She looked down for a moment. "All right," she said at last. "But I won't ever care what you look like."

"Thanks," I said. I really did believe that *she* believed it. And who knows, maybe she would've been able to handle the sight of me, but I wasn't ready to go there.

"I do love you, you know," she said, looking back up.

"I love you, too," I said. "I have probably since the first time I saw you."

"Isn't it strange that way?" she said. "How you know before you know?"

I kind of laughed. But the funny thing was, I knew exactly what she meant.

"Oh!" she suddenly said. "I almost forgot. I have a present for you."

She pulled a small box wrapped with red ribbon from her jacket pocket and handed it to me. "I got it last weekend when we went away. I was too mad to give it to you earlier."

Nobody had ever given me a present before. I opened the box and looked inside at the little silver square. "What is it?" I said.

"It's a cell phone," she said, laughing. She took it out, unfolded it, and handed it to me.

"Now we can talk to each other no matter where we are. See, my cell number's already in here—just press this button," she said. She showed me how to answer a call, and how to make one. "Don't worry, it's already paid for. And look, it even takes pictures."

She scooted up beside me and held the phone out in front of us as far as she could.

"Say cheese," she said, and laughed. The next thing I knew, there we were, the two of us smiling together on the little screen.

I turned it over. There was an inscription on the back, engraved in fine letters: "Gabriel."

"What's this?" I asked, holding up the back of the phone.

"That's your name," she said. "I thought you needed one of your own, so I made one up for you. Gabriel. You know, like the archangel?" When I didn't respond, she quickly added, "If you don't like it, we can choose another."

"No," I said, finally finding my voice. "Gabriel is perfect. Even better than the phone."

"I'm glad you like it," she said. "I was a little worried you wouldn't. I wasn't even sure if you wanted a name."

She smiled and leaned back so that she was resting on her elbows. I could tell she was relieved. A breeze came up and blew a strand of hair across her face.

I held the phone up so that she was framed in the tiny screen and pressed the button like she showed me. The strand of hair, blazing red in the sun along the edge of her smile, froze on the screen.

"Perfect," I said, and closed the phone.

"Could you pass the mac and cheese?"

Echo handed the bowl over to me.

"Does anyone else want some?" I asked, holding up the bowl. Everyone shook their heads, so I shoveled the rest out onto my plate and dug in.

"Jesus, you're hungry tonight," said Barry.

I looked up and realized everyone had pretty much finished their dinner and was watching me. I shrugged. "Didn't really eat lunch today," I said. Of course it wasn't true. The picnic lunch Amber had made more than filled me at the time, but all of a sudden when I sat down at dinner, I realized I was starved. It was weird—it felt like I hadn't eaten in days. I think I was using so much energy to keep my form, my body just couldn't keep up.

"He always eats a lot when it's yellow meal," Echo said.

"Chris, if that rash isn't better by Monday, we're taking you to the doctor," Sheila said. I looked up and saw the worry on her face.

"I'm all right," I said. The last thing I wanted was to see the doctor. Who knows what kind of tests they'd try to do.

"Well, the way you keep squirming, even I'm starting to itch," Barry said. "Looks like you rolled in a patch of poison ivy or something."

I looked down and realized my knee was cycling up and down like a piston. I forced myself to be still.

"So," I said, to change the subject, "hot date tonight, huh?"

Barry glanced over at Sheila, who blushed slightly. Echo giggled.

"Just going to a movie," Barry said, lighting up a cigarette. "No big deal."

Barry and Sheila looked at each other for a second but didn't say anything. Barry went back to his cigarette.

"Dad, could I borrow your car?" I said, finishing my plate. "Josh and I are going out tonight. I'll probably stay over at his place. I'll have it back tomorrow."

Before he could say anything, Sheila stepped in.

"I don't know, Chris. You look really tired. Maybe you should just stay home and go to bed early."

"I feel fine, Mom," I said. "It's been a long week, that's all."

Barry shrugged. "Just don't do anything stupid," he said.

"I won't."

Barry stubbed out his butt, and we all got up. The two of us cleared the table while Mom and Echo loaded the dishwasher, our new nightly ritual.

A half hour later, I came out from my room just as Barry and Sheila were putting on their coats. Echo came out too, and we all stood together in the hallway for a moment.

"Here you go," Barry said, handing me his set of keys.

"Thanks," I said.

Sheila came over and kneeled down before Echo.

"You going to be okay by yourself?" she asked.

"Of course," Echo said. "It's only a few hours, anyway."

Sheila smiled and gave her a quick hug and a kiss. Then she stood up and gave me a hug.

"Bye, sweetie," she said. "Have a good time."

"Yeah, I'll see you tomorrow," I said.

I watched them head out, then lingered by the door, looking through the window as they got into Sheila's car, backed out, and drove off.

"I've never seen them go out before. Not together."

I turned around to see Echo standing in the hallway watching me.

"Me neither," I said.

"It's good, isn't it?"

"Yeah, it's good."

I went and took a shower. Afterward, as I stood in the bathroom and wiped away the steam from the mirror, I could see parts of the rash along my torso had turned white and the skin was starting to flake away. And there it was, underneath—the greenish gray of my old self, my real self, veiny, opaque, glistening. At that point I knew it was almost over. Chris was coming to an end.

It kind of made me sad all over again. I mean, even though I knew he was gone, in some ways it was like he wasn't really dead—not totally, anyway. But once I let his form go, or once it let me go, it would be over for good.

I dressed in fresh clothes and headed out into the living room to say good-bye to Echo, but she wasn't there. She wasn't in her room, either.

"Echo?" I said.

She didn't answer, but then I heard her voice, real faint like it was far away. I followed the sound into the kitchen and saw the cellar door was open, the light on.

I crept down the steps, then paused halfway down. The corner was gone—the sheets were piled on the floor, the tea set put away, the bunnies and bears piled on top of the toy box in the corner. And there was Echo, removing the pictures from the wall, singing to herself.

Before I could say anything, she turned around and, seeing me, started.

"Sorry. Hope I didn't scare you too much," I said, coming the rest of the way down the stairs.

"No," she said. "Well, maybe just a little."

As soon as I got closer, she cocked her head and gave me this look.

"What happened to you?" she said in this little voice. I could tell she was worried.

"What do you mean?" I murmured, as my heart started to pound. I reached up and felt my face and neck. It was a little bumpy, but the skin seemed to be holding.

"You look really bad," she said, then added, "You're all pasty."

"I'm just tired," I said.

"Oh," she whispered. I could tell she didn't really believe me—not completely anyway—but she wasn't going to give me a hard time. She never did.

"Anyway, I'm heading out now. I just wanted to say good-bye."

"Have fun with Amber."

I froze. "What?" I said, forcing a laugh.

A little smile crept across her face. "You're all spiffied up," she said. She sniffed the air a couple times. "And you're wearing cologne."

I shook my head and smiled. "You're too smart for your own good."

"Don't worry," she said. "I won't tell."

"Thanks," I said. "So what are you doing?" I asked, looking around.

She shrugged. "Putting things away," she said, looking around as well. "I don't know, I just felt like it. Do you think it's okay?"

"It's fine, Echo," I said.

She turned back to the pictures on the wall.

"Can I have one?" I asked, seeing her take down another drawing.

"'Course you can. You made them. They're yours."

She handed me the paper she was holding, the one with the bears dancing in the sunny meadow.

Then something really weird happened. The next thing I knew, I was crying. And not just a little. I mean, I was really bawling. I still don't know why. Like I said before, doppelgangers don't cry. We're not supposed to be able to. At least, that's what my mother had always told me.

Echo didn't say anything. She just came over and gave me a hug, and for a minute we stood there while I collected myself.

"Thanks," I said, wiping my eyes as she stepped back.

"Don't get your picture wet," she said.

I folded the paper up and put it in the back pocket of my jeans.

"You're a good sister," I said.

"You're a good brother."

We just stood and looked at each other. Then I gave her a little wave and headed up the stairs. I could still hear her singing when I left the house.

CHAPTER NINETEEN

I have to admit I was a little nervous getting back behind the wheel. I'd driven only that one time a week ago. Not only that, this car was a little different from Amber's, and it took me a few minutes to figure out where everything was. But I finally managed to turn the lights on and get the car started. Before long I was on my way to Amber's.

As I made my way through town, I was so focused on trying to drive, I didn't realize how jacked up I was until I was almost to her house. Then it hit me all at once—this weird combination of excitement and nervousness all wrapped into one. My knuckles turned white along the edge of the steering wheel, my heart pounded in my ears, and all of a sudden I felt like one of those big meteors streaking in from outer space, skipping across the atmosphere, disintegrating in a trail of fire, burning up in one long, exhilarating rush.

The problem with meteors, though, is that they crash. Whatever's left smashes into the earth and dies, becomes a lump of cold, melted rock.

I had just turned the corner onto Amber's street and could see her house up ahead when a pulse rattled against my chest, a double charge that nearly sent me off the road. A second later it came again. I put my hand on the source of the vibration.

It was the phone. I turned into Amber's driveway, pulled it out of my pocket, and laughed in relief. Here Amber was calling me, and I was right outside her door. I decided to answer it and sneak up on her while we talked—I'd seen them do that sort of thing on TV all the time. It would be a funny trick.

But when I answered the phone, the trick was on me.

"Yes?" I quipped, stepping out of the car.

"So you decided to skip class again, I see," a voice purred. "You're a naughty, naughty boy."

It took a second before I realized who it was. I froze, unable to speak.

"What's the matter?" the sheganger teased. "Cat got your tongue?"

I got back into the car and shut the door as quietly as I could.

"How did you get this number?" I hissed.

"Oh, I just had a nice long chat with that girl of yours. You know, a little heart-to-heart. Could hardly get her to shut up, in fact. Still, I understand the attraction. She's certainly got the goods, a perfect specimen."

"I told you before to leave her alone."

"I'm happy to. After all, I've got the teacher. She's more than adequate. Only you need to cooperate. I can't wait forever, you know."

"I told you I'm not interested."

"Of course you are, you silly boy. You think I can't tell seeing you, *smelling* you. So stop all this dramatic non-sense—it's disgustingly human."

"Sorry, the answer's the same," I said, trying to keep my voice from quavering. "I've got to go."

I started to close up the phone, when I heard her call out, "Wait!" I hesitated, then brought the phone back up to my ear.

"What?" I snapped.

"If you won't come to me as I am, then I'll take a form that I *know* you'll find appealing."

My stomach fell, and for a second I just closed my eyes. I knew who she was talking about. Until this moment I'd been trying to fool myself into thinking that it wasn't going to come to this, but really I knew. The second I caught her scent in the air at school, I sensed deep down that it meant trouble.

I glanced through the windshield at the big house. Amber was somewhere inside, waiting for me. And I could go in there, I could protect her tonight, even tomorrow. But not forever. Somehow the sheganger would find a way. After all, it's what we're good at. It's what we're made for.

That and one other thing. Suddenly I knew what I had to do.

"You still there?" she said.

"All right," I said. "You know Parson Woods? The forest outside of town where you ditched the Subaru?"

There was a pause. She was trying to figure out how I knew. "Sure," she said at last.

"Meet me there at eight thirty."

"I knew you'd come to your senses."

"Let's just get it over with," I said. "Half an hour."

"Sounds good," she replied. "I've got some business to take care of anyway."

"So do I."

I closed up the phone before she could say good-bye. I didn't want to hear her say another word.

I started up the car and backed out of the driveway as fast as I could. Trying to keep one eye on the road as I headed down the street, I flipped the phone open again and pressed the button Amber had showed me earlier. It wasn't easy—I almost dropped the stupid thing my hand was shaking so hard. A few seconds, later Amber's voice was in my ear.

"Hi, Amber," I said.

"Chris?"

"No, it's Gabriel," I said, trying to laugh.

"Sorry," she said. "I can't believe I forgot. It's going to take me a while."

"That's okay," I said. "Listen, Amber, I'm going to be late."

"What's wrong?" she said. She wasn't dumb. She could tell something was up.

"Nothing serious. There's just something I've got to do first. I'm sorry. I'll tell you all about it later."

"You promise?"

"I promise," I said.

There was a pause on the other end. "Okay," she said at last. "Oh, by the way, did Ms. Simpson call you yet?"

"No," I whispered.

"Well, we had this long talk. It was really weird, but it was good. And that whole thing that happened yesterday—when I saw you two—we cleared it all up. Sorry again that I overreacted. Anyway, there's a quiz you need to make up. She said she'd get a hold of you."

"Thanks, Amber," I said. "I'll see you soon."

"See you soon," she said.

I glanced at my watch as the headlights appeared through the trees. Eight thirty. She was punctual, all right. Somehow that didn't surprise me. I leaned against the hood of Barry's car and tried to seem steady, tried to seem cool as the headlights came around the corner and flashed onto me as she pulled up.

She stepped out of the car and walked toward me.

"Hey, gorgeous," she said.

"Did you take care of your business?" I asked. I had an idea what it was, but I wanted to make sure.

"Just needed to tie up some loose ends. Write a few letters, that sort of thing. It seems Ms. Simpson has abruptly resigned and left town for unknown parts so she can—how do they like to put it?—go find herself."

"So you're dropping her just like that?"

"Why not? After tonight I won't need her anymore. Besides, think of it as a public service—should supply this town with enough gossip to get them through the next few years," she said. "Then again, who knows? Maybe she won't even be missed."

"She will be. I know I miss her."

The sheganger sighed. "Ms. Simpson? You've got to be kidding me. And all this time I thought you didn't like the teacher."

When I didn't say anything, she took another step closer.

Even in the shadows, I could see her eyes sparkle as she smiled at me, her breath coming in little puffs of steam in the night air. My nostrils flared as her scent started to reach me through the cold.

"Well, I brought her along if you want to say hello. She's right back there in the trunk."

"No thanks," I said, taking a few steps back. I needed to get away from her smell.

She laughed. "Look at you. Even now, you're still fighting it. All because of some human female. Some silly little girl."

"She's not some silly girl," I said. "And I'm doing this for her."

She sniffed. "How noble of you. You know, I might just kill the pathetic little thing anyway when this is over."

"Why do you have to go and say something like that?"

"Well, somebody has to teach you a lesson. You can't get all involved with these people. Otherwise, how can you be what you are? It's not good for you. It's certainly not good for them. You need to understand."

"I understand, all right."

"Good. Now, let's get down to business, handsome. Which backseat do you want, yours or mine? Mine's more comfortable."

I pulled the pistol from my pocket and raised it. It was Barry's gun. I'd gone back for it after leaving Amber's. I wasn't sure I'd use it, I wasn't even sure I could. Now I'd find out.

The gun shook slightly in my hand as I pointed it at her.

She squinted for a moment, as if she was trying to figure

out what I was doing. Then she started to laugh.

"A gun?" she said. "You've got to be kidding me."

I didn't say anything.

"You can't seriously be thinking about doing this," she sneered.

"I told you to leave her alone. You wouldn't listen to me."

"What the hell is wrong with you? I mean, just for the sake of argument, so what if I did take the girl? It's no different from anything you've done."

"It *is* different!" I shouted.

She shook her head in disgust. "All right, enough. Put the gun away and let's go. It's time."

"No," I said. The gun lowered slightly. "I told you before, it isn't going to happen. I don't want it to."

It wasn't completely true. A part of me still wanted to, even after everything. And seeing her there right in front of me, her scent so close, didn't help. But it wasn't what I'd come here for.

"Of course you want to," she said. "You have to. That's just the way it is. You can't fight nature."

"I'm going to try," I said, raising the gun again.

"By killing me?" she said, her voice rising slightly. I could tell she was starting to get a little worried. "You don't want to couple, fine. But you can't *kill* me. We don't kill one another. We never have."

"Why not?"

"We just don't. There are too few of us to engage in that sort of nonsense."

"I don't care," I said. "I can't let you hurt her. I can't let you hurt any of them. Not anymore."

"But that's what I *do*. That's all that I am, you know that. I kill. I'm a doppelganger."

"So am I," I whispered, cocking the gun.

She shook her head again. "They really got to you, didn't they? You know, it's kind of ironic if you think about it. I mean, you talk about defying nature, resisting me, resisting your urges, but if you hadn't given in to them, if you hadn't killed Chris, you never would've gotten to this point."

"Life's funny, I guess," I said.

"It certainly is." She smiled and looked down at the ground.

"Turn around."

She took a step toward me. "I know what this is about," she said. "You think that if you do this, it'll be over, right? All the conflict you feel, the guilt, the self-loathing, it'll all come to an end by killing me. Isn't that so?" She took another step.

"Stop it!" I shouted. "Turn around!"

"Well, it won't," she said, then paused. "It won't ever end, because the urge will always be there. In fact, it's there right now, isn't it? It's been a while since the last time, after all. Since you took Chris."

I was shaking pretty bad now. She started walking toward me again.

"Please don't do this, Chris," she cooed. "I know you can't. You can't kill your own teacher."

"I'm not Chris," I whispered. "And you're not her."

"I can be whoever you want me to be," she said.

Her arms reached out.

Nothing can prepare you for the first time. No matter

what you've seen on TV, no matter what anyone tells you, there's something about shooting a gun—the noise, the recoil, the muzzle's flash—that takes you by surprise.

I don't doubt that the look of shock on my face matched her own as we both stared down at the hole in her chest. She reached up and put her fingers to the spot, then pulled them back to gaze at the blood blackening her hand.

When she looked back up at me, the shock was beginning to fade and the slightest smile had settled in.

It lasted only a moment.

Soon she began to twitch, then bubble and blur as her human face slowly dissolved and her true features emerged, starting with the eyes—the wide bulbous orbs mingling with Ms. Simpson's nose and mouth. At that point I turned away. I just couldn't watch.

When I looked back, she had crumpled. The transformation was complete.

I walked over to where the sheganger lay sprawled across the gravel and watched the slit of her mouth as it opened and closed a few times. Then, in the headlights' glow, she went still.

CHAPTER TWENTY

For a long time, I just kind of sat there, crouching in the gravel beside the body. I was starting to feel really lousy—headache, nausea, hot flashes, cold flashes. It was like my body was turning against me, a sort of biological rebellion. I'd been holding on for so long that I think my whole system was going into toxic shock. And then seeing the sheganger lying there like that with her head turned toward me, it was almost enough to push me over the edge.

In the end I just focused on being Chris. That's what got me through—keeping my will bent on holding the form and thinking like a doppelganger.

The first thing I did was stick the sheganger in the trunk of the Jetta. It wasn't easy. Sure enough, Ms. Simpson—the real one—was back there, looking none too good, and it took a bit of cramming to get the doppelganger in beside her.

After that, I got in and drove off, out of Parson Woods and back through town. I needed to get rid of the bodies—both of them—and I needed help to do it.

It was after nine by the time I reached Amber's. For almost an hour, I just sat in the car, trying to control the shaking that had come over me. I was all screwed up. I wanted to go in there so badly, to see her and smell her and hold her again, even though it had been only a few hours since we were last together. It was like I *needed* her. But at the same time, the idea of going in there and asking her to leave with me and help do what she'd already done for me once before—well, it made me sick, to be honest. I mean, tonight was supposed to be special. It was supposed to be our night, and now it was ruined. Everything was ruined.

I couldn't do it. I couldn't ask her to help me. In fact, the more I sat there thinking about things, the more I realized I couldn't ask *anything* of her, no matter how much she might want me to. I couldn't put her through the awfulness that lay ahead of me, that would always be there. I mean, she didn't deserve it. And on top of all that, what would I do if another sheganger came calling?

I looked back at the house. Television light flickered from the living room windows. I knew I had to go in there. Not to ask her to help me, but to say good-bye.

I forced myself out of the car, went to the door, and knocked.

Amber didn't say anything when she saw me, but I could see her eyes widen as she opened the door. For a second I was afraid I'd lost Chris and reached up and felt my face. Everything seemed to be in place, no monster eyes that I could tell. Then I realized it wasn't fear on her face, just worry for the pale, trembling wreck standing there in front of her.

She pulled me inside and shut the door. Before I could say a word, she threw her arms around my neck and pulled me into a long, deep kiss. It was the first time we'd kissed since she discovered who I really was, and maybe that was why this time I didn't feel afraid. This time I felt like it was for real. At that moment it seemed to be the *only* thing that was real.

At last she released me, and as we stepped back and looked into each other's eyes, I discovered I'd stopped shaking. All of a sudden, I felt real still inside and free, like I'd suddenly escaped.

"I'm glad you're here," she said, putting her head against my chest.

"Me too," I said. "I'm sorry I'm late."

"It's okay. It doesn't matter. None of it matters. Like you said this afternoon, we can worry about things later. Tonight we can forget."

I didn't know if she was saying it for me or for herself, but it didn't matter. At that point, I couldn't have told her about what had happened with the sheganger anyway, let alone say what I'd come to say. Not after the kiss. I mean, she was asking me to join her in a place I'd always wanted to go, a place where everything was normal, where the truth didn't matter or maybe even exist. I just couldn't say no. I would forget about all of it for her.

For a while we just lay together on the couch in the living room watching TV, like we were just another couple, like it was any old night. Except that I wasn't really watching. I was too busy caressing her arm, her hair, taking in her scent. I wanted to take in all of her, to breathe it all in and hold it so that it would never leave me.

Then she asked me to come upstairs with her, and I did.

I had been nervous before about the idea of sex, and on the way up the stairs the feeling came right back, even more so since the sheganger had gotten me all stirred up. But when the moment actually came, the nervousness went away. Amber helped me through. It was tender, gentle—I don't know, it just felt right. After all the killings, after all that had happened with Barry and everyone else, this was as far away from that as you could get. And for the first time, being with her, being a part of her, I forgot about the monster that I was. I felt human to the core, not just on the surface. I remember wishing I could stay that way forever.

Afterward I held her in my arms. We didn't say much. It was like we both felt a little shy, but in a good sort of way. It was all okay.

"Don't worry, Gabriel," she murmured. "We'll figure it out. We'll figure everything out tomorrow."

"Tomorrow." It was the last word she said to me before she fell asleep. I wish she hadn't. For some reason it stuck in my head, and all of a sudden I started thinking of Macbeth, of that sad, terrible soliloquy at the end: "Tomorrow and tomorrow and tomorrow . . ." The words kept echoing through my brain, and after a while I began getting the itchy feeling all over again, along with the hot flashes, and I knew that I hadn't really escaped. Chris was falling away.

And that wasn't all. As I lay there beside Amber, I began to feel the urge. At first I thought it was just the strain of holding on to Chris, but pretty soon I could tell that it was coming back, the old familiar clenching. It was the goddam sheganger again—she'd cursed me by mentioning it right before I shot her. That had to be it.

For the rest of the night, I lay there as still as possible, trying to ignore it, hoping it would go away, that it would all go away. But it didn't. If anything, it got worse, slowly building with each beat of Amber's heart against my chest, like grains of sand falling through an hourglass onto an ever-climbing pile, beat after beat, grain after grain, tomorrow and tomorrow and tomorrow. It was as if, in the act of being with Amber, I had used up the small part of me that was human. All that was left was doppelganger, and I'd been a fool for thinking it could be any other way.

At last I couldn't take it. I detached myself from Amber, climbed out of bed, and headed for the bathroom. I thought I was going to be sick. After a few steps, though, I felt so dizzy I just sat right down at the end of the bed. I put my head in my hands and took some deep breaths, and soon I started feeling a little better. So I picked my head up.

And that's when I saw him.

I almost cried out at the sight of the creature staring at me in the dim glow of the nightlight. I looked away and rubbed my eyes, and when I looked back at the mirror hanging on the bathroom door, all I saw was Chris. The doppelganger was gone. I glanced down at my hands, at my arms. Sure enough, they were still human.

Get a grip, I told myself. But there I was, shaking all over again, worse than ever. I'd forgotten how ugly I was. You'd think seeing the sheganger earlier would have softened the blow, but I guess it's different when it's yourself.

I reached up and felt my neck. This time pieces of skin

came off in my hands, big, dry flakes, and I wondered how much time I had left. Probably only a few hours, if that. I looked over at Amber, lying there under the covers, her hair fanned out across her pillow. She looked so peaceful. So perfect.

I stood up and started putting on my clothes. I couldn't stay, I couldn't let her see me as I really was. And now that the urge was creeping back, I knew for sure that I had to go. It wasn't so much that I was afraid of hurting her. I just didn't want to feel that way around her. It wasn't right. The whole thing was one big mess.

I finished dressing, then removed the medallion from around my neck and took one last look at good old Jude, patron saint of lost souls, before placing it on the pillow beside her. I supposed I needed him more than she did, but I wanted her to have something to remember me by. I needed her to.

Then I left. I didn't even say good-bye or kiss her or anything like that. I probably should have. I mean, that's what I'd come there for. Besides, that's what they do in the movies, right? But I just didn't want to risk waking her. I admit it, I was afraid.

Gray was just starting to creep into the sky as I drove away in the Jetta. Even though it killed me to leave, deep down I felt like it was the right thing to do. But I didn't feel free or at peace or vindicated or guilty or anything like that as I headed down the road. I just felt tired and alone. It was strange feeling alone again. I'd almost forgotten what it was like.

At least I knew where I was going. The idea had come

to me as soon as I left the house.

Though I made it to the lake well before sunrise, the morning sky was bright enough that I didn't need any headlights to guide me as I gunned the car up the winding road toward the lookout. Before long, I was closing in on the top. Then nothing but early gray sky before me.

A big rock did the job. I'd seen it done in the movies lots of times. It's easier than you might think—just drop it onto the pedal, jump back, and hope the car doesn't turn on you. Of course, if you're smart, you tie the steering wheel down first. But it was okay—the Jetta went straight and true, with enough speed to hit the water a good ways out.

I hobbled over to the edge and watched it sink. It was about all I had left in me to do. After that I just sort of collapsed onto the wet grass and watched the sun come up over the hills. As the light hit my skin, I looked down and saw the last remnants of Chris fade until there was nothing left. As much as I'd resisted these past few days, it felt good to let go, to be myself again. Ugliness and all.

I'm on a train crossing back over the plains. The fields of wheat I saw coming through the first time have been harvested. There's nothing left but stubble now. Still, when the sun sets on the shaved plain, it's just as pretty, only in a different sort of way.

I guess I'm going home, if you want to call it that. I think I remember the way. Back to the mountains, back to the cabin. No one lives there anymore. I figure I might as well go there, far away from everyone. Just me and the crickets.

Over these last few days, curled up in the dark corner of my boxcar, I've been thinking a lot about what happened. I mean, I try not to, but there isn't anything else to do. And so I end up thinking about all the things I could've done differently, how I might have avoided hurting everyone the way I did. In the end, I really don't know that I could've. After all, fate brought me and Chris together. The rest just happened.

But the sheganger was right. If I hadn't killed Chris, if our paths hadn't crossed, I wouldn't have met Amber. I wouldn't have fallen in love. The worst thing is not knowing if that's good or bad. For the most part, it feels pretty bad. It hurts a lot—even more than it did being Chris—and so I try to bury it. But every once in a while, a little piece will break free, will surface and blossom, and I'll remember what it felt like when I saw her face for the first time each day, or the sound of her voice, or her scent. If I'm really hard up, I'll even pop the cell phone open and look at her face, smiling on that little screen. Then I'll think maybe it wasn't so bad, maybe some good came of it—not just because I might have given her something she'd never had before, but because I'm a better person for it. I feel more like a person because of her. That's the truth.

Maybe it doesn't even matter. All I know is that I miss her. A lot. And I miss the Parkers. Not just Echo, but Sheila and Barry, too. I hope they'll be okay. I'd like to think they will. Who knows, maybe someday I'll go back and find out.

And every once in a while I think about the sheganger. She taught me things—about our race, about myself—that I hadn't known before. It's strange, but I feel a little bad that she's gone. Don't get me wrong—I don't feel sad for her the way I do for the others who died, and I'd probably kill her all over again, given the chance. But she was a class act in her own twisted, doppelganger way.

That's the other thing she was right about, by the way—she said I wouldn't feel better for killing her, and I don't. Once the numbness faded away, I didn't feel like I'd broken free one bit. It was just another part of the burden. But I'm learning to accept it. There isn't anything else I can do.

Most of all, I miss Chris. We hardly spent any time together, and none of it was good. But in the end I think I got to know him pretty well. You can't be somebody for a month and not come away without at least a little piece of them staying with you. And deep down, a part me feels that if Chris could see how I tried to live his life, he wouldn't be too upset with me; he might even be okay with it. I'm not trying to justify anything, and who knows, maybe it's just wishful thinking. But what I'm trying to say, I guess, is that sometimes, you've got to make the best of a bad situation.